The Suspension Bridge Robbery

A Gilded Age Legal Thriller

G. Reading Powell

Chapter 1

As Catfish Calloway ascended the iron staircase, the last thing on his mind was defending another murder case.

He stopped on the landing, caught his breath, then ducked through the swinging door into His Honor's private comfort station. After almost four decades of climbing courthouse staircases, he was finding the stairs more formidable and answering nature's call more urgent. He'd even started using a walking cane because his disloyal knees wouldn't always support him. Once done with his private business, he mounted the final flight to the second floor and stopped outside the door on the right. McLennan County badly needed to touch up the chipped gold-stenciled lettering on the door—the Honorable Levi Walcott Goodrich. Catfish dropped his satchel and rapped on the door, but there was no answer. He pressed his ear against it and waited a heartbeat or two. Still, nothing stirred inside the judge's chambers.

Catfish checked his pocket watch. Almost eleven fifteen. He'd intended to send their new apprentice—he just needed the judge's signature on a judgment—but the youngster hadn't even shown up yet, and he'd had to do it himself. A sorry first impression. How was he supposed to teach the boy to be a lawyer if he didn't even bother to be on time for his first day in the law offices of Calloway & Calloway?

It was fast turning into a wasted morning. He started to leave but stopped short to straighten the portrait of President Cleveland on the wall. Hard times—Grover the Good should've retired after his first term in office. Heading back toward the stairs, he noticed lights on inside the Nineteenth District Court. Peculiar. It was the first day of the October 1894 term of court, but Judge Goodrich didn't typically begin the opening session until afternoon.

He peered through the window in the door; court was in session. Judge Goodrich's head was propped on his knuckles, still as a statue to boredom, but it probably wouldn't be long before he got peeved at somebody for not moving things along. The first qualification for anyone aspiring to the district bench was impatience. Twelve citizens good and true pondered the squeaking wheels of justice from the oak-banistered jury box. The only public spectators were two men and a woman seated together in the middle of the gallery. The older man looked familiar.

It probably wasn't a criminal case since Tom Blair wasn't at the table closest to the jury where the prosecutor always held forth. Catfish hadn't heard of any civil cases going to trial that week. And the plaintiff's lawyer was a fella he'd never seen before.

The defense lawyer was none other than Joseph Birdsong Jaye, known around the McLennan County bench and bar as Jaybird, not because he signed his name *J. Birdsong Jaye*, but because he'd achieved that *nom de guerre* fair and square by habitual courtroom ineptitude, often fueled by demon rum. It was too far to see for sure, but he was confident Jaybird's plaid sack coat was badly wrinkled.

He didn't recognize Jaybird's poor client—young man, maybe in his twenties, short hair, only the back of his head visible, rocking forward and back incessantly. Peculiar.

2

Between the judge's bench and the jury, a fella sat in the witness chair, facing away from Catfish. A black bowler rested on the rail beside him. The crook of a cane extended above the rail. Was it a blackthorn cane? Catfish's jaw clenched.

Then the witness turned, showing his face, and Catfish's grip tightened on his own walking stick.

He crammed his ear against the glass, but the witness's voice didn't carry through the heavy courtroom doors. Catfish didn't need to hear his testimony, though. He knew. Whatever the case was about, he knew.

Without the slightest forethought, a closing argument formed on his lips. *Gentlemen of the jury, Thaddeus Schoolcraft stood before you, raised his right hand and swore on the Bible to tell you the truth, and sat in that witness chair and lied to you as if lying was righteous.* He'd made that very argument eight years earlier. Then, just three months ago in his last murder trial, they'd been thrown together again in this same courtroom.

The burning, souring bile rose once more, pricking his conscience until he turned away. This wasn't his fight.

Before he took a single step, however, something beyond his control stopped him, something inexplicable. He slowly exhaled and slipped inside the courtroom. The closest seats were directly behind the defense table, where he was more at home anyway. The plaintiff's lawyer and the judge were exchanging words, but he couldn't focus on them yet. Not with Schoolcraft on the stand.

He studied the man, even though he needed no reminders of his appearance—horseshoe mustache, thin arched eyebrows, dark eyes. Short hair, precisely parted on the right side. Just like eight years ago. Brown coat, buttoned at the top only, beneath his winged collar and four-in-hand tie. Catfish couldn't see below the witness rail but didn't need to. He knew. There'd be a sterling silver watch chain hanging from his third vest button sagging into the bottom right vest pocket. A fob would be dangling from the button, but he'd never wanted to get close enough to determine whether it was Masonic or Demonic. His shoes would have button gaiters. French calf. Black.

Catfish lit a White Owl cigar and spat the butt into the spittoon at his feet. The smoke whirled up until it was dissipated by the electrified fan whopping overhead on the long shaft dangling from the two-story ceiling. Open windows admitted the cool October air along with the clanking of street cars and the whinnies of carriage horses.

The bailiff, his head back, his eyes shut, his mouth open, snored softly. He always napped after his labors during a jury's morning break. Following the afternoon break, the nap would deepen; the snoring would intensify; the judge would softly tap the edge of the bench until he awakened. McLennan County justice had its rhythms.

"You may proceed, counselor," the judge said to the plaintiff's lawyer.

Catfish turned his attention to the man striding back to his table. Why'd he never come across this lawyer before? He knew all the members of the local bar, as well as those of all the surrounding counties, but he'd never even seen him. Not a fella he'd likely forget.

The lawyer made a grand gesture toward the jury box. "Tell the gentlemen of the jury why you went to the suspension bridge on September fifth, 1894."

Whoa, less than a month ago. Quick trial setting. He checked his watch again. And a quick trial today—not even noon yet, but they'd already picked a jury, made opening arguments, and were well into witness testimony. Must be a trifling case to move so quickly.

Schoolcraft turned in his chair and eyed the jurors directly. "I received a telephone call from the local agent for the American Express Company. He said their express wagon was stolen while crossing the bridge, and the driver and guard were murdered."

Murder? Catfish yanked the cigar from his mouth. He remembered a robbery-murder last month on the bridge but didn't even know they'd arrested anybody. County Attorney Tom Blair should be prosecuting this case. And why in the world would Judge Goodrich appoint Jaybird, of all the lawyers in the bar, to defend a murder case? But he must have been appointed because no person with means, when accused of murder, would even consider hiring a bootless, no-count lawyer like him.

Catfish tapped ashes into the spittoon.

Underneath his wavy white hair, Jaybird's double chin rested on his chest, rising and falling gently with his breathing. His suit was indeed wrinkled, and his arms dangled lifelessly from over his swivel chair. Eyes probably closed. He'd be in a chorus with the bailiff before long. To his right, his client rocked back and forth. Whoever he was and whether he murdered somebody or not, that man deserved better than J. Birdsong Jaye. No wonder the prosecution got it to trial in only a matter of weeks.

Schoolcraft must have orchestrated this haste.

Catfish cleared his throat loudly, and Jaybird startled but settled back. Judge Goodrich watched him nod off, then looked directly at Catfish. He'd probably already warned Jaybird several times.

"What time of day did this robbery occur?" the prosecutor asked.

"The agent said it was about seven forty in the morning."

Catfish tensed. *Jaybird, be on your toes now.* He shouldn't let that lying carpetbagger sneak any more hearsay into evidence. Catfish blew smoke toward Jaybird's table. He coughed but didn't waken.

"Why did the American Express agent call you, being a KATY Railroad detective?"

Not a man to miss an opportunity to spew self-laudatory drivel, Schoolcraft wheeled his chair from the prosecutor toward the jury. "The express wagon was carrying a mail bag of cash which just arrived in town by one of our trains. The express agents unloaded it from our express car and were transporting it to another train depot for transshipment. American Express has no detective in Waco, but they were aware of my reputation and asked me to investigate for them. I was happy to, of course, American Express being a good customer of the KATY Railroad."

The prosecutor shuffled through some papers. "How much cash?"

"Twenty-five thousand dollars."

Whew! Ten times more money than the entire jury likely earned last year.

"What did you do after you got this call from American Express?"

"I went to the bridge."

"Describe for the gentlemen what you saw there."

Schoolcraft crooned to that jury like it was an opera audience. "There was a swelling crowd gathered. I cut my way through them and on the right side of the bridge, about midway across the river, I found two bodies. Both had bullet wounds to the chest. The express wagon was gone and so was the money bag."

"Did you see anything else there that struck you as important?"

"Gentlemen," Schoolcraft said, "on the south side of the bridge near the bodies, I found something singular, a bicycle. This evidence proved quite illuminating."

"Describe it."

"It resembled any other bicycle except the tires were both patched in a number of places, and there was a wicker basket strapped to the front of the handlebars."

Sounded like Toby Topper's bicycle. Catfish darted a look at the man beside Jaybird at the defense table. He still rocked, head down. Toby? He'd never watched the boy up close.

"Was the accused there?"

"No."

"Did you find a weapon?"

"Other than the driver's pistol, which was still in his holster, and the guard's shotgun, which lay beside him, I did not."

"What happened then?"

"Sergeant Quinn of the Waco Police was there, and not much later Lieutenant Palmer arrived. I left matters to them."

Catfish smiled, recalling his cross-examination of Palmer last July in Cicero's trial. The young pup police detective had been so proud of his bloody finger-smudge science until Catfish showed the jury how he'd stolen it directly from a Mark Twain yarn.

The prosecutor peered over his papers at Schoolcraft. "Did you ever learn who did this?"

Catfish's eyes shot to the defense table. *Jaybird, perk up!*

Toby's guardian was out cold.

Catfish gripped the handle of his cane. He could picture the carved inscription on its shaft without even looking at it. He fought to suppress a raging impulse.

Not his case. Not his client. Not his fight.

"Yes, sir," Schoolcraft answered. "An eyewitness told me—"

Dang it! Catfish flicked his cigar into the spittoon and struggled to his feet. "Hearsay!"

Schoolcraft's head jerked toward him.

The prosecutor whirled around. "Who are you?"

Before Catfish could respond, Judge Goodrich said, "Catfish, we'll have no *amicus curiae* out of you, please."

"Sorry, Your Honor," he said as sheepishly as he could manage. "Couldn't help it."

"Would the court please instruct the jury to disregard that man's outburst?" the prosecutor asked.

"Gentlemen of the jury, Mr. Calloway isn't involved in this case. You'll disregard his comment. And Catfish, you'll keep your place." Then, he glared at Jaybird.

"Of course, Your Honor." Catfish took his seat. His eyes fell on the words carved into his cane, but he quickly rotated them out of his sight. Not his case.

Jaybird was awake but not on his feet. He blinked and gazed around like a chick just out of its egg and eased back in his chair. His client rocked back and forth, still looking down. Hadn't reacted to any of the disturbances. Just as oblivious as his lawyer.

Catfish peeked at Schoolcraft, who still stared back at him.

"Proceed, Mr. Chitty," Judge Goodrich said.

Chitty? Hilton Chitty from Dallas? The celebrated railroad lawyer? Above his high forehead, his dark, slightly graying hair swept back like a norther blew it there and froze it in place. Imposing figure of a man.

"Yes, Your Honor. Thank you." He eyed the jury knowingly. "Now, Detective Schoolcraft, you were telling us what you learned about the identity of the killer."

Catfish cut his eyes from the prosecutor and witness to

Jaybird, who was now awake but bent over the table, cradling his head between his hands. It must have been pounding from last night's binge. His client rocked back and forth, seemingly unconcerned about his attorney's abysmal performance.

"An eyewitness said the killer was a man people called Toby Topper," Schoolcraft said.

Catfish clamped his eyes shut. *Hearsay, Jaybird, hearsay!*

"Who, sir, is Toby Topper?"

"I don't know that anyone knows his real name. Quite a mysterious chap. Always bicycling around town, tipping his hat to passersby. I understand a business employs him to make deliveries."

Chitty, tall and thin, cocked his head quizzically. "He tips his hat?"

"Yes, sir. He always wears a gray top hat. It's a bit tattered. While riding his bicycle he constantly doffs it to people he passes on the street. Over and over again. Off and on. Off and on. Off and on." Schoolcraft stroked his horseshoe mustache as if he were about to spout scripture like a Christian. "It's queer, really, but it's exceedingly distinctive."

"Is he the man sitting beside Mr. Jaye? The accused?"

"That's him."

Chitty cast an accusing glance at Toby. "Did you find the defendant's top hat at the scene of the crime?"

"No, sir."

"You said you've seen him riding about town on a bicycle. Can you tell the gentlemen of the jury whether the bicycle you found near the bodies was the one ridden by Mr. Toby Topper?"

Objection! Catfish leaned forward, still clutching his cane. Jaybird was stuck to his chair like Brazos River mud.

"I believe it was," Schoolcraft replied.

"Pass the witness."

"Mr. Jaye," the judge said. "You may cross-examine."

Catfish's gut tightened.

"Oh, yesh, Your Honor," he said with a slur, not even rising to address the court. "Thank you, indeed. Quite happy to. I will do just that very thing."

Jaybird been drinking already. Catfish rested his forehead on his hands which he'd folded over the handle of his cane. Couldn't watch.

"Missster Ssschoolhouse ..."

Catfish winced.

"Oh, I misspoke, I'm sssorry. *Detective* Ssschoolhouse ..."

The jury burst into laughter, forcing Catfish to look.

"Are you quite sssure about all that testimony you testified to?"

"Yes, counselor, quite certain."

"Oh." He sounded surprised. "Is there any posssibility you might be inco-correct about sssome of it?"

"None."

"Oh, oh, I sssee. Thank you, ssso much." He steepled his hands and tapped his fingers.

The jury snickered.

The judge covered his forehead with his hand.

The accused rocked back and forth.

Catfish sagged back in his seat. Not his case. As he dragged his glare from Schoolcraft, his eyes swept across the words on his own cane: *Audi Alteram Partem.* Dang it, he couldn't sit back and let this happen. If only he could cross-examine that scoundrel. Of course, he'd tried that before. Eight years earlier. In this same courtroom. The jury had believed Schoolcraft anyway, and Houston Calloway—Catfish's precious elder son— was hung for murder.

When Schoolcraft left the witness stand Judge Goodrich recessed for lunch and motioned for Catfish to follow him back into chambers. Catfish only wanted his judgment signed, but the judge had no way of knowing that. He had something else on his mind, and Catfish had a good idea what it might be.

Not his case!

***

Judge Goodrich took off his robe, dropped into the chair behind his desk, and gave Catfish an unsettling, melancholy look. "Have a seat."

It was coming.

"Thanks." Catfish took a chair. "Sorry I interrupted out there."

"I knew exactly what you were up to." The white-haired, white-mustached Goodrich pulled off his spectacles. "I thought about doing it myself but repeated cautions to Jaye have accomplished nothing."

"Yes, sir?"

Goodrich hunched over this desk, fidgeting with a fancy silver dip pen. "This whole thing bothers me."

Catfish braced himself for it.

The judge hesitated a second, then pointed the pen at him. "I'd like to appoint you to assist in the defense."

His rational mind had already rejected the possibility. The trial had begun, and he didn't know what had happened already; he knew nothing about the facts of the case; he hadn't even spoken with the client; and anyway, he'd resolved not to lead any more murder defenses. "Oh, Judge, I don't know anything about the case."

"Jaybird doesn't either." Goodrich stuffed the pen in its stand. "At least you'd be sober."

Why'd he appointed Jaybird in the first place? Judge was likely feeling remorse because he knew how worthless Jaybird was, but Catfish wasn't about to touch that. "How'd Chitty come to prosecute? What happened to Tom Blair?"

"He has a conflict of interest. His law partner in his private practice represents the widow of one of the deceased men. You probably saw Mrs. Hook in the gallery with her father and brother."

"Was that Old Man Stanek?" Catfish asked.

"Her father. Anyway, Tom recused himself, and the express company asked me to appoint Chitty special prosecutor. Jaybird didn't object."

"No surprise." Catfish scraped his fingers through his hair, causing it to fall over his forehead. "Did he at least file a motion for continuance?"

"No, as a matter of fact, there was a joint request, signed by both Chitty and Jaybird, asking for an immediate trial. I had no choice."

"I don't understand Jaybird at all."

"I don't either." The judge leaned back in his chair, drumming his fingers on the desk. "He's no match for Chitty. Toby doesn't stand much of a chance against the railroad, the express company, and the state of Texas."

The judge's gaze fixed on the engraving in Catfish's cane: *Audi Alteram Partem*. Goodrich certainly understood it—*Hear the Other Side*—and Catfish knew exactly what the judge was about to do. He covered the words with his hand. Not his case; not his client.

The judge loosened his collar. "I'd feel better if I knew you had a steady hand on the defense."

His gut rebelled at the idea. "Judge, you saw last term my

hand's not so steady anymore." He'd lost the Cicero Sweet murder case in July. Cicero was an old friend's son, and it was a case he should never have taken. The judge knew Catfish was still embarrassed by it. Goodrich had seen him go to pieces in the middle of trial—lost his temper, screamed at witnesses, cursed, got emotional. Imagined things that didn't happen. When it was over, he'd resolved it was time to let his law partner and younger son take the lead in murder cases. He'd ride shotgun for Harley. So, now was not the time to jump into the middle of another one. Not his fight. "I'd respectfully ask permission to decline the appointment."

The judge sighed. "I suppose Schoolcraft will have his way then."

Schoolcraft. Bile still burning his throat, Catfish couldn't expel the image of that grin beneath the horseshoe mustache, of the bowler hat, and of the blackthorn cane. Schoolcraft had a hand in Cicero's case as he had in the trial of Catfish's elder son, Houston. Catfish stroked his pounding forehead. He couldn't step aside and let Schoolcraft wreck another young man's life. There was no one else to defend him, despite the bitter taste of it. And the judge knew it.

Judge Goodrich checked his pocket watch. "Toby probably killed those men, but I don't want a trial like this on my conscience." He spoke more softly. "As a personal favor to me, Catfish, I hope you'll accept my appointment."

His head throbbed in protest, but despite all reason, deep within him some irresistible, primal impulse roused. His eyes met Goodrich's. "Of course. I'll do it, Judge."

It was his fight now.

Chapter 2

Catfish gazed out the open second floor window of Judge Goodrich's chambers wondering why in the world he agreed to defend Toby Topper. A trolley, its electrical wires crackling impatiently, whisked past a plodding mule cart. The mule dumped a mound of fresh dung in protest against modernity. Catfish snickered. *Me too, Old Beast.* He leaned out the window to see below to the courthouse entrance where his hound dog, Colonel Terry, stood watch bothered neither by mule nor machine. He whistled; the colonel bayed in reply and stood, eying him hopefully. "Stay!" he yelled, and the noble critter settled on his haunches like the Sphinx of the Brazos guarding the Temple of Justice.

The judge had gone to fetch Chitty and Jaybird for a conference in chambers. By the time the others arrived, Catfish had dispelled the sour taste of Thaddeus Schoolcraft but not his doubts about taking the case.

Once everyone was seated, the judge made an entry on his docket sheet and looked at the lawyers. "I've appointed Mr. Catfish Calloway to assist Mr. Jaye in the defense."

"I object to that," Chitty said, almost coming out of his seat.

The judge shook his head. "Too late, I've decided."

Chitty took on a new shade of disagreeable. "Something like this wouldn't happen in Dallas County."

Judge Goodrich was generally an even-tempered man, but his face reddened. "Well, sir, it just did happen in McLennan County and that's where you find yourself."

Chitty became suddenly deferential again. He was probably in his late forties, much younger than the judge. "I'm sorry, Your Honor. I didn't mean to be disrespectful. I feel ganged up on by these gentlemen." He cut them a sideways glance. "A catfish and a jaybird. Are all McLennan County lawyers from the barnyard?"

"Beg pardon, mister," Catfish said, smiling. "Don't know much about barnyards in North Texas, but I'm fish and he's fowl. Neither one's likely found in a barnyard in this county—"

Chitty smirked.

"Unless a varmint dragged 'em there."

"Your honor," Chitty said, ignoring him, "I have the proposed jury charge for your signature." He slid it across the judge's desk.

"Judge," Catfish interrupted, "I'll need a continuance to get up to snuff on this case."

"I object, they joined in a request for this tri—"

"I didn't," Catfish interjected.

"Hold on, gentlemen," the judge said. "After I empanel a jury, I go to verdict, no matter what. No continuances. We'll proceed with this trial in due course. Now, Mr. Chitty, who did you plan to call after lunch?"

"My next witness is a policeman who went to the scene. Sergeant Quinn, I believe. We also have eyewitnesses who'll identify the defendant as the killer. First is"—he thumbed through his notes—"Robert Lazenby."

Bob was an eyewitness? Catfish glanced at his co-counsel. *Jaybird, we've got a guilty client.*

***

Toby Topper was peculiar. He didn't look Catfish in the eye, just rocked back and forth with his head down.

"Toby?"

He kept rocking. Blank face.

Catfish had never paid much attention to the young fella before. They'd never spoken, but he'd seen the boy countless times riding around town on his bicycle, tipping his hat repetitively. Everybody knew him by sight and called him Toby Topper. Likely not his real name.

Catfish took a chair at the defense table across from Toby and Jaybird. If he was to defend the boy, it might help to know what the defense was.

Toby never stopped moving, bending at the waist, dipping forward, then jerking back in an invariable rhythm.

"Toby, you understand me?"

He was a big boy with a puffy face, probably in his early twenties. No facial hair. Maybe didn't even shave. Despite the question, his gaze never left the tabletop.

"He doesn't sspeak much," Jaybird offered, his own speech still slurred. "Not sso ssure he's all there, you know."

Catfish leaned closer. "Mr. Topper?"

No reaction.

What had he gotten into? "Mr. Jaye, looks like we're in the same bed on this one."

Jaybird belched. "Indeed."

"What's our defense?"

Even across the table Jaybird smelled of liquor. "We don't have one. I think he did it. That's what everyone sssays."

"Has Toby said?"

"He can't."

Toby rocked.

"I see." No, he didn't see at all. Was there some underlying intelligence in Toby Topper? Was this odd behavior just a mask to cover his crime? Or was he just a fool easily bent to another's will? "Well, we'll come up with a defense. I'm meeting my law partner for lunch, and we'll figure something out. Meet you back here afterwards."

The only defense appeared to be that Toby wasn't capable of defending himself. Couldn't try a man who was unable to testify or even help his lawyers with the defense. Catfish had seen lying clients, clients who scared him, clients who disgusted him, clients who'd lost their memories, and downright guilty clients, but they were all ready, willing, and all too able to tell him some tale of innocence or justification. Toby Topper couldn't even say his own name.

Eyewitnesses, including his friend Bob Lazenby, were apparently about to testify Toby gunned down two men.

Jaybird blinked. He was a furlong or two beyond useless.

They needed reinforcements.

Chapter 3

As she waited for Mr. Calloway, wondering why he'd summoned her, Miss Peach watched the busy town square through the front window of Sam Kee's Chinese restaurant. Electric trolleys, wagons, carriages, horses, mules, and pedestrians by the score circulated on the streets surrounding the spired clock tower of City Hall. A dear man, known widely as Bootblack Ben Moon, had set up his shoeshine operation outside the window on the sidewalk under Sam Kee's awning. He was always either there catering to the city hall business or at one of the train stations.

She periodically glanced down the sidewalk for Mr. Calloway. He always ate at Sam Kee's when in trial because it was right around the corner from the courthouse. It was odd he wanted to meet there today since he wasn't in trial, and she knew of no reason so urgent he would ask the district clerk to telephone her to arrange a lunch meeting. Neither he nor Mr. Harley had any matters scheduled for hearing before the district courts this week. After a worry-filled, emotionally-draining, and physically-exhausting murder trial last summer, they'd all looked forward to a more peaceful fall.

Their new apprentice had accompanied her to the restaurant because she didn't know what else to do with him. He'd finally gotten to the office over two hours late on his first day, long after

Mr. Calloway had left to do what the apprentice could have and should have done himself. He would learn. She could hear Mr. Calloway say *Better three hours too soon than a minute too late.*

He was fresh-faced—quite handsome—with a thin mustache and wavy light-colored hair, slightly younger than her, but still past twenty. "Miss Peach, how long have you been a clerical worker for Catfish?"

He was certainly familiar for one who'd never met their employer. She cleared her throat. "I always address him as Mr. Calloway."

"Sure." Then he smirked. "Is that what you call his son too?"

"He's Mr. Harley." She craned her neck to see down the sidewalk. Still no Mr. Calloway.

"And how old is *Mr.* Harley?"

"Twenty-eight."

"Ah," he said with a grin, "not so much older than me."

She tugged wrinkles out of the sleeve of her blouse. Harley had been on her mind, but she didn't care to be interrogated about him. "He's quite intelligent."

"And what about you? How shall I address you?" He cocked his head with a thin smile. "I assume your Christian name is acceptable?"

"Mr. Calloway and Mr. Harley call me Miss Peach."

He shrugged.

She glanced down the sidewalk again. "To answer your question about my employment, I've served as the stenographer for Calloway & Calloway over three years now."

"You must have posted quite a few letters in that time."

Off-putting as he was, she tried not to judge him. He leaned back in his chair, hands in his trouser pockets, legs extended and crossed as if he was much older.

She smiled politely. "Mr. Harley tells me you graduated from Dartmouth College."

"Of course." He brushed a piece of lint from the sleeve of his well-tailored serge coat. "It's expected in my family."

"I went to Baylor University."

"Really?" He pulled his watch, inserted a fob key, and wound it twice. "Girls aren't admitted to Dartmouth College."

The front door flew open. Mr. Calloway whisked in, winking at her as he went straight to the counter to place his order. Colonel Terry, tail wagging, trotted at his heels. Very quickly, he came to the table, cane under his arm, bowl and cup in hand. The steaming, savory rice overpowered the air around their table, but she preferred that to the cigar smoke Mr. Calloway usually generated. When in trial he always had fried rice and ginger tea, but he wasn't in trial. How odd.

He was focused on something so intently that he must not have even noticed the young gentleman seated at their table. How could he not? Even Colonel Terry gave the new face a glance before he plopped at his master's feet.

"Mr. Calloway, this is Mr. Hampton Boswell."

Boswell had straightened himself by then and wore a smile she hadn't seen earlier. They exchanged greetings.

Mr. Calloway started devouring his lunch silently. His mood was jovial generally—a delightful gentleman to work for—but his work occasionally demanded great intensity, and this must have been such a time. His lovely blue eyes, which seemed to change their hue to suit his disposition, were almost gray.

In no time he'd gulped the rice and wiped his mouth.

"Here's the situation," he said in a lower voice, eying the men at a nearby table. "We've got a new client who's probably guilty of robbery and murder of two express agents. Bob Lazenby apparently saw him do it. Judge Goodrich appointed us to defend him because for some reason he'd appointed Jaybird before, and Jaybird turned out to be himself. I expect Judge feels bad about his choice. Anyway, I couldn't turn him down, so now we've got to make a defense. Like as not somebody must have put the boy up to the robbery, but we don't have time to do a thorough investigation."

Miss Peach bit her lip. Boy? Who might it be?

"Why give him a defense?" Boswell asked. "I mean, if he's guilty?"

Mr. Calloway studied the boy and tweaked the ends of his long, white mustache until they attained their proper curl. "I don't have time to explain that to you now, son, but—"

"Please, sir, call me Hamp." There was that smile again.

"Hamp, we'll talk about why we represent folks accused of crimes when we have more time."

Boswell's face lit up as if he finally understood. "Oh, I see. He's wealthy, and the firm will earn a big fee."

"The judge appointed us to represent him because he's indigent. County doesn't pay big fees for that work." Mr. Calloway turned to her. "You may know him—Toby Topper?"

"Oh, my heavens above!"

"I don't know how I got us into this, but there we are." When he raked his fingers through his snow-white hair it flopped over his forehead, and, as if he'd brushed off an elixir's lid, boyish passion spilled over him, his eyes now deeply blue. "We can win this fight, but it'll take every trooper to his mount."

She'd follow the old cavalryman anywhere. "Just tell me what to do."

"Where's Harley?"

"He's on his way. He was meeting with Mr. Rotan about the

Cotton Palace opening. I telephoned over there and left a message."

Mr. Calloway stroked the colonel's head, then hunched over the table. "Listen, I don't have much more time. I need you to do some things for me. Tell Harley I want to know everything there is to know about objecting to trial of a defendant on the ground he's a lunatic. We'll talk about it tonight. I think I can stall things that long."

She jotted a note.

"After that, go back to the office and get on that talking-phone."

He was such an oldster about modern marvels like the telephone.

"Contact Senator Coke," Mr. Calloway continued. "I want to know if he can associate with us in a murder trial. Tell him the trial's already started though."

Boswell brightened at the mention of Coke. "I could speak with the senator for you, sir. My father knows him from when he was governor."

"Thanks, but Miss Peach can handle it."

"Then what would you like me to do, sir?" he asked, wide-eyed.

Mr. Calloway sipped his tea. "If you're reading the law under us, then maybe you better get at it. I left some books for you."

A frown flashed across his face, then vanished into a slow nod.

Miss Peach had made a place for him near the bookshelves in the back of the office. She'd showed him the books Mr. Calloway set aside. There were standards such as Judge Clark's treatise, the Texas Penal Code, and the Code of Criminal Procedure, but some weren't law books at all: the Bible, Bleak House, Treasure Island, The Apology, and the brand-new edition of Pudd'nhead Wilson which Mr. Calloway had purchased after it played such a role in Cicero's trial. A lawyer needed a broad education, he'd said. Boswell had shown little interest in any of them.

"I'm more keen for action than reading, sir. Maybe I could help you in court?"

She folded her hands on the table. *Oh my.*

Mr. Calloway answered immediately. "Let's start with reading."

Boswell's head dropped.

Mr. Calloway finished his tea and rose to leave. "Colonel, get." The hound led the way to the door, but his master turned back. "Hamp, you know anything about lunacy?"

He hesitated for an instant as the word *no* began to form on his lips, but before it came out, he brightened. "Yes, actually, I studied it in college."

"Good, maybe you can help with that. I gotta be smart as Dr. Rush by tomorrow morning."

After Mr. Calloway left, Mr. Moon came in. "Sorry to bother you, Miss Peach, but I just hear from a gentleman they's trying Toby for murder, and Cap'n Calloway's defending him. That true?"

"It is."

Mr. Moon wiped his brow, hat in hand. "Lordy me."

"Is he a friend?" she asked.

"Oh, I just knows him, you know. He rides around the square ever day and tips his hat to me ever time. Sure is friendly. Tuesdays, he takes his lunch at the church, so Maudie, she tells me about him. Ain't seen him in a spell though." Mr. Moon looked around the room. "I hope the Cap'n know, Toby just different. Ain't no murderer."

"I'm sure he's not, but as Mr. Calloway says, sometimes being different gets you in trouble. I'll tell him what you said about Toby."

Mr. Moon backed away. "I didn't mean to be no bother to

you folks, but I's sure sorry for that boy."

"You're never a bother." She smiled. "It's so nice to see you. Give my regards to Mrs. Moon."

"Yes'm, Miss Peach." He bowed his head to Boswell and went back to his stand.

"Who is that?" Boswell said with a look of disbelief. "Is he permitted in this part of the establishment?"

She recoiled at his attitude. "Yes, of course. He's our friend and Mr. Kee's too."

Boswell shrugged and rocked back in his chair again. "He called Mr. Calloway 'Captain.' Was he an officer in the war?"

"I don't think so, but he was in the war. He doesn't talk about it much."

He inspected his cuticles carefully. "You know, I'd like to brush up on lunacy some. Get Dr. Rush on the telephone for me when we get back."

What?

She rose from the table to cover her smile. Dr. Benjamin Rush, the country's first expert on diseases of the mind and a signer of the Declaration of Independence, had been dead a very long time. "Perhaps I can find a book for you."

Chapter 4

Sergeant Quinn, with his keystone hat under his arm and solemnity across his face, lumbered to the witness stand. Catfish had known him for a long time. A good copper. Honest fella. After taking the oath he settled into the witness chair.

Chitty led him through his experience on the police force, and then came to the murders. "Sergeant, were you called to a shooting on the suspension bridge on September fifth?"

"I was."

"Explain for the gentlemen what you found there."

"Yes, sir." Sergeant Quinn turned to the jury. His voice was calm and matter-of-fact as he always was. "About mid-point on the bridge a crowd had gathered around two dead bodies. Both had been shot. Blood was soaked into the decking around the bodies. One was on his stomach, the other his side. They were more toward the south side of the bridge. I was told he pushed them off—"

"Objection!" Catfish rose quickly, his chair screeching. "Hearsay as to what he was told by others."

"Sustained," the judge ruled. "Sergeant, only what you know yourself, please."

"Yes, Your Honor."

Jaybird leaned over and whispered to Catfish—or tried to,

anyway, being incapable of speaking quietly. "Capital work, Calloway. Nicely done." He seemed to be sobering with food in his belly.

Judge Goodrich eyed Jaybird disapprovingly.

Chitty twisted his chair toward the jury, crossed his leg over his knee and extended it so his foot pointed at the jurors. Light from the dangling bulb overhead glinted off the highly polished shoe. "No need for what others said." He brushed some invisible speck from his pin-striped trousers. "Can you tell us the identity of these two poor men you found shot to death?"

"One was Lawrence Hay and the other was Bill Hook. They both worked for American Express Company. Mr. Hay lived in town. Mr. Hook lived on a farm north of here."

In the gallery, Mrs. Hook wailed, and her brother tried to console her. Old Man Stanek sat quietly, arms crossed, brow furrowed.

Chitty's gaze lingered over them, then back to the witness. "What did you do after you inspected the bodies?"

"I noticed there was a bicycle lying on the bridge beside the rail near the bodies. I examined it, and I recognized it. It belonged to Mr. Toby Topper. I knew that because the tires were patched, and he'd tied a wicker basket onto the handlebars. That's where he carried goods he delivered about town for Mr. Risher's drugstore. And there was a tin cup fixed to it that customers dropped coins in."

Catfish peeked at the jury. The hostler from the stable on the town square had probably seen Toby on that bicycle every day.

Chitty examined a paper on the prosecution table. "Sergeant, I'd like to move forward in time to your subsequent investigation. Did you ever obtain any information as to the whereabouts of the express wagon?"

"Yes, we were told." He eyed the judge and didn't say what he was told.

Catfish pushed his chair back a little so he could see the fourth juror on the front row, John Darden. He was the head clerk at the Hotel Palmo. His eyes fixed on Quinn.

"Based upon that information, but without going into what was said, where did you go?"

"It was late afternoon of the same day, Wednesday. I went to Taylor Street in East Waco. I found the wagon there, parked to the side of the street outside of the old cotton mill. It was empty."

"The money bag was missing?"

"Yes."

"Was anyone around?"

"Only the watchman at the mill. We found him sleeping by the gate."

Chitty stood. "At that point . . ."

As the testimony droned along, the bailiff got up from his chair near the jury box and glanced at the judge, who motioned him on, and then he went to the southeasternmost window of the courtroom. Catfish checked his watch. Right on time. The bailiff pulled the window shut, then did the same to all the others on the south side. He left the north ones open.

Chitty, the out-of-towner, didn't even notice.

" . . . and that's all I saw," Quinn finished.

"Were you ever able to recover any of the stolen money?"

"By Wednesday night, we found some of it."

Catfish yawned. Pray God Toby didn't have it on him.

"Explain for the jury, please."

"The express company offered a reward the morning of the robbery," Quinn answered. "That afternoon, somebody contacted us and gave information that led to its discovery."

27

Chitty eyed Catfish, showing the slightest hint of a smile. He edged closer to Quinn. "Without going into what this person said to anyone, what did you do?"

"Another officer and I went to an abandoned shanty in East Waco. We found Mr. Topper sleeping inside."

The money bag was coming.

Catfish checked his watch again, then pinched his pince-nez spectacles onto his nose, pulled out his magic pencil, and yanked on the chain until the lead popped out the other end. Then he held it up, examined the point from every angle, wrote his name on his notepaper, closed and returned the pencil to his vest pocket, careful not to look at the jury, but confident they were watching him. Juries always watched the defendant and his lawyer.

Chitty pointed an accusing finger at Toby. "You discovered the defendant?"

"We did."

"All right," Chitty said as if the time for truth's revelation had finally come. "What happened when you went in?"

"He woke up and became agitated. We put him in handcuffs and then searched the area."

Chitty paced beside the prosecution table, hands folded behind his back. "Did he say anything?"

"Just gibberish. Nothing we could understand."

Chitty reached under the prosecution table and pulled a gray stove-pipe top hat from a box. While everyone watched Chitty and the hat, Catfish tried to sneak a peek under the table for a money bag, but there wasn't anything else there.

Chitty handed the hat to Quinn. "Did you find this hat now marked for identification as Exhibit Three?"

"Yes, sir, it was hanging on a nail."

"We offer State's Exhibit Three."

Catfish prodded Jaybird, who said from his seat, "No objections at this time from the defense, Your Honor."

"Exhibit Three is admitted," the judge ruled.

Catfish leaned near Jaybird's ear. "Get on your feet when you address the court."

"Oh?" Jaybird said in his loud whisper. "Yes, why, of course I will, if you want."

Chitty displayed the worn, dirty hat to the jury. About eight inches of the gray ribbon from the edge of the brim was torn loose and dangling. Catfish had seen it flying from Toby's hat like a tail when he rode fast on his bicycle. No doubt that was Toby's hat. The hostler nodded as Chitty paraded it before him.

Next to Jaybird, Toby rocked back and forth. Didn't even look at the hat.

"Tell the jury what was on the floor next to Mr. Topper."

Expecting to hear about the money bag, Catfish leaned back and gazed at the ceiling fan whopping over the defense table. Shadows on the tin ceiling tiles high above danced in circles to its beat.

"We found a Colt pistol."

Almost as bad as money. Catfish checked his watch. When he looked up, several jurors were staring at Toby, and one crossed his arms.

"Did you check the cylinder to see if it had been fired?" Chitty asked.

"It had three live rounds and two spent cartridges."

"Sergeant, what I'm going to ask you about now is important." Chitty reached into his briefcase and pulled out a leather pouch. He started toward Quinn.

Catfish checked his watch again. The prosecution had built a head of steam: Toby's bicycle, Toby's hat, a pistol fired twice. Probably money in that pouch, too. Time to vent that steam before the conviction engine chugged on too fast to stop.

He clattered up. "Your Honor, I hate to interrupt."

Chitty whirled around and scowled.

Catfish ignored him. "May we approach the bench?"

"Come," the judge commanded.

Catfish grabbed his cane, pausing halfway to the bench to check his watch again. Just two more minutes.

Chitty waited, already at the bench, still glowering.

"What is it, Catfish?" the judge asked.

"I was wondering, judge, if Mr. Chitty has the stolen money, I'd like to see it before the jury does."

Judge Goodrich eyed Chitty. "That acceptable to you?"

The veins in Chitty's neck were about to burst. "Your Honor, that's absurd. He doesn't have a right to see my evidence in advance."

Catfish shrugged. "I just thought it might be better to look at it first, while we're already up here, in case I have an objection the jury shouldn't hear."

"What objection?" Chitty almost screamed.

Probably less than a minute now.

Catfish shook his head. "Not sure till I see it."

"All right," Chitty spewed, his hand shaking as he ripped open the pouch and thrust a small stack of money at him.

Catfish carefully examined each of the hundred-dollar treasury notes one by one, front and back. Each bore the image of Admiral Farragut, damn him. He handed them back. "Thank you, counsel. Judge, looks like they're in order after all. No objections. Sorry to interrupt things."

Chitty glared at him.

"Let's move along," the judge said, sounding impatient. But was that a subtle twinkle in his eye when he looked at Catfish?

When they turned away from the bench, Chitty pressed close to Catfish and hissed at him. "Cheap parlor trick." The peacock strutted back to his table.

Parlor trick? Catfish didn't yet have any facts to defend his client with or any law either for that matter, but he'd defend him any way he could till he did.

He checked his watch. Dang. It must be behind schedule.

Chitty, pouch in hand, leaned on the witness rail. "Sergeant Quinn, before you were interrupted you were about to tell the jury . . ."

The rumbling of a train sounded faintly.

His watch must've been fast.

". . . if you found anything else of importance?"

A train whistle shrieked so loudly it rattled the light bulbs hanging over the counsel tables. Chitty flinched; Catfish smiled.

"Wait a minute," the judge said, turning to the jury. "Gentlemen, that's the afternoon Santa Fe. It'll take about five minutes for it to back up on the switch, and we won't be able to hear a thing, so we'll patiently wait."

Chitty turned on Catfish, his eyes furious.

The train lurched into its daily, agonizing, squeaking, scraping, hissing switch to a different track less than a block away from the courthouse. How many times had Catfish waited out that disturbance during trial?

Chitty hunched over the prosecution table the entire time, his head down, his arms bracing himself on the table, his pearl cufflinks sparkling, his Grand Army of the Republic watch fob dangling from its gold chain. Figured.

When it finally ended, all the steam was out of the prosecution case.

Chitty's eyes slowly lifted from his table and fixed on Quinn. "What did you find in the shanty next to the defendant?"

"Stuffed into his coat, which he was using as a blanket, was a wad of cash money."

Catfish looked up from his notetaking. No bag?

"What denominations and how much?"

"Hundred-dollar treasury notes. We found twenty."

Chitty displayed the notes the jury. The jurors eyed Toby. He didn't return their gaze, just rocked back and forth.

Where was the rest of the money? And the bag?

"Are you aware what denominations the express money was in?"

"It was hundreds."

Chitty started to sit but caught himself halfway. "By the way, what color was the coat he had?"

"Brown."

"Thank you, Sergeant. No further questions."

Jaybird spoke from his seat. "No ques—"

Catfish clamped a hand on his arm and jumped up. "May I cross-examine, Your Honor?"

"Proceed."

Catfish smiled at the officer. "How do, Sergeant. Nice to see you today."

Quinn nodded politely.

"I take it you didn't find the money bag in that shanty?"

"No, sir."

"Or any more money?"

"No, sir."

Catfish scratched his head. "So, there's at least twenty-three thousand dollars still missing?"

"There is."

"So, if I'm following you, you think the man stole twenty-five thousand dollars—let's see, that's two hundred and fifty notes—but you only found twenty notes?"

"Correct."

"Don't know where the rest is?"

"I don't."

"Think he spent it all?"

"I doubt it."

Catfish shrugged. "Maybe buried it on Treasure Island?"

A teacher on the jury hid a smile behind one hand.

"I doubt that too. He hid it someplace, though."

"You know whether Mr. Topper owns that shanty?"

"No."

"And you don't know of any other property he might own?" Catfish gazed toward the windows thoughtfully. "Maybe a big ranch out in the country somewhere where he could have buried the loot?"

The hostler chuckled.

"No, sir."

"I assume you asked Mr. Topper if he stole that money before you arrested him?"

"I did."

"Didn't say he did, did he?"

"Nor did he deny it. My superior also questioned him after we brought him in."

"Who's that?"

"Lieutenant Palmer."

Catfish broke into a grin. "Palmer? You mean that young fella who looks for finger smudges on things?"

"He's done that before." Quinn undoubtedly remembered how Catfish had humiliated Palmer on cross-examination during Cicero Sweet's trial.

"He didn't find any of those finger smears on the bicycle, did he?"

"No, sir."

Catfish inched closer to his client. "When you talked to Toby, was he rocking back and forth like he is now?"

"Yes, among other odd behaviors."

"Peculiar fella?" he asked in a lower voice.

"Yes, sir, in my opinion."

Catfish watched Toby rock back and forth. "Doesn't look much like one of the Dalton Gang, does he?"

"I've never seen them."

Catfish winked at Schoolcraft, who sat stoically on the front row of the gallery, hands resting on the crook of his blackthorn cane. Schoolcraft's eyes narrowed.

"Pass the witness," Catfish said.

Chitty leaned back in his chair. "Nothing further."

The courtroom door opened, and Catfish's heart sank. It was Bob Lazenby, a friend of his and a man as honest as the day is long—and apparently the next witness against his client.

Chapter 5

Why hadn't Bob Lazenby looked Catfish in the eye even once since he'd entered the courtroom? His demeanor was deadly serious, out of the ordinary for him. They'd been pals for years, socialized together. Met most Friday afternoons with the rest of the fellas at the bar of the McClelland Hotel. In fact, Bob was a founding member of the McClelland Hotel Bar Association. But today it was as if they'd never met.

"Would you kindly state your full name for the jury, please?" Chitty asked.

"Robert Sherman Lazenby."

Chitty questioned Bob about himself first, but Catfish already knew all that: twenty-eight years old, married two years, expecting a child any day. Bob was superintendent of the Artesian Manufacturing & Bottling Company.

"Where were you, sir," Chitty said, "at approximately seven forty on the morning of September fifth?"

"I was headed for the Texas Central depot."

That train depot was across the Brazos River in East Waco. He'd have to cross the suspension bridge to get there.

"Were you alone?" Chitty asked.

"No, I was taking a business associate to the depot to catch a train."

"Who was he?"

"Mr. Sam Prim."

Catfish didn't know him, but he'd heard Bob talk about him many times. Prim was president of the Dublin Bottling Works, a company that bottled Dr. Pepper and Circle-A sodas for Bob's company.

"Where was he going?" Chitty asked.

"His home in Dublin. If I recall correctly, the train was scheduled to leave just after eight o'clock that morning."

"Why was he here in Waco?"

"He'd been here to work with me on an exhibit we're planning for the Cotton Palace."

"What's the Cotton Palace?"

Some jurors chuckled. Chitty must not have read any local newspapers. The Cotton Palace was the talk of Waco these days—indeed, around the region—and had been for months.

"The Cotton Palace is a fair we'll hold over at Padgitt Park celebrating King Cotton and every other commercial and cultural endeavor as well. The fair's to be an annual thing and opens November eighth."

"I see," Chitty said. "So, you expect people to come in for the fair from around the county?"

Bob smiled. "No, sir, from around the whole country."

"Well, quite ambitious, I'm sure." Chitty tossed his hand in the air, flashing his pearl cuff stud.

Catfish discreetly pulled his coat sleeve back to reveal his tarnished brass cuff button. Martha would be horrified.

"Back to Mr. Prim," Chitty said. "You testified you were going to the train depot. What route did you take?"

"I picked him up at the Pacific Hotel, and then we went on Franklin to First Street, then over to the suspension bridge."

Chitty went to the jury box, placing a hand on the rail in front of the hotel clerk. "Tell the gentlemen what happened as you turned from First Street onto the bridge."

"I'd just gotten to the bridge approach, past the old tollbooth, when Mr. Prim cried out, and I looked ahead on the bridge where he pointed."

"What did you see?"

"Not very much, actually. I've been afflicted with poor eyesight since childhood, so it was all a blur to me. But then I heard two gunshots."

The jurors watched him closely. Catfish hoped they'd picked up the poor eyesight comment. Maybe he hadn't seen Toby there at all.

"Could you see the shooter?"

Bob shook his head. "I could make out the express wagon, but that's about it."

Good man, Bob. Catfish rocked his chair until it screeched, then squinted at Chitty to drive home the point to the jury. He could feel them watching.

"You mentioned Mr. Prim cried out. What did he say?"

"Objection!" Catfish cried, rising to his feet. "Hearsay."

"Prim was witnessing a robbery and murder, Your Honor," Chitty replied calmly, lifting a law book. "His exclamations are trustworthy by virtue of the spontaneous utterance exception to the hearsay rule."

"Judge—"

"And besides," Chitty added, "Prim's our next witness."

"Overruled. You may answer."

"He said, 'Look, robbery' or something to that effect, and the first gunshot was almost the same instant."

"Did he say anything else?"

Catfish jumped up again before he could answer. "Judge, note our exception—and may we have a running objection to hearsay?"

Judge Goodrich seemed inclined to let in all the hearsay—maybe a point of appeal for Harley.

"I'll grant your running objection. Proceed, Mr. Chitty."

"What did he say?" Chitty repeated.

"After the second gunshot, he said somebody had shot two men."

"Somebody shot two men," Chitty echoed, gazing at the jury before returning to his table. "Did he say anything about the man's appearance?"

"I don't really recall, except he did mention a top hat."

Chitty pivoted and glanced toward Toby, as did several jurors. "A top hat, eh? Do gentlemen in Waco wear top hats often these days, Mr. Lazenby?"

"Not generally. Maybe to the opera house but not at breakfast time on Wednesday mornings."

The courthouse clock struck two. Colonel Terry bayed in response from the courthouse steps.

"What did you do after Mr. Prim mentioned the top hat?"

"I hesitated at first, but he said the shooter escaped the other direction in the wagon, so I eased my buggy toward where it happened."

"What did you find when you got there?"

Bob looked down. "Two dead men."

A streetcar outside the south windows honked its horn, and somebody started yelling something unintelligible. Chitty waited until it finished. "Did you see anything else?"

"Toby Topper's bicycle."

"How'd you know it was his?"

"He's made deliveries to me before. I've seen that bicycle many times."

Chitty stepped closer to Bob. "Do you have any doubts at all it was Mr. Topper's bicycle?"

For the first time, Bob eyed Catfish. "No."

"No further questions."

Catfish ambled to the bar and leaned against it. He'd cross-examined so many witnesses from there that the finish on the rail was worn. "How do, Bob."

"Good afternoon, Catfish."

"You know," he said with a slow smile, "I think I've heard you say before—tell me if I misquote you—you're blind as a bat."

Bob smiled back. "I am. At a distance."

"Like that morning?"

"Sure."

"Never were close enough to see the face of the shooter?"

"Nope."

"So, Mr. Lazenby, you can't swear to the jury Toby Topper was the killer?"

"I can't."

"Thank you. Pass the witness, Your Honor." Catfish sank into his chair.

"Anything further, Mr. Chitty?" the judge asked.

"Briefly." Chitty approached the court stenographer's desk. "Mr. Lazenby, have you ever seen anyone other than the defendant wearing this hat and tipping it to passersby while riding on that bicycle you saw on the bridge?"

"No."

"That's all."

"Now wait a minute, Bob." Catfish stood quickly. "You

didn't actually see anybody tipping his hat that morning, did you?"

"I didn't."

Catfish sat.

"That's all. And now we call Mr. Sam Prim." Chitty shot a glance at Catfish. "Who saw it all."

Chapter 6

"Do you have a recollection of the killings that occurred on the bridge at approximately seven forty that morning?" Chitty faced Prim across the witness rail.

"I do." Prim had a friendly way about him.

Catfish rested his jaw on his palm.

"How long had the sun been up that morning?"

"Oh, probably an hour and a half. People were beginning to stir, but there weren't many out on the streets yet, except for wagons hauling cotton. In fact, just before we got to the bridge, Mr. Lazenby pulled his buggy around a convoy of cotton haulers ahead of us."

Chitty leaned on the witness rail. "What did you first see after Mr. Lazenby turned his buggy onto the bridge approach?"

"In the distance, about halfway across the bridge, I saw a wagon ahead of us. There was a man on a bicycle coming toward us, next to the rail, on the same side of the bridge as the wagon."

Catfish pulled himself up. "Your Honor, may we approach the bench?"

"What now?" Chitty asked.

"Up here, gentlemen," the judge said.

Catfish pressed close to the bench and lowered his voice. "I'm real sorry to interrupt, Judge, but could we take a short break?"

"Why?" Chitty demanded. "I obje—"

"Hang on," the judge said. "What for, Catfish?"

"I'm so sorry, Judge, but my ginger tea has run its course."

Chitty put on a show of incredulity. "What're you talking about?"

Judge Goodrich smiled. "I believe Mr. Calloway needs to answer the call of nature."

"That's utterly absurd. He's stalling again. More parlor tricks. He can wait like everyone else."

The man was like a teakettle. Heat him up and he simmered and simmered till he boiled, then he whistled until somebody paid attention to him.

"I can't always answer for things I can't control." Catfish turned his whole body to face Chitty. "Why, you're in pissing range, counsel."

"That's outrageous!" Chitty said.

The court ordered a five-minute recess, the jurors to remain in the box. Catfish grabbed his cane and charged out as quickly as a three-legged man could. By the time he returned, almost ten minutes had elapsed. As he reentered the courtroom, he noticed Hampton Boswell was sitting inside the bar, behind the defense table. What the dickens was he doing away from the law books?

Catfish passed through the swinging gate at the bar. "Thanks, Judge."

"You may proceed now, Mr. Chitty," the judge said.

Chitty planted himself near the witness, feet spread and hands on his hips as if he was the Colossus of Rhodes. "Mr. Prim, I apologize for the defense lawyer's interrup—"

"Sorry, Mr. Prim," Catfish blurted as he took his seat. "Being older, I can't hold it in like my learned friend from the city of Dallas."

Several jurors cackled.

Chitty was still at the boiling point despite the recess. "I obj—"

"Gentlemen, enough!" the judge said. "Move along, Mr. Chitty."

While Chitty started the questioning again, Catfish rolled his chair back until he was beside Hamp and whispered to him. "Thought you were going to read some law?"

"I found something important I thought you needed to know."

"What?"

"I researched lunacy in one of the law books. The forty-first law says an insane man can't be punished."

The forty-first *law*? Maybe Article Forty-One of the Code of Criminal Procedure? Or Section Forty-One of the Penal Code? Or of the Civil Statutes? Or the Constitution? Or did Moses maybe hand down more than ten? "All right." Catfish went back to his table. No harm in letting Hamp stay.

Chitty went to the stenographer's desk. "Were you able to see the person riding the bicycle?"

"I was. At least I could see what he was wearing on his head. He had a light-colored top hat, and he repetitively took it on and off. It appeared to me he was doffing his hat to the men in the wagon, but he did it repeatedly. It was so odd it caught my eye."

Chitty flourished the hat and fired the next question as if from an artillery battery. "Is this the hat you saw the murderer wearing when he gunned down two innocent men?"

"It appears to be."

Catfish half stifled a yawn.

Chitty returned the hat to its place. "Tell the gentlemen what you saw."

Prim glanced at the jury, then back at Chitty. "The man on the bicycle pulled something black out of his belt and pointed it at the wagon. I think I cried out at that point because I thought maybe it was a gun because of the way he extended it. Sure enough, it was, and he fired two shots which killed the two men in the wagon."

"Then what happened?"

"He threw the bicycle down, grabbed the dead men, and pulled them out of the wagon. He jumped onto the wagon, whipped the horses into a trot, and escaped across the bridge."

Out of the corner of his eye, Catfish watched Toby rocking incessantly. Was all this peculiar behavior in court just play-acting? The witnesses seemed sure it was him.

"Your Honor," Chitty said, "may we ask that the defendant stand and put the hat on his head so the witness can see him?"

Catfish jumped up. "Whoa now, I object to that, Judge."

"Overruled." The judge turned to Toby. "Mr. Topper, stand if you please."

Toby didn't look. He rocked back and forth.

"Catfish, please help him," the judge said.

"Yes, Your Honor." He grabbed Toby by the right arm, pulled him up and had him stand between the defense table and the bench.

Chitty placed the hat on his head. "Mr. Topper, pleas—"

Toby grabbed the hat by the front brim, tipped it toward Chitty, put the hat back on his head, and then repeated it. Over and over.

Chitty let him do it for what felt like an eternity. "Thank you, Mr. Topper." Chitty took the hat from him.

Catfish led Toby back to his seat. The boy was a puzzle.

"Mr. Prim, did the defendant appear to be the man you saw doffing his hat before he shot the express men?"

"Yes."

Chitty eyed the jury. "That's all."

Catfish held his cane under the table and yanked the rubber tip off, slipping it into his satchel.

"Catfish," the judge said.

"All right, Mr. Prim, let's talk about what you saw." Catfish rose slowly to his feet. "I believe you said you couldn't ever see the gunman's face?"

"Not well."

"Well, sir, you were . . . what"—Catfish gestured off into the distance—"probably a hundred yards from him?"

"Probably."

"Couldn't see the details of his face?"

"I couldn't."

"Can't really swear it was Toby Topper's face?"

"No."

Catfish appreciated at least he was honest. "So, the only thing you saw that connects the shooter to Mr. Topper is his tipping of the top hat?"

"I remember seeing that very well."

Time to prove lunacy. Catfish went over to the stenographer's desk and retrieved the hat. "Mr. Prim, what Mr. Topper just did in front of the jury"—he imitated Toby's repetitive hat tipping—"that look normal to you?"

"No, sir."

He lowered his voice as if he didn't want Toby to hear. "Look like maybe something wrong in his head?"

"Objection!" Chitty shouted. "That's speculative."

"Sustained."

A different point occurred to him. Catfish took the hat back to the stenographer's desk and retrieved his cane from the defense table. "Let me ask you some questions about whether what that shooter did seemed wrong in the head." He rapped the wood-tipped cane on the floor, arresting everyone's attention. He stopped in front of the jury, tucked his cane under his coat, brought it back out holding it like a long pistol. "He pulled a six-gun from his coat?"

"Yes, sir."

"Pointed it at the wagon?" He aimed the cane at the windows.

"Yes, sir."

"Shot who first? The driver or the guard?"

"Well, let me think." He pondered the question a moment, then looked at Catfish. "The guard, I believe. The one seated on the right, anyway."

"So, the one who was holding a coach-gun in his hands?" He gripped his cane like a shotgun.

"I suppose. I didn't see what he held, but I did see a shotgun lying on the bridge when I got closer."

"The driver held the reins"—he shifted his cane to his left hand and held up the flat of his right—"not a gun?"

"Probably, right."

"So, the shooter shot the one who was better able to shoot back?"

"I suppose," Prim said.

Catfish paced in front of the jury, head down, his cane rapping the hardwood floor. Not sure the jury was getting the point he just reached himself. "If a robber intended to rob two men and first shot the one holding a gun before he could shoot back, that wouldn't exactly be wrong in the head, would it?"

Chitty popped up halfway. "Objection!"

"Sustained."

"All right." He paced away, his back to the jury—*rap* . . . *rap* . . . *rap*, his cane echoing his steps—then returned to where he'd been. "When he fired, that man was riding a bicycle, true?"

"True."

"On the rickety plank bridge, true?"

"I assume."

Catfish hoisted his cane sideways, gripped both ends as if it were handlebars, and wobbled his upper body. "Not exactly a steady surface?"

"Probably not."

"And the man he shot was, what"—he indicated the distance between himself and Chitty—"about ten feet away?"

"More or less."

"In a moving, bouncing wagon."

"Yes, sir."

Catfish thrust his forefinger to his heart. "Shot him dead with one shot?"

"Apparently."

Catfish crossed the courtroom toward Toby. *Rap . . . rap . . . rap . . .* "Mr. Prim, you been watching Mr. Topper here in court?"

"Some."

He stopped and stared at his client. He was incapable of doing what Prim had just described. "Seem like a steady fella to you?"

"I'm not sure what you mean. He's constantly moving."

"Exactly." Catfish started to sit. "Oh, by the way, this killer jumped in the wagon and took off?"

"He did."

He jabbed his thumb over his right shoulder. "Left the bicycle behind for anyone to find?"

"Well, I—yes I suppose he did. I don't know why he left it."

Catfish cocked his head. "For the life of me, I don't either." He gazed off toward the windows a moment. "I don't either."

He turned to the judge. "All I got."

The judge looked at Chitty.

"Mr. Prim," Chitty said, "Sergeant Quinn previously testified Mr. Topper was sleeping on a brown coat when he was arrested. I'll ask you, what color was the shooter's coat?"

"Brown."

Chitty pressed faster. "What size of man was the shooter in comparison to Mr. Topper?"

"He was the same size."

"Despite all the questions Mr. Calloway posed to you, do you still believe it was Mr. Topper who was on the bridge?"

He looked over at Toby and turned back to Chitty. "I do. He moved the same way. Yes, sir, I'm sure."

"No doubt?"

"No doubt."

Chapter 7

Bill Forsythe, a string bean of a boy in overalls with holes in the knees, grinned as if exceedingly pleased to be on the witness stand. No more than sixteen, the towheaded lad answered Chitty's interrogation with unwarranted relish. The last thing Catfish needed was an eager eyewitness.

About the time Bill finished answering questions about himself, the courtroom door creaked open. Harley bounded in, law books under his arm, his thatch of black hair flying, followed by Miss Peach. As relief swept over Catfish, he motioned for Harley to join him at the defense table and made a writing gesture to Miss Peach. She took station behind the defense table against the bar, her usual post during a trial where she could take notes of the testimony and serve as Catfish's extra eyes and ears.

"Bill," Chitty said, "were you on the suspension bridge in the early morning last September fifth?"

Bill grinned as if he'd done a good deed. "I sure was, mister."

"Did you see the robbery and murder?"

"Not rightly, but I heared it."

"What do you mean?"

"I was fishing from the bridge. I wanted to catch me a big ol' channel cat for supper." He flashed a grin at Catfish as if he was poking fun at a chum. "Anyways, I heared two shots, and then I turned around and seen this wagon scurrying off toward East Waco."

"Were you able to see who was driving it?"

"I seen he was wearing a top hat"—he nodded Toby's direction—"like he does."

"Do you know the defendant?"

Bill craned his neck around to gawk at Toby. "Seen him around, you know. Fellas make fun of him 'cause he's scary."

"Just a minute, young man," Judge Goodrich interrupted. "Answer only what you're asked."

"Yes, sir, Judge," he said contritely.

"Bill," Chitty said, "what did you do after you heard the gunshots?"

His eyes bugged out, and his mouth flopped open. "I seen these two fellas laying on the bridge, and I run over to 'em."

"Were they dead?"

"One of 'em was. He was stone cold dead. The other one looked me right in the eye." His own eyes popped wider as if to demonstrate. "St. Peter ain't got hold of him yet."

The widow Hook jumped up and scampered out, sobbing, her brother at her side trying to console her. Old Man Stanek stayed put.

"Did I say something wrong?" Bill said innocently.

"Not at all," Chitty replied. "The express man who looked at you: Was he conscious?"

"Huh?"

"Was he awake?"

"Like I told you, mister, he looked me square in the eye."

"All right, did he say anything?"

Catfish shot out of his chair. "Object to hearsay!"

"The man made a dying declaration, Judge," Chitty

responded, swatting at the objection as if it was a horse fly.

Harley tugged on Catfish's sleeve. He leaned over, and Harley whispered in his ear.

After conferring, Catfish addressed the judge. "If the court please, my son will argue for the defense on this."

"What do you have to say, Harley?" the judge asked.

Harley had a steady, sincere countenance—he didn't yet know enough about the case to be worried—as he hoisted a weighty calfskin tome. "Your Honor, under Article Six Hundred Sixty of the Code of Criminal Procedure, the prosecution must lay a predicate that the declarant was conscious of his approaching death and believed he had no hope of recovery. The State hasn't proved that." He took the open book to the bench and shoved it over to the judge.

Catfish retreated to Miss Peach's side, opposite young Boswell, while Harley argued. She already began to draw daisies on the top of the page above her shorthand notes. When she joined the firm and took over the note-taking job in court, it freed him to keep a better eye on the witnesses.

"The man had just been shot, Judge," Chitty said in response to Harley's argument. "He was spilling blood all over the bridge, and this witness will say he died right after he spoke. That's circumstantial evidence to support the predicate."

"It doesn't prove he had no hope of recovery," Harley shot back.

"Your Honor," Chitty answered, "this kind of hearsay statement is trustworthy because a man on his deathbed knows he has nothing to gain by lying since he won't be alive to reap the fruits of a lie."

The judge began to read the code provision to himself.

Miss Peach held her pad for Catfish to see. She'd written:

King John, Act V, Scene IV. He flashed her a puzzled look, and she smiled knowingly. Expect he'd later hear Shakespeare's take on it.

"Well, I'm not sure about this one," Judge Goodrich said, "but I'll overrule it. Gentlemen of the jury, you're about to receive in evidence a hearsay statement. It's your job to decide if it's trustworthy or not and give it weight accordingly."

Several jurors nodded.

"Note our exception, Your Honor," Catfish said, returning to his place. He winked at Harley discreetly. *Maybe the Court of Criminal Appeals will have the last word.*

"So noted," the judge said.

"What did the dying man say?" Chitty asked.

"He said, 'Topper,' then he went dead as a doornail." Bill pointed a scrawny dirty finger at Toby. "Topper's what he said, sure as I'm a Christian."

Chitty eyed the jury. "Nothing further."

Catfish stood and faced the boy for cross-examination. "'Topper?'"

"Uh-huh, that's what he said." He grinned toward Toby. "Toby Topper."

"Now, he didn't actually say 'Toby,' did he?"

He shook his head. "I don't recall that, but it's what he meant."

"Well, sir, the judge doesn't want you to speculate about what he might have meant." He ran his fingers through his hair, studied the floor a moment, and fixed his eyes back on young Bill. "You testified you'd just seen a man driving away wearing a top hat, didn't you?"

"That's true as true can be."

"And then the express man said 'topper'?"

"True again."

"Sure he didn't say 'top hat' or maybe 'top'?"

"Nope, he said 'Topper' plain as day. Then he croaked."

No shaking that boy. "That's all," Catfish said.

Bill sauntered out, gawping at Toby as he passed.

"The State rests," Chitty announced, gazing at the jury as if he proved Jesus ascended into Heaven.

***

During the recess that followed Bill's testimony, Catfish called Harley and Miss Peach together for a talk. Hamp Boswell pulled a chair too. Jaybird snoozed at the far end of the table, and Toby rocked.

Harley leaned in. "Papa, I read up on insanity challenges."

"Good, that's great," Catfish said. "I want to move for a continuance of this trial and for a separate jury to try the issue of his competence to stand trial, if your research supports that."

"It does," Harley said.

"I'd hoped so," Catfish said. "This jury is tainted by hearing things they shouldn't. If we have to go to verdict with them, we'll lose. I want a fresh jury to try lunacy, and I want time to get ready. I expect Judge Goodrich will do that. He was troubled with the way the trial was going with Jaybird defending." He glanced down the table. Jaybird's head was on his chest.

"I think that could work," Harley said.

"I don't know how long a delay he'll give us, but any will help." Catfish turned to Miss Peach. "You get anything set up with Senator Coke?"

"I'm afraid he's not available, sir. He's in bed, and they're worried it might be scarlet fever."

That's a blow. He wanted Coke to help with the insanity

defense while he focused on the robbery. Catfish eased back in his chair. "I was counting on him."

"I told him briefly about the case," Miss Peach said, "and he mentioned he had an idea that might help us anyway. I have his telephone number, and he'll be home tonight."

"I think I know what he has in mind," Catfish said, stroking his whiskers.

Hamp pulled his chair closer. "What can I do, Mr. Calloway?"

Did that boy need to be told again he was supposed to be reading the law? On the other hand, Catfish appreciated enthusiasm. "There is something you can help me with."

"Anything at all."

"I'm thinking the foreman of this jury is going to be a man named Bonner, Joseph Bonner. I don't know much about him, but I'll need to before closing argument."

"How do you know he's going to be the foreman?" Miss Peach asked.

"Just a prediction, but watch him. He's the one with the high collar and gray hair." He stabbed his cane at the right rear corner of the empty jury box. "Only one who talks much to the bailiff. Bosses the others around. Always paying attention in court."

"What do you want me to do?" Hamp asked.

"Go back to the office and look him up in the city directory. Find out everything you can about him."

"That's all?" His shoulders slumped.

"Important work, son."

Hamp didn't protest but didn't rush to leave either. He departed only when the judge returned to court. The jury was still out on break.

"Judge," Catfish said, "if it please the court, I have a matter to take up."

"Proceed," the judge said, settling back on the bench.

Catfish leaned on his cane. "Since I just got into the case today, we'd like some time to prepare our case. I haven't even had the opportunity to speak with my client much."

"That seems reasonable. I think—"

As expected, Chitty started to boil. "We object to any delay, Your Honor. They agreed to this trial setting and should be ready to proceed. Mr. Calloway has obfuscated and procrastinated long enough. He's hindering justice."

Catfish eyed the judge. Better go ahead and play his cards now. "Your Honor, we move for continuance of this trial, so you can impanel a separate jury to try the issue of Mr. Topper's competence to stand trial for murder. We contend he's in a state of lunacy, and we need time to gather evidence from other sources."

"That's ridiculous, Judge," Chitty said indignantly. "They waived any competence challenge by failing to make it before trial. They even asked the court to set the case for trial on the murder charges. Mr. Jaye did that." Chitty pointed an accusing finger at Jaybird.

Jaybird flinched at the sudden attention and eyed Catfish like an errant child.

Chitty ignored him. "Then when you called the docket this morning, he announced ready for trial."

"Mr. Jaye," the judge said, "did you file an insanity plea?"

He started to stammer an answer from his chair, but Catfish dragged him up.

"Let me see here." Jaybird shuffled through some papers. "Did I file a what now?"

The judge rubbed his hair backward with both hands.

"Your Honor," Catfish began.

Without looking, the judge held up his hand to stop him and studied the court's file. "The docket sheet doesn't show any such insanity plea filed by the defense. What I do find is a joint request, signed by both Mr. Chitty and Mr. Jaye, asking me to set the case for trial on the merits in this term of court. I did so at the request of both parties, and I don't intend to continue the case."

"Well then, Your Honor," Catfish said, "we ask leave of court to withdraw our request, and we ask for a hearing on competence. Mr. Topper's entitled to have a separate jury decide the lunacy question."

Judge Goodrich yanked off his spectacles and aimed them at Catfish. "So, you're asking me to put this trial on hold, set a sanity hearing on another day and summon a new jury to decide that?"

"Yes, sir."

"That's absurd," Chitty said, boiling over. "That's what they're really after by this maneuver. The jury's going to convict him, and they're trying to avoid that by country chicanery."

Catfish huffed. *Well now, Mr. Dallas Lawyer, of course I'm trying to avoid a conviction, but accusing me of chicanery and insulting our local bar is unkind.*

"We demand the court deny their motion," Chitty said.

The judge's face turned sour. "I'm not going to grant a continuance once I've started a trial, and we'll finish by Friday, gentlemen. I have other cases set Monday. I find the defendant waived any claim he's not competent to stand trial. You will proceed with your defense and not mention to the jury anything about insanity. We will follow the law in this court. Understood?"

He must not be as troubled about Toby's plight as Catfish thought. A quick glance at Harley drew only a shrug. "Yes, Your Honor, we understand."

The bailiff brought the jury back in. Catfish stared blankly at the defense table in front of him. He glanced over at his client, who rocked back and forth as if he had no concern in the world. Couldn't put him on the stand, not in that condition. Their best chance was to get a different jury—one not tainted by evidence about the murders—to find him incompetent to stand trial, but the judge wouldn't permit that.

"Gentlemen of the jury," the judge said, "you will now hear the defense opening remarks."

Jaybird, wide-eyed as a frightened child, looked at Catfish. "Shall I open?" he whispered in a voice all could hear.

Catfish gave a single, discreet shake of the head. "I'll do it."

Slowly and deliberately, he made his way to that familiar place where he did his work. It was a sacred place—ten feet in front of the jury rail, dead center, between his client and a jury ready to convict. A man's life in the balance. It had been as comfortable a place to him as was a field to a farmer or a forge to a blacksmith. It was where he contributed to mankind the best he had to offer. For almost four decades he'd lived and breathed to stand in that place.

Now he stood between Toby Topper and the scaffold, but his client couldn't tell him what had happened, he didn't have any time to investigate, and the judge wouldn't let him prove Toby was a lunatic. Silently, he leaned with both hands on the handle of his cane until the oak floor creaked.

The twelve waited.

Over his right shoulder Judge Goodrich's chair squeaked. "Catfish?"

Words were Catfish's stock-in-trade, yet at this moment, in this place, he had no idea what to say.

Chapter 8

It was like standing in the muddy shallows of the river, sinking slowly into the mire with nowhere to go but down. A couple of the jurors no longer looked Catfish in the eye.

His client rocked while Harley buried his head in a law book. Miss Peach watched him expectantly.

"Gentlemen of the jury," he began, "the State of Texas has the burden of proving Mr. Topper's guilt beyond all reasonable doubt. That's a heavy burden. They've not done so, and now it's time you hear from us."

He stared at the floor, tapping it once with his cane. "We will . . . We will call witnesses."

But who and what would they say? He paced toward the bar—rap . . . rap . . . rap—then stopped and slowly turned. Going only on instinct, he edged into deeper water. "Look at Mr. Topper, gentlemen. Does he seem to you like a man who was capable of planning a robbery? Of gunning down two men while riding a bicycle? We'll prove he's ... too simple-minded to do that."

Chitty leapt to object, but before he could the judge roared. "Up here, gentlemen!"

The four lawyers hurried to the bench.

Judge Goodrich was red as a beet. "What are you doing? I

instructed you not to go into insanity."

"Respectfully, Your Honor, I'm not. You told me not to go into his competency to stand trial—that he's insane today. My point is that he wasn't capable of committing this crime because of his mental condition. He's innocent."

"They waived any claim about his mental condition," Chitty railed.

"Respectfully, Judge Goodrich," Harley interjected, holding up the open Penal Code of Texas. "Our defense to the merits of the charges is insanity. That's Article Forty-One. Insanity at the time of the crime is independent of a competence challenge on grounds of present insanity to stand trial for the crime. We're entitled to prove he was in a state of insanity on September fifth."

Once again, Chitty simmered. "They waived that defense by not filing a special plea of insanity before tri—"

"If I might, Your Honor," Harley said, eyeing Chitty defiantly and grabbing another book from the table, "Article Four Hundred Ninety-Seven of the Code of Criminal Procedure says a plea of not guilty is sufficient to raise the insanity defense."

Catfish didn't even realize that. That boy knew law like Jaybird knew drinking. *Keep after him, son!*

"No special insanity plea is required," Harley concluded.

The judge, calmer now, examined the code provision. "It looks like the defense is entitled to go into insanity at the time of the murders, Mr. Chitty."

Steam hissed from under Chitty's lid. "But—"

"Your objection is overruled."

Chitty stomped back to his table, but the judge ignored him. "You may proceed with your case, gentlemen."

Catfish returned to his place before the jury. "Gentlemen,

Toby Topper was insane at the time. He was incapable of planning and carrying out these crimes. We'll bring you witnesses to prove he was in a state of insanity on September fifth. Thank you."

The judge turned to the jury. "All right, gentlemen, you will now hear whatever evidence the defense chooses to present. Mr. Calloway, proceed."

Saying it was one thing, proving it was another. "Respectfully, Judge, may we at least have until in the morning to begin?"

Chitty leapt up. "And I object to that!"

Catfish shrugged. "Judge, they've had a month to get ready, and I've just had a few hours. It's not fair to make us present our case until we've had time to prepare."

Chitty glared back at him. The kettle was shuddering. "Jaye had plenty of time."

The judge glanced at Jaybird and back at Catfish. "We'll begin at nine o'clock sharp, Mr. Calloway," the judge said. "I remind you, however, we will finish trial this week one way or the other. Court will be in recess." Judge Goodrich exited by the side door after the bailiff led the jurors out.

Chitty whirled on Catfish and boiled over. "You'll regret your hubris."

Hamp Boswell's jaw dropped. Chitty stormed out.

"Well, let's see," Catfish said, turning to Harley and Jaybird and counting off their sins on his fingers, "we're guilty of cheap parlor tricks, obfuscation, procrastination, chicanery, and hubris. Not a bad day's work for country lawyers."

Pray God they'd have more than that tomorrow. The only way to save Toby was to prove he's a lunatic incapable of committing the crime. Coke had to come through for them by morning. He could get them the witness they needed. Catfish pulled the rubber cap from his satchel and pressed it back onto his cane.

***

Harley was the first one downstairs and out to the steps of the courthouse, where Colonel Terry was dutifully waiting for Papa. The townspeople knew if the colonel was guarding the courthouse steps, then Catfish Calloway was in court. Despite his age, the colonel hopped up, wagged his tail, and reported to Papa for orders. An ear rub put him at parade rest.

Papa gazed toward the western sky. "We got about an hour or so of daylight. Harley, let's go over to the bridge and walk through what happened. I need to see it with my own eyes now we've heard the witnesses."

"Right."

"Miss Peach, we'll meet you back at the office by seven for that talking-phone business with Senator Coke."

She hesitated. "Mr. Calloway, I have a longstanding engagement at six, which I would hate to miss, but I think I can get back to the office by half-past-seven, if that would be acceptable?"

"Of course," Papa said. Then he grinned, flashing that blue-eyed twinkle. "Meeting a suitor?"

She flushed and glanced at Harley. She didn't get embarrassed often, but when she did her face glowed. "No, sir, not at all."

"I know how to operate the telephone, Papa," Harley said.

"No rush," Papa said, waving him off. "Miss Peach, get on with your business, and we'll see you at seven thirty."

She walked briskly off, heading up Franklin Avenue.

"Miss Peach got a fella?" Papa asked.

Unexpectedly, Harley's own face warmed. It was something

he wondered lately too. She was too pretty not to, but some fellows might be put off by her assertiveness. He found it appealing. "I've seen her several nights going somewhere near my boarding house."

"On Franklin? Doesn't she board over with Mrs. Sparks?"

"On Columbus."

Papa gazed over toward Columbus Avenue, the opposite direction from Franklin. "I wonder what she's up to? You know, Harley, I wager that young lady has a beau after all."

Harley had seen her walking with a young man once. A Baylor professor, he thought, but he wasn't sure. It had bothered him a little, but it frankly wasn't any of his business—or Papa's for that matter. She was their employee, and their relationship with her was strictly business.

Harley lifted his briefcase. "Don't we need to go on over to the bridge while there's daylight?"

***

The bridge was suspended from parallel steel cables, both enormous in circumference as well as length, sagging between castle-like towers on both banks of the Brazos River. Harley probably stood close to the spot where the express agents had fallen. There was a large area of discoloration in the timber planking of the bridge's deck, but he couldn't be sure it was blood. Because the cables sloped upwards toward the opposing towers almost equally in both directions from where he stood, he concluded the robbery must have taken place about halfway across the bridge.

Papa waited at the far west end of the bridge, next to the old unused toll booth, about where Lazenby and Prim were when the robbery occurred. He waved his cane and began stepping off the distance. The colonel trotted beside him.

Papa reached Harley's position and looked back to the toll booth. "That's about a hundred twenty or twenty-five yards."

Harley had thought it was less. "I didn't have much trouble seeing you, and the sun's going down now."

"You can't make out faces at that distance," Papa added.

Harley wondered why it mattered. Prim saw Toby's top hat and brown coat, and Quinn identified Toby's bicycle. "You're right, but I didn't have any trouble seeing your hat or the color of your coat."

Papa glanced back toward the toll booth. "Seeing a face is different. But then again, nobody claimed he saw Toby's face, did he?"

True, but nothing they'd seen at the bridge so far changed Harley's feeling that Toby killed the express men.

Papa walked over to the south bridge rail and pointed his cane at the bridge deck. "And Toby's bicycle was about here. Wasn't any doubt in anybody's mind it was Toby's bicycle."

"It's very distinctive."

"So, the witnesses are probably right about the top hat and the bicycle. Probably the brown coat too. And that all matches Toby." He turned around and rested his forearms on the rail, gazing at the water.

Harley did the same. By then, the sun was below the horizon over the city to their right, leaving only the receding light of dusk. The dark water of the Brazos River rushed by thirty feet below. Fish jumped near the east bank. Colonel Terry curled up against the rail for a nap. It was a peaceful place for such violence to occur.

Harley finally spoke. "It seems to me our defense is insanity. Maybe somebody put him up to the robbery. And if he did, Toby was too simple-minded to refuse. Our only possible defense is an insane man isn't responsible for his actions."

Papa bit the tip off a White Owl and spat it into the river. "I wonder why they're in such a hurry to try him. Almost like they want to execute him before anybody has a chance to think about it."

"Maybe because it's so clear-cut."

Papa lit the cigar. "The boy seems mighty odd to me, but I don't know if that's insanity in the eyes of the law. Never in over thirty years had a client I thought was insane." He blew smoke back across the bridge and faced Harley. "What'd you find out about legal insanity?"

"Texas follows the M'Naghten Rule." He opened his notepad and flipped through the pages. He read aloud as he held the pad to the dwindling daylight. "The accused can only discharge himself from responsibility by proving that his intellect was so disordered that he did not know the nature and quality of the act he was doing and that it was an act which he ought not to do. If he had sufficient intelligence to know what he was doing, and to know that the act was wrong, and had the will and power to refrain from doing it, he is in contemplation of law, responsible for the act committed."

Papa scratched his head. "Sufficient intelligence to know what he was doing."

Harley tapped his notepad with his forefinger. "If he didn't know right from wrong, he's legally insane."

Off in the distance to the south a whistle shrieked. Colonel Terry's head shot up. The grinding, clanking, squeaking of a northbound train sounded through the dusk. It must have been the evening Cotton Belt heading toward the nearer of the two railroad bridges. Down the river beyond the Cotton Belt bridge, in the dusky light, lay the KATY Railroad bridge. Harley checked his watch—it wasn't even six thirty yet. No, it was more likely the KATY. The headlamp of the locomotive popped into view on the west bank, a trail of billowing gray smoke arcing into the sky, and the train rumbled across, rattling the giant wooden trestle bridge of the Missouri-Kansas-Texas line, gaining speed as it reached the east bank and finally vanished to the north. The tranquility of the river slowly returned.

Harley looked at Papa. "Do you think we can prove he didn't know right from wrong?"

"I have an expert witness in mind." Papa stared off the bridge as if he was thinking out loud. He puffed on his cigar until the orange tip glowed brightly in the fading light. "If Dick Coke can just get him for us on short notice."

Harley waited to hear his name, but after a minute or two, Papa went a different direction. "What do you think of our new apprentice?"

The honest answer was *not much,* but he hadn't been around the young man enough to make an accurate judgment. "It's probably too early to tell. He asked to see what I found in my insanity research."

Papa chuckled. "I thought so."

Harley must have missed something Boswell had said. "Why'd you ask him to investigate that juror?"

"Oh, give him some reason to feel useful mainly. Seems eager enough."

"Maybe too eager."

"We'll see," Papa said. "I promised his family we'd make a lawyer of him. They're good folks."

Harley looked over his shoulder at the sunset. Except for the faint gray clouds, the western sky had a glow. By his side, Papa gazed off toward the courthouse rising high above the riverbank. The warm evening light illuminated its north face as its clock tower stood watch above the city.

"Son."

"Yes, sir."

Papa nudged him with his elbow. "Nice work in court today."

"Thanks."

"You were clearheaded, knew the law, and knew exactly what to argue. Your old man almost got outflanked by Chitty."

Two ducks glided into a wing-flapping landing on the river below.

Harley inched his elbow over until it touched Papa's. "You did just the right thing."

In the faint light of dusk, Papa's blue eyes were misty gray.

Chapter 9

"Dick!" Mr. Calloway bellowed into the telephone as if he and the senator were conversing from opposite riverbanks. "Dick!"

Miss Peach covered her smile, and Harley looked away.

Mr. Calloway shouted again into the mouthpiece. "Dick, can you hear me?"

Boswell gaped at the senior Calloway. Even the colonel found the racket objectionable and lumbered to the other room.

"Sir," she whispered, "you don't need to yell. He can hear you."

She and Harley exchanged glances, both stifling grins.

Mr. Calloway, resting on the corner of her desk, finally settled on the proper volume of conversation, the proper way to hold the mouthpiece, and the right proximity to the ear for the receiver. It was only the second time she'd ever seen him talk on a telephone. Bit by bit he revealed Toby's story to the senator. He actually enjoyed using the *talking* phone.

She'd heard all about Richard Coke from Mr. Calloway before. The two of them were quite close in age. With Sam Houston's encouragement, Coke had come to Texas from Virginia long before the war and settled in Waco to practice law. Later he served as a judge, then as governor, then as senator. She'd seen him only once. He had a bushy gray beard below a shiny dome of a head, was over six feet tall, and must have weighed in excess of two hundred fifty pounds. He was such a powerful stump speaker.

His voice was still big. "Catfish, if I were you . . ."

Mr. Calloway winked at her, holding the receiver away from his ear again as Coke's voice boomed through the wires—"So when you see David"—and slid off the desk and moved the other way until the telephone wire pulled him back.

Mr. Calloway ended their conversation with profuse thanks and felicitations. He plopped into her desk chair, lit a White Owl, and propped his feet. "Sounds like Dr. David Wallace is our man."

"Is insanity his field?" Harley asked.

"He specializes in diseases of the mind. Coke says if anybody can prove the boy's a lunatic, it's David Wallace. I figured Coke could help us with him. They're old friends. He promised to have Wallace at the courthouse first thing tomorrow."

Mr. Calloway checked his watch. "Miss Peach, while we're in court, you wait outside and intercept him. Take him to the county courtroom on the first floor and wait there until we send for you. When he examines Toby, go with him."

She nodded.

Mr. Calloway blew smoke at the front door. He must have remembered Boswell. "Hamp, since you've studied lunacy, you can go along with her to Wallace's examination."

"Yes, sir," Boswell replied eagerly. "And, sir, I discovered some things about Mr. Bonner."

"Who?"

"The jury foreman. You asked me to investigate him, remember?"

"Of course," Mr. Calloway said. "Write it up so we'll have it before closing argument."

"Sir," Miss Peach said, "I've never heard of Dr. Wallace. Can you tell me something about him before we meet?"

Boswell snapped to attention. "I can ask my father about him."

Mr. Calloway tapped ashes into a tray. "Wallace had a general medical practice here in Waco with Dr. Sears about twenty years ago. He and Coke got to be friends. When Coke was elected governor, he appointed Wallace to be the first superintendent of the new state lunatic asylum in Austin, and about ten years ago he headed the new lunatic asylum in Terrell. He's been back in Waco awhile in a consulting practice."

"He's well thought of in statewide medical circles," Harley added.

"He does seem to be an impressive person," she said.

As Mr. Calloway headed back to his office, he hesitated by the door. "Might ask him if the story's true he treated Carlota."

She didn't know anyone named Carlota. "Who?"

"Empress Carlota of Mexico."

How thrilling—a physician who treats royalty. She couldn't wait to meet him.

Chapter 10

Catfish should have expected this. Chitty came to court the next morning ready to march through Georgia. He had a grim disposition and ranks of law books arrayed on his table. He was now flanked by a slight, bookish clerk and a second lawyer, an equally imperious man in his thirties. That young fella was balding with a fleshy face and a huge drooping mustache, like a belligerent walrus.

Chitty swaggered toward the bench. "Your Hon—"

The judge held up his hand. "Hold on!" He started fidgeting with his gavel. He'd acted particularly agitated ever since he took the bench that morning. "Gentlemen, something has come to my attention we need to address right away. One of the jurors"—he checked his notes—"Mr. Bonner, came to my chambers first thing this morning and told me somebody showed up at his home yesterday afternoon while we were in session here and interrogated his wife about him. Wanted to know about his politics and such. This man told her he was from this court."

"What?" Chitty exclaimed.

Furious, Catfish cocked his head at Chitty's table. Was it the walrus or their scrawny understrapper?

"He was a young man, apparently." Judge Goodrich consulted his notes again. "He said his name was Boswell."

No! Catfish whirled around. Hamp was white as a sheet.

It couldn't have been—what was he—"Judge," Catfish stammered, avoiding Chitty's gaze, "this is my apprentice, Mr. Hamp Boswell of Austin. It sounds like—"

"Mr. Boswell," the judge said, scowling at Hamp, "did you go to Mr. Bonner's home yesterday?"

Hamp got to his feet unsteadily. "Yes, sir." His eyes were wide.

It must've been a mistake. Catfish raked his hair back. "Your Honor—"

"No, I want to hear from this young man first," said the judge. "What were you up to?"

"Well, I was investigating the jury foreman. Mr. Calloway told me to go there."

Catfish's chest tightened.

Harley jumped up. "That's not—"

Catfish threw his hand in front of Harley. "Wait!" He struggled to dampen his tone. "Judge Goodrich, I take responsibility for this, but I believe there's been a misunderstanding."

Out of the corner of his eye, Catfish caught Chitty, hands braced on his hips.

The judge glared.

Catfish took a slow, deep breath. "I told Mr. Boswell to do some checking on Mr. Bonner, because I didn't know him." And the young fool was only supposed to check the city directory. "It's entirely my doing. I'm afraid I wasn't very clear about what I wanted him to do. He was just trying to be helpful."

"That's jury tampering," Chitty roared.

Catfish turned on him. "You don't accuse my people of law-breaking, mister!"

Rap! Rap! Rap! Goodrich rarely used his gavel. "Back down, gentlemen." He faced Hamp. "Young man, you're learning a mighty hard lesson, hopefully not too late."

"Yes, sir?"

"What you did could well be a crime."

Hamp's mouth dropped open. "I didn't—"

The judge held up his hand. "Mr. Bonner told me some things you said to his wife, and I want to be sure of what you said."

"Judge—" Catfish edged forward, but the judge's glare froze him in place.

Hamp's voice cracked. "Yes, sir?"

"Did you tell her you were from the court?"

My God! It hit Catfish like a sledgehammer.

"I'd just left here and—"

"Did you tell her that?" the judge demanded.

Hamp nodded.

The judge made a note. "Did you tell her you were investigating her husband?"

"I was—"

"Did you tell her that?"

"Yes, sir."

His head spinning, Catfish braced himself on the back of his chair.

The judge jotted something else and looked up. "Did you ask her how her husband felt about crazy people?"

He nodded again and cast a pleading look at Catfish.

"And what his politics were?"

"Yes."

"Anything else?"

"Not that I recollect, sir."

Shame flooded over Catfish. The judge had done everything he could to help them, and now he thought they'd taken advantage of him.

Judge Goodrich's head went down, his hand over his forehead. After a silence that nearly outlasted the century, he peered at Chitty. "Do you want a mistrial? If you do, I'll grant it."

Chitty and the walrus exchanged glances. "No, no, Your Honor, I'm confident Mr. Bonner wasn't intimidated by the defense's tactics. We prefer to deal with their misconduct in another way. In fact, these revelations support a motion we'd already planned to make."

"Very well, it's your choice," the judge said. "Let's hear what you have in mind."

Wilson's walrus jowls quivered as he spoke. "Your Honor, on behalf of the State of Texas, we move to disqualify Calloway & Calloway from representing the defendant."

Catfish clutched his chair. Chitty was a back-alley fighter.

"On what basis?" the judge asked.

The walrus eyed Chitty and proceeded. "Besides jury tampering, the elder Mr. Calloway has threatened violence to a prosecution witness."

Catfish swatted the air. "Nonsense."

"Quite the contrary," Wilson shot back. "He threatened to kill Detective Thaddeus Schoolcraft, who is here today ready to testify about it, should the court desire."

Catfish twisted around. Sure enough, Schoolcraft was coiled on the back bench, and he hadn't even noticed him enter. Killing was too good for the likes of him. "Your honor, I dispute that. It's true I despise the man on grounds of general and pervasive despicability. His genus of reptile isn't even classified by science yet. But I've never found it necessary to kill a man just because I disliked him."

The judge looked at the walrus. "Even if he did make a threat,

73

how does that disqualify him? Schoolcraft's already testified."

"We may need to recall him in rebuttal. Mr. Chitty and I have come to understand that in a murder case in this very court last July, Mr. Calloway became distraught and angry with a witness and threatened him. It is apparently in his nature. Witness intimidation is most unprofessional and is grounds for disqualification."

"In addition to jury tampering," Chitty added.

Catfish and Chitty glared at each other.

The walrus continued. "I ask the court to protect our witness from this man by removing him from the case."

"The defendant doesn't need three lawyers anyway," Chitty said.

That was the nub of it—they preferred to face a single jaybird.

"Judge," Catfish said, "this has nothing to do with Schoolcraft or that juror and everything to do with trying to deprive Mr. Topper of a proper defense in this trial."

"May we recall Mr. Schoolcraft to the stand?" the walrus asked.

The judge exhaled. "All right. Let's hear him."

Catfish took his chair and glanced at Harley, who gave him one subtle head shake.

Schoolcraft slithered to the witness stand. Honest Texas rattlesnakes at least have the decency to rattle before they strike, but he didn't even look Catfish's way until he settled in. His black eyes spewed venom before his words.

"You're still under oath, sir," the judge said. "Proceed, counsel."

"Detective Schoolcraft, how do you know Mr. Calloway?"

"I was witness to a murder at the train station committed by one of his sons. He represented the young man in court and cross-examined me."

Catfish's collar tightened. Memories flashed like lightening—another day in court, Schoolcraft's hideous grin, his own failures, the terror in Houston's eyes.

The gallows.

With an unsteady hand Catfish brushed lint from his coat sleeve. Harley pressed closer.

"Can you describe that cross-examination, please?" the walrus asked.

"Certainly. It was actually quite similar to Mr. Calloway's cross-examination of Mr. Orman in the murder trial last July. I'm sure Judge Goodrich remembers it well. On both occasions Mr. Calloway became irrational and lost control of himself. At any rate, after I had testified about the murder of an innocent man by his son, he became angry and threatened to kill me."

Catfish scrawled a note—they weren't even words, but no one could see them. As he wrote, he exhaled so slowly his breath betrayed no sound at all. Harley tried to read it, but Catfish pulled it back.

"Do you fear he might lose control again and do harm to you if you testify in our rebuttal case?"

"I do indeed."

Catfish blotted the nib of his pen with his thumb. The black stain spread. He hadn't been in the business of killing since the war, but if anyone could force him out of retirement, it'd be Schoolcraft.

"That's all," the walrus said.

"Catfish, any questions?"

"Not a one." He tossed his pen down as he rose. "His presence here today, obviously alive and unharmed, is proof I'm not a threat to him. I give the court my word this man has nothing to fear from my hand. He's bound for Hell without any help from me." He pulled back his coat for the judge to see. "Not even armed."

The judge turned to Jaybird. "Mr. Jaye, are you ready to proceed with the defense of this case if I disqualify Mr. Calloway?"

Jaybird remained seated, gaping at the judge. Catfish pulled him to his feet.

"Me, sir?"

Judge Goodrich glared at Jaybird. "I'll take the motion under advisement and give you my ruling in fifteen minutes. Court is in recess until then."

Chapter 11

As soon as the judge was gone, Papa spun toward Boswell, shoving his chair out of the way. Harley grabbed it before it crashed into something but stayed clear of the fray.

"Young man," Papa said, his face crimson, his blue eyes ice cold, "don't you ever do anything like that again."

"But I—"

"No buts!" Papa cried.

Chitty and Wilson stood by gawking. Schoolcraft joined them.

Harley grabbed Papa's arm. If only Miss Peach had been there to help. "Let's step outside."

The three hurried downstairs to the landing between floors where they found some privacy.

Papa pressed Boswell against the stairwell corner. "I have nothing further to say to you right now." He stabbed a finger at the boy's face. "You will march yourself back to the office. You will go to the bookshelf and find Dallam's Texas Reports, volume one. You will open it to page one, and you will start reading. Every word."

"But—"

The extent of Papa's rage took Harley by surprise.

"And you will *not* take your nose out of that book until I personally tell you it's time."

"Sir—" Boswell pleaded.

"If you finish volume one before I return, you'll start the next." He turned his back on the boy and pounded up the stairs, not even using his cane.

Boswell remained pasted against the wall. The color had not yet returned to his face.

Harley waited until Papa was out of hearing. He didn't like what Boswell had done, but he knew exactly how he was feeling. "Look, you made a mistake. He'll get over it. Don't dwell on it. Just do what he told you." Harley put his hand on Boswell's shoulder and managed a smile. "You'll be fine."

Boswell swallowed hard. "I was just trying to do what he instructed. He shouldn't be sore at me."

Harley had expected more remorse. His smile vanished. "Hope the judge doesn't disqualify us."

When he returned to the courtroom, Papa was sitting silently at the defense table, filling his fountain pen with an ink-filled eyedropper. Somehow, he didn't spill any. He didn't look up and it was no time to disturb him. Goodrich surely wouldn't disqualify Papa after he'd gone to the trouble of appointing him.

It seemed like only moments later when the door opened, the bailiff shouted, "All rise," and Judge Goodrich returned.

Once on the bench he adjusted his spectacles. "I've known Mr. Calloway for many years and there's nothing for any witness to fear from him. As for the matter with juror Bonner, based upon Mr. Calloway's assurances, I trust his apprentice will neither be seen nor heard in this court again this term nor will he disturb any juror or his family outside of this court. So Mr. Wilson, I deny your motion."

"Your Honor," Chitty said, stepping forward, "I beg you to reconsider."

"I've ruled."

Chitty didn't move. "Respectfully, we may find it necessary to seek a writ of mandamus in the Court of Criminal Appeals."

"You just go right ahead, Mr. Chitty," the judge replied calmly but growled, "Motion denied!"

Chitty retreated and dropped into his chair.

Harley let out a breath. A lawyer as experienced as Chitty should have known better than threatening a judge with reversal.

***

"We call Mr. Toby Topper."

Catfish wasn't sure about putting him on, but he had no other witness and there was little risk as long as Toby acted as he had up to that point. While Harley escorted Toby to the stand, Catfish craned his neck to see Dr. Wallace sitting by himself on the back row of the spectator gallery. He wanted his expert to watch Toby's public behavior before they met privately over lunch, but he didn't want Chitty to know about Wallace and have time to prepare for cross-examination.

When asked to place one hand on the Bible and raise the other, Toby rocked back and forth, staring straight ahead. At Catfish's direction, Harley rushed over to help. He positioned Toby's hand on the Bible and raised the other for him.

"Do you solemnly swear to tell the truth, so help you God?" the bailiff asked.

Toby didn't respond.

"Mr. Topper, I need you to answer out, please, sir," the judge said.

Toby rocked.

"We waive the oath, Your Honor," Chitty said.

Catfish eyed Chitty. Why was he being so helpful?

Judge Goodrich motioned Toby toward the witness chair. "Very well, the oath having been waived by the State, the witness will take the stand please."

Harley guided Toby to the chair.

As soon as he sat, Toby began to rock, staring straight ahead at the floor in front of the jury box.

"Mr. Topper, can you say your name?" Catfish asked.

Toby rocked.

"Toby, can you hear me?"

Toby rocked.

"Mr. Topper, do you know where you are?" Catfish asked.

Toby rocked.

"Do you understand you're in court?"

Toby rocked.

"Did you understand, on September fifth, 1894, it was wrong to take a man's life?"

Toby rocked.

Not much else he could do. Toby's want of competence was on full display both for the jury and for Dr. Wallace. "Pass the witness."

"Mr. Chitty, you may cross-examine."

"Thank you, Your Honor." Chitty went to the court stenographer's desk and retrieved the top hat.

"Is this your hat?"

Toby rocked.

Chitty carried the hat to him. Toby grabbed it, popped it on his head, and tipped it toward Chitty, over and over. He stopped rocking.

"So, it's your hat?"

Toby tipped the hat.

"Well, Mr. Topper—and by the way, is that your real name?"

Toby tipped the hat.

"Isn't the name you were born with actually Budge? Toby Budge?"

Catfish didn't know that. He looked at Jaybird, who shrugged in reply.

Toby tipped the hat.

"Let me change subjects, Mr. Topper, if you prefer that name for some reason." He glanced at the jury. "Have you ever delivered goods to the man who manufactures Dr. Pepper soda?"

Toby tipped the hat.

Chitty consulted his notes. "Robert S. Lazenby?"

"Six-One-Oh North Tenth," Toby said distinctly, neither tipping nor rocking.

"Excuse me?"

Toby tipped the hat.

Catfish eyed Harley. What had just happened? Those were the first words he'd heard his client utter.

Chitty went to his associate, leaned down, and the walrus whispered in his ear.

"Robert S. Lazenby," Chitty repeated after their conference.

"Six-One-Oh North Tenth," Toby answered.

Chitty watched him for a moment. "Artesian Manufacturing and Bottling Company?"

"One-One-Eight North Fourth," Toby said.

Catfish stiffened. What was happening? The bottling company was across Fourth Street from his law office, and that street number was about right. No one could remember addresses like that.

"So, you can speak after all." Chitty glanced at his associate, who flashed a note to him. "Risher Drug Store?"

"Five-One-One Austin Ave," Toby said, neither tipping nor rocking.

Catfish chewed the tip off a White Owl and lit it. It was as if a different fella had dropped into the witness chair from nowhere.

The walrus searched his papers and handed one to Chitty.

Chitty grinned at Catfish. "William Calloway?"

"One-Three-One-Six Washington Ave."

Catfish tried to hide his shock, but how could Toby know his exact home address?

"Harley Calloway?"

"Four-Two-Oh Franklin Ave."

That's right too. *My God!* Harley's report on the law of sanity rattled in his head: *Did he have sufficient intelligence to know what he was doing?*

"Levi Goodrich." Chitty glanced at the judge.

"Three-One-Three North Twelfth."

Judge Goodrich shifted in his chair.

Chitty lifted a document and paraded in front of the jury. He looked at juror Holcomb and at his paper. He uttered the next name confidently. "William T. Holcomb."

Holcomb glanced to his left and right, as his fellow jurors stared at him.

"Seven-Oh-Four South Eleventh."

Holcomb nodded.

Catfish had to stop this. Chitty was making Toby look like the smartest person in the room. "Your Honor, I object to the relevance of these questions."

"I'm exploring the defendant's intellectual capacity," Chitty replied smugly, "as Mr. Calloway requested."

"Overruled."

"I think one more will suffice anyway, Your Honor." He studied the document and looked at a juror on the back row. "Samuel E. Stewart."

"One-Three-Two-Oh South Twelfth," Toby answered and began tipping his hat.

Stewart's expression affirmed the address.

"Nothing further." Chitty retrieved the hat.

Harley helped Toby back to his seat.

"He murder my Duša's man," Mr. Stanek yelled from the gallery.

Judge Goodrich gave a warning look to Stanek. The old man's ruddy face tightened, and his large hands clutched the seat in front of him as he bent forward to glare at Toby.

Toby rocked.

Catfish blinked at Harley but dared not look at Wallace. Their goose was cooked.

Chapter 12

Miss Peach loathed the county jail. It was such a sad place, and the jailers did nothing to make it less so. There was little to it but brick walls, iron bars, clanking keys, coughing inmates, and the sickening stench of vomit and human excrement. Even the cell doors moaned when the jailers opened them. Confinement in such a miserable place would drive anyone mad.

Over the lunch recess she accompanied Dr. Wallace to the jail for his examination of Toby while both Mr. Calloway and Harley went elsewhere to talk with potential witnesses. Long ago, because of his relationship with the sheriff, Mr. Calloway had obtained the right to meet clients in the private visiting room rather than in their cells. The guards resisted, but she threatened to go to the sheriff if they refused her. After a few less-than-ladylike words from her, they relented.

Mr. Calloway had instructed her not to reveal the doctor's true identity to anyone including the jailers. After watching Toby's testimony, Dr. Wallace said he wanted to withhold final judgment on Toby until after his examination. Mr. Calloway was worried if he concluded Toby was sane, Chitty might call him as a prosecution expert witness, but even if he found Toby insane, Mr. Calloway wanted to keep the doctor a secret so Chitty wouldn't have time to prepare for cross-examination.

Consequently, the gray-haired, bearded, erudite Dr. Wallace was just "David," a friend of Toby's.

She and the doctor sat across a bare table from Toby in the dreary, drab, little room. The horrid jail guard refused to leave and planted himself by the door.

The jailer's hands were filthy and had dirt under every nail. Leering at her, he looked as brutish a man as any on the other side of the bars. "Don't get too close, missy. Topper's a murdering mad man."

"I'm fine, thank you."

There was something familiar about the jailer, though she couldn't quite put her finger on it. When he started picking his nose, she distracted herself by looking through her handbag.

"Don't worry none," he said, leaning back against the wall of the visiting room. "I'm here to watch after you."

It was impossible for Dr. Wallace to conduct a medical examination in front of the guard without revealing what he was doing. He tried to keep up the ruse and converse with Toby as friends might, but Toby didn't converse.

The deputy shifted his weight. "Men like him ain't born like us normal folks. They's spawned off in the woods somewheres by a witch-woman." He discharged tobacco spittle into a corner spittoon.

Dr. Wallace sighed, removed his spectacles, and locked eyes with the guard. "Please be respectful of my friend."

The hulking man shrugged indifferently. His eyes met hers, and he grinned and winked at her. She looked away, stifling a shudder. She was certain she'd seen him before, but where?

After a few minutes he yawned, ran a hand through his close-cropped curly brown hair, and opened the door to leave. "I'll lock it. If your *friend* tries to hurt you, just holler."

When the door slammed shut, Dr. Wallace began the examination in earnest. "Can you tell me your name?"

Toby rocked silently.

"I'm Dr. Wallace. Your lawyers asked me to see you."

Toby rocked but didn't meet his eyes.

Wallace gently questioned him about who he was, where he lived, where he was at the present time, and why he was there. He rocked to and fro but made no response to any of the questions. There was no indication he even understood Wallace was speaking to him. The doctor asked him about the day of the robbery and where he was, but he still didn't react. Never once did his eyes leave the tabletop.

What an odd creature Toby was. It was so terribly frustrating that nothing they did or said changed his reaction in any discernible way. How could they possibly get through to him?

Wallace began a physical examination. Toby acted oblivious to the doctor's poking, prodding, and peering at him from every angle. He rocked and stared at the table except when restrained by the doctor's firm hands. Wallace measured the size of Toby's head with a tape.

She recorded his observations as he dictated them to her.

"Physical examination reveals a normal head shape and size. There is no asymmetry of the cranium. No physical defects or abnormalities. No apparent lesions from a forceps injury in childbirth."

Dr. Wallace bent over Toby's head and held it still. "Examination of the scalp reveals a left parietal hematoma approximately the size of a silver dollar." He eyed her over his spectacles. "Has he suffered a recent blow to the head?"

She shrugged. "Maybe when he was arrested. That was about a month ago."

Dr. Wallace released Toby and stood back to observe him. "There are no common features of the feebleminded such as imperfections of sight or obtuseness of hearing as far as I can tell. No ear abnormalities. No unusual hair growth." He pried open Toby's mouth and held his tongue with a depressor. "His palate is not vaulted." He helped Toby to his feet and examined his trunk and extremities. "No defect in height or weight. In fact, he is quite large."

Toby stood in place, rocking as before.

"You may take your seat." When he didn't do so, Dr. Wallace guided him into the chair.

Wallace glanced at her and back at Toby. "David R. Wallace."

Toby spoke distinctly but without looking up just as he had in court. "One-Oh-Oh-Nine Austin Ave."

The doctor continued his dictation. "No defects of speech, though the content of his speech is quite limited in degree. Correctly recites my address when my name stated."

She recorded his dictation exactly.

Wallace turned to her. "Has Toby made deliveries to your home?"

"To my boarding house, yes."

"Say your full name to him, as it appears in the city directory."

At his suggestion she'd borrowed the District Clerk's directory. She examined her own entry. "Peach, Zipporah."

Toby rocked silently.

"Try it again," Wallace said. "Reverse the names."

"Zipporah Peach."

Toby rocked silently.

She wrinkled her face. "You know, it lists my address as 'boarding with Mrs. Sparks' rather than by a street address."

"Say her name exactly as it appears in the directory."

She found the entry for Mrs. Sparks, leaned toward Toby and spoke softly. "Sparks, Mary E."

"Fifty-one, thirty-one, two."

Wallace's eyes darted to her. "That's not her street address, is it?"

She shook her head.

Wallace stroked his long, gray whiskers. "Very curious."

She tried again. "Mary E. Sparks."

"Fifty-one, thirty-one, two."

"Not a street address." Dr. Wallace was thoughtful and matter of fact. "Make a thorough record of these answers please."

She summarized the exchange, noting the names and numbers precisely.

Wallace leaned over her shoulder and flipped some pages in the directory. He stopped at page 164. "Holt, Benjamin."

Toby rocked but didn't say anything.

Why did Dr. Wallace ask that name? There were three Holts in the directory, but none named Benjamin.

Then he flipped more pages and did the same thing. "Rider, Peter."

There was no Peter Rider in the directory either.

Toby rocked.

"You try some names," Wallace said to her, returning to his seat.

She flipped through some pages. "Emma Reed."

"Seven-Oh-Nine Barron."

She smiled at Toby as demonstrably as she could. "Good."

His demeanor changed ever so slightly. Was he starting to rock a little faster?

"Charles W. Farrell."

"Three-One-Three South Second." He rocked faster, with more energy in his motion and in his own queer way, perhaps with more enthusiasm.

She projected a big smile.

For the first time he glanced at her out of the corner of his eye as he rocked.

Oh my! There was a person inside that body. She was positive of it. "Hannah Tyson."

"One-Three-One-Eight-One-Half South Fourth."

She clapped and grinned even more demonstrably than before.

He still didn't look at her directly, but he was watching her reaction.

She bent closer to him and spoke in a softer tone. "Joseph H. Hutcherson."

"Six-One-Six North Twelfth." He rocked but still watched her.

She nodded enthusiastically. "Yes, Toby, that's so good." She clapped again.

He rocked faster.

There was a sweetness in Toby even if it was generally hidden. He didn't seem to want to stop their game, but their time was up, and Dr. Wallace said he was done.

She hugged him. "Very good, Toby."

He didn't hug her back, nor did his flat expression change.

The deputy dragged him back down the hallway to his cell. A nagging thought was lodged in her mind—how could a boy like this be capable of robbery and murder? She'd met killers Mr. Calloway had represented, but insane or not, Toby Topper wasn't like them in any way.

***

Catfish met Dr. Wallace in the first-floor county courtroom after his examination of Toby. He wanted to be sure of the doctor's opinion before they took him to the district court and put him on the witness stand. "Doctor, the issues for the jury will be whether he's the killer and if so whether he was insane or not at the time of the killings. We're hoping you can help us somehow. I'd like to put you on the witness stand later this afternoon."

Harley and Miss Peach flanked Wallace at the big courtroom table. Catfish had conferred with both, and they disagreed on strategy. Harley favored a defense that Toby might have committed the crimes, but he didn't know right from wrong. Harley's reasoning was they didn't have any other witnesses to support his innocence, and the prosecution witnesses were convincing. After meeting with Toby, however, Miss Peach didn't think him capable of the crimes and believed an insane asylum was little better than prison.

Harley referred to his notes. "The precise question we'll ask you is whether Mr. Topper has such a defect of reason from a disease of the mind that either he doesn't know what he is doing, or he doesn't know the difference between right and wrong."

Catfish knew they needed other witnesses but wanted to find a way to prove Toby was innocent. "Doctor, I was convinced Toby's too simple-minded to commit robbery and murder, but I've got to confess, after his performance on cross, I'm not so sure. We're wondering what your opinion would be."

Wallace removed his spectacles. "Are you familiar with the work of Dr. J. Langdon Down?"

Chapter 13

"We seem to be short some lawyers," the judge said when court reconvened at one thirty.

Only Chitty and his bookish clerk occupied the prosecution table. "Mr. Wilson won't be joining us until later, Your Honor."

Harley noticed that Schoolcraft was missing too. Had Wilson—the walrus as Papa called him—gone back to Dallas? "Judge, my father is interviewing witnesses and will be here a little later. I'll be putting on our next two witnesses." The only thing they knew for sure about Toby was that he made deliveries for Risher's Drug Store, so Papa went there.

Papa wasn't ready to call Dr. Wallace as a witness yet. Toby's mental condition was more complicated than they'd imagined, and they wanted to ask Wallace more questions about it that night when they'd have more time. Papa wanted to pursue both the innocence and insanity defenses. They had lined up Ben Moon to testify as a character witness, and Bob Lazenby agreed to be recalled about Toby's mental state.

"Very well, Mr. Calloway, you may proceed," the judge said.

Harley waited until Moon was sworn. "Tell the gentlemen of the jury who you are, please."

"I be Ben Moon. Some folks calls me Bootblack Ben." Mr. Moon's back was straight as an arrow as he awaited Harley's next question. He fingered the tattered brown hat in his lap.

Harley smiled back at him. "Why do people call you that?"

"Mostly 'cause I shines shoes."

"Where?"

"Oh, most days I be at the square. Some days I goes over to the train station when the train due in. Travelers, they always needs a shine, you know."

Harley had known the old gentleman all his life. One summer when he was a boy, Mr. Moon showed him where to pick mustang grapes, and they sat in the shade of the tree for hours talking and eating until his mouth burned from the tart grapes. Other than his parents, most grown-ups didn't pay any mind to boys; but Mr. Moon did, and they became pals. He shared incredible stories about growing up a slave in East Texas. He bore the scars on his back—Harley even touched them through his shirt—but he never would show them. "Don't you bother yourself none about them stripes, Mr. Harley. I be a free man now, and they ain't no pain no more."

Papa had said despite all Mr. Moon had endured, he kept a gentle soul. He was about ten years younger than Papa. They had some connection from before Harley was born, and Papa always treated him with the same respect he did white people, but he had never talked about why. Harley suspected it had something to do with the war, which Papa rarely mentioned.

Harley hoped the jurors would feel the same way they did about Mr. Moon. Most men in town had probably gotten a shoeshine from him. His word might carry weight because he was such a keen observer. He knew everybody, saw everything, and remembered most of what he saw. He knew more about what happened in Waco than the police did.

A quiet had settled over the courtroom when Mr. Moon took

the stand. The bailiff had opened a newspaper. About half the jurors had started looking at the floor rather than the witness. Maybe they'd just been showing him respect in their own way.

Harley pointed to Toby. "Mr. Moon, do you know this gentleman over here, Mr. Toby Topper?"

Toby rocked.

"Yes, sir. I sure does."

"How do you know him?"

"Well, just seeing him around town, you know. He ride that bicycle all day long. I expect I sees him maybe ten, twelve times a day most days. Leastways, that I notice him."

"Have you ever given Mr. Topper a shine?"

"No, sir, not as I recollect."

One of the jurors leaned over the jury rail, apparently trying to see Toby's shoes. The man next to him closed his eyes; his chin drooped to his chest.

Harley cleared his throat, but the juror didn't stir. "Has Mr. Topper ever spoken with you or communicated with you in any way?"

"Mr. Harley, sir," Moon said, "I don't know as I's ever heard Mr. Toby say nothing. But he do tip his hat to me ever time he passes by. He's right friendly."

"When he tipped his hat, did he ever smile at you?"

Moon wiped his forehead with a big leathery hand. "Not on the outside, no sir. But I knows he does on the inside. That boy got a sweet, sweet spirit." He smiled, exposing some missing teeth. "And the Lord, he know too. He take care of Mr. Toby. He just different, you know?"

"Yes, sir," Harley said. Harley wrote the answer on his notepaper.

"Did he ever look you right in the eye?"

"Well now"—he scratched his head with a single finger—"No, sir. I don't believe he ever did."

"Are you familiar with Toby's reputation in the community as a peaceable and law-abiding citizen?"

"Oh, yes, he is that for sure."

"One last thing. Do you have an opinion about whether Mr. Topper is sane or insane?"

Chitty jumped up. "I object. He's not competent to give such an opinion."

The sleeping juror roused. All eyes darted to Chitty.

"Any person with first-hand knowledge of Toby is competent to give this opinion, Your Honor." Harley reached for Clark's treatise. "I have three cases if you want to see them."

"That's not necessary. Overruled."

The jurors settled back in their seats, not even one facing Mr. Moon. It was as if he wasn't even there. What was the matter with them?

"What's your opinion, sir? Is he sane or insane?"

Mr. Moon gaped back at Harley and at Toby.

Harley edged closer. When he met with Moon earlier, he'd been hesitant. Harley had explained that saying Toby was insane wouldn't be speaking ill of him but would help him.

"Well, sir, I reckon he's slow-like."

That wasn't enough. "Do you think he's right in the head?"

"You know, the Lord, he looks after Mr. Toby, but Mr. Toby do need looking after."

Harley leaned in. "Because he has a defect of the mind?"

Mr. Moon's head drooped. "I reckon that must be what it is. Like he's simple, you know? I can't think of no other reason."

"This is my final question then. In your opinion does Mr. Topper have such a defect of the mind that either he doesn't know what he is doing, or he doesn't know the difference between right and wrong?"

"Oh, I don't know about his mind and such, but it do seem like he don't keep up with what's going on around him."

Harley scribbled the answer in his notes. That was probably the best they could get from Mr. Moon. "Thank you, sir. Pass the witness."

None of the jurors would look at Harley. It was as if they wanted him to know they wouldn't even consider Mr. Moon's opinion. Harley's grip tightened on his pen.

Chitty's chair squeaked. One juror's head shot up.

The prosecutor rocked back, smiling. "Ben, I'm not sure our court reporter has had a chance to note this, so I'll ask you for the court's record—are you a colored man?"

"Well, sir." Moon said, expressionless. "Yes, I is. That's what the Lord done made me, for sure."

"No further questions," Chitty said to the judge, rising halfway.

Harley wadded his notes and crammed them into his briefcase. Expecting the jury to listen to Mr. Moon had been a big mistake, and the old gentleman didn't deserve such treatment. With Papa and Miss Peach still gone and the jury slipping away from him, he couldn't have felt more alone.

Chapter 14

While Harley put on Ben Moon, Catfish took a hack to Risher's Drug Store. He leaned over the back of the driver's seat. "Samson, you know Toby Topper, don't you?"

"Oh, sure enough, Mr. Catfish, but just by sight." He popped the horsewhip. "He's a damned odd fella."

Colonel Terry sank to the floor of the buggy.

"Know anything about him?"

Samson yanked the reins. "Whoa, now!" The hack turned right from Franklin onto Fifth Street. "Well, I know he killed dead them two express agents, if that's what you mean."

"We think he's innocent of that. Anything you know that'll help us prove it would be appreciated."

"Wish I could help. I just seen him peddling around the streets, not much else." He doffed his hat like Toby did. "Tipping his hat, you know."

"You didn't happen to see him the day of the robbery, did you?"

"Can't recollect that far back. Sorry."

"Ever seen him with anybody?"

"Haw!" Samson turned his buggy onto Austin Avenue. "Only one time as I think back. Him and some woman was riding side by side somewhere. I don't remember where. I thought it was curious at the time is why I remember it. She was talking to him like they was having some kind of conversation or something, but that's really all I remember."

"That's very helpful." Catfish hooked his arm over the seat next to Samson and bent closer to him. "Who was she?"

"Don't know that," he said looking sideways from behind a big curly beard. "Never saw her face. She was wearing one of them straw hats with flowers or something in it like womenfolk does."

"Would you know her if you saw her again?"

"Nope. Like I say, never seen her face. I couldn't begin to tell you what she looked like." He pulled to a stop in front of Risher's.

***

Though he knew Harry Risher, and the store was right around the corner from his law office, Catfish had never been inside. Like the Corner Drug where he traded, this shop was deep and narrow, brightly lit, with long counters on both sides and towering oak shelves behind them stocked with cures and remedies. Glass cases on the countertops displayed sundries, toiletries, and ladies' notions. The store was bustling with customers.

Risher wasn't anywhere in sight, and so he approached a clerk. "Harry not in today?"

"Sorry, he's gone to Mineral Wells to bring back a stock of crazy water," the young man replied. He was neatly dressed, his hair parted in the middle and slicked down with sweet-smelling hair tonic. "How can I help you?"

"I wanted to ask Harry about a boy who used to work for him, Toby Topper."

"I vaguely remember him. He made deliveries on his bicycle,

but I didn't see him much and never spoke with him. Actually, I didn't think he was able to speak. He was a strange sort."

"He doesn't talk much." Catfish leaned on the counter. "Did you ever hear anything about his family or where he lived?"

"Not really. I vaguely remember Mr. Risher saying he was an orphan."

"You ever recall seeing him in the company of a woman?"

"Sorry, I never paid much attention to him." He pointed across the store to a lady behind the opposite counter. "You might ask Miss Gussie. She knows everybody."

Catfish made his way through the customers to the other counter and browsed down the product displays until he reached the woman in her fifties. "How do, ma'am, I was wondering if you recommend Brilliantine," Catfish said, tweaking his whiskers.

"Most gentlemen prefer Rowland's instead." She opened a box of Macassar Oil, unscrewed the bottle cap, and handed it over for him to sniff. "Less gummy, you know."

Smelled like a whole garden of flowers. Judging by the picture on the box, it was for ladies too. "I'll take it, thank you." Maybe he'd try it on Colonel Terry's tail. "By the way, do you happen to remember a young man who used to make deliveries for Mr. Risher by the name of Toby Topper?"

"Bless his heart, what a queer child. That'll be twenty cents, please."

Queer seemed to be the prevailing sentiment about Toby. Catfish handed her a quarter. "Know anything about his family?"

She shook her head and slid a nickel across the counter. "Didn't he wind up killing someone?"

"He's accused of that, but he didn't do it. I'm his lawyer."

"Oh," she said, dropping the amber bottle back in its box and handing it over the counter. She was suddenly less talkative. "What else might I do for you?"

"Believe that does it, thanks." He checked his watch.

He'd better get back to court in case they had to call Dr. Wallace this afternoon. He hoped Harley had learned a thing or two from him about stalling a trial, there being an art to dawdling without appearing to dillydally and drawing the court's ire. He'd had a good deal of practice, but Harley hadn't.

On his way out, as he passed by the counter with newspapers and periodicals, something caught his eye—a thin paper-wrapped book published by Beadle's in New York. It was the title in large red letters that he noticed: *The Adventures of Thaddeus Schoolcraft, Railroad Detective.*

He laughed. That pompous reptile. Then the subtitle hit him: *The Waco Train Station Murder.* He stopped smiling. What murder?

The cover of the dime novel bore an engraving of a train station—good, it didn't look anything like the old MOPAC depot in Waco—and a man standing over a body with a smoking six-shooter in his hand. The drawing of the sneering shooter didn't resemble Houston in the least. Maybe it wasn't about his son after all.

The drawing showed another man rushing to the scene of the shooting. He wore a bowler hat, had a horseshoe mustache, and carried a Blackthorn cane in one hand and a revolver in the other. This part of the drawing looked like real life, the spitting image of Thaddeus Schoolcraft.

Inside, the text of the story appeared more like a newspaper article—three columns of densely packed words, bold black titles at the top of the left-hand column: *The Adventures of Thaddeus Schoolcraft, Railroad Detective—The Waco Train Station Murder—BY MIRIAM GARTRELL GISELLE.*

Never heard of her.

He read the first paragraph.

The locomotive pulled into the Missouri Pacific Train Station at Waco. It was a Tuesday morning, March 23, 1886—his gut tightened—Thaddeus Schoolcraft watched the kindly cotton merchant gather his belongings and leave the passenger car. The famous detective's steely eyes went to the tall, angry young man who had sat across from the merchant, staring at the merchant's back as he made his way down the aisle and out the door of the passenger car. Fury rumbled in the young man's cold heart like the molten depths of Krakatoa. Detective Schoolcraft sensed an eruption was imminent. The angry young man stood to his full height, still stabbing the merchant's back with his piercing, furious eyes. He brandished a Colt. He was the desperado, Sam Houston Calloway.

***

As he strode back down Austin Avenue toward his office, Catfish's mind couldn't erase what he'd read: *the desperado, Sam Houston Calloway.* Schoolcraft's voice—the *desperado, Sam Houston Calloway*—pounded inside his head. He skimmed the pages as he walked, looking up only at street crossings but not always even then. The more he read, the more the passersby faded, the horses and the mules and the buggies and trolleys all disappeared, everything melted away but the partly true tale. He walked some and stopped to read, over and over, causing Colonel Terry to stare at him in perplexity. When the story came to the murder trial, he paused reading and crossed Third Street.

"Watch where you're going, mister!" shouted a farmer from his buckboard.

The colonel growled back at him.

In front of City Hall, he dropped onto a bench and read more.

> *A local lawyer showed up to defend the desperado. He was a crafty old white-haired courthouse law-dog who called himself Catfish. His whiskers curled at the ends from his constant preening. Once a legendary lawyer, age and whiskey had taken their toll. Would he prove a match for Detective Schoolcraft?*

That was enough. He flipped to the last page, inspected the concluding vitriol against Houston. He pulled a match, lit it with one strike, and held it to the bottom corner of the paper cover until it ignited. When flames scorched his shirt cuff he let go and the blazing pages burned and floated to the street. He flicked the burnt match at the smoldering residue.

Colonel Terry trotted beside him as Catfish pounded down the sidewalk toward the courthouse. *Desperado— courthouse law-dog—a match for Detective Schoolcraft.*

When he turned the corner onto Second Street a hack was departing the courthouse entrance, leaving the walrus on the curb. He disappeared inside. As the hack rounded the corner Catfish caught a glimpse of the carriage's remaining passenger.

Hamp Boswell, their apprentice.

Chapter 15

"Mr. Lazenby," Harley said, "you're still under oath from testifying yesterday. Remind us what you said then about how long you've been acquainted with Mr. Toby Topper?"

"I'm not sure. Probably three or four years."

Harley's chair screeched as he scooted back from the table. "How would you describe his behavior when he made deliveries to you?"

"It was unusual to say the least. For one, I don't recall him ever speaking. He would ride his bicycle to our home, come to the front door and knock. He wouldn't even look at me directly, only out of the corner of his eye. And he'd tip his hat constantly. I would take the delivery from the basket on his bicycle, drop some money in a tin cup tied to the handlebars, and he'd leave. That was it."

As Lazenby finished his answer the courtroom door creaked open. Billy, the Western Union boy, rushed in with an envelope. Wilson, who just returned to court, met him at the bar and snatched it.

Harley refocused on Lazenby. "Did you speak to Toby when he came?"

"I'd usually say hello, you know, or something like that. And goodbye. Thank you, probably."

Harley stood by the end of their table opposite the jury from Toby. He wanted the jury to watch his client rocking mindlessly as if he was off somewhere in his own world even though he was the center of attention in this one. But between Toby and the jury, the prosecutors seemed more intent on the telegram than anything. They exchanged looks, and Chitty nodded.

Harley half expected Chitty to interrupt, but he didn't. "Did Toby ever respond or even acknowledge your greetings?"

"Never."

Harley bent over the table. Toby went back and forth right in front of his nose, never altering his pattern, never changing his gaze. "What did you think about that?"

"I'm not sure. I suppose I thought something was wrong with him, but I had no idea what. He just seemed simple-minded."

When the door opened again, Schoolcraft slipped in and settled into a gallery seat behind the prosecutors. Chitty whispered to Wilson, who went to sit with Schoolcraft.

Harley, trying to ignore all the distractions, decided to finish quickly. "Mr. Lazenby, I need to ask you a very important question. Based on your observations of Mr. Topper, do you have an opinion about whether he had such a defect of reason from a disease of the mind"—Chitty stood but didn't yet speak—"that either he didn't know what he was doing or he didn't know the difference between right and wrong?"

"If it please the court," Chitty said, his nose aimed high, "for the record, I object. This man is not qualified to opine upon sanity."

"Overruled." The judge had overruled the same objection to Mr. Moon opining. "Answer the question, Mr. Lazenby," the judge said.

"In my opinion, Toby didn't have the remotest idea what was

happening around him. Of course, I'm no medical man, but he certainly had something wrong in his mind. Anybody can see that."

Harley smiled at Lazenby. "Thank you, sir. That's all, Your Honor."

"Mr. Chitty?"

"Mr. Lazenby," the prosecutor said from his chair, "if I understand you correctly, Mr. Topper would pick up something for you at the drugstore and navigate his bicycle to your home?"

"Yes, it's about seven or eight blocks away."

"Just finding your address is a mark of some intelligence, isn't it?"

"I suppose."

"He didn't wander about town in a mental daze?"

"He did his business."

"Exactly." Chitty rose an inch or two in his chair as he addressed the judge. "Your Honor, nothing further."

***

As Miss Peach turned away from Chitty, her eye caught the telegram on his table, no more than ten or twelve feet away but too far to read. When her gaze lifted, Mr. Wilson—the walrus—brushed by her as she returned from the gallery and quickly stuffed the telegram into a briefcase.

He peered at her and settled back into his chair.

Judge Goodrich released the jury for a recess. As the others began dispersing for the break, Mr. Wilson caught her eye again and approached. If he ever smiled, no one would know it because the walrus-whiskers covered his mouth almost entirely.

"You are Miss Peach, I understand," he said, his jowls waggling with his words.

"I am. May I do something for you?"

"I was marveling at why a . . . girl would be seated inside the bar." His eyes were utterly expressionless. "Are there no social events on the calendar today?"

Even a genuine walrus would be more agreeable. "Why, Mr. Wilson, I'm at the bar to see that justice is done, of course. Are there no etiquette lectures on your calendar for today?"

He snorted, tilting his balding, bewhiskered head to look down at her as he followed Chitty out. Through the open door she watched the two prosecutors deep in conversation with Schoolcraft in the waiting room.

She joined Mr. Calloway and Harley, who were chatting with Mr. Lazenby at the defense table.

Mr. Calloway had been quiet and stared off into the distance since he returned from Risher's. Whatever it was that troubled him, however, he kept it to himself. "Bob, you ever see Toby with a woman in a hat?"

Mr. Lazenby shook his head.

"Or know anything about him being an orphan?"

"Sorry," Mr. Lazenby said.

Mr. Calloway thanked him, and he left.

"What now, Papa?" Harley asked.

"I suppose we've got no choice but to put on Dr. Wallace this afternoon." The doctor was still tucked away by himself downstairs in the county courtroom in case they needed him. "I'd hoped to visit more with him about his opinions, but the judge wants this wrapped up, and he's not likely to grant us any more delays."

"I think the jury will find Dr. Wallace very convincing," Harley said.

"Son, I'd like you to question him. You've got a better grip on the medical science and insanity law than me."

Harley brightened. "Are you sure?"

Mr. Calloway smiled warmly. "I'll ride shotgun for you."

Miss Peach knew putting on such an important witness was something Harley had longed for. He'd finally have a chance to prove himself in front of a jury.

"I'll do my best."

Before Mr. Calloway could say anything else, Chitty and Wilson returned.

"Excuse me, gentlemen, Miss Peach," Chitty said politely. "Something has come up back in Dallas that requires my immediate attention, and I was hoping you might agree to a recess until the morning."

Mr. Calloway didn't look nearly as astonished as she was. This was so unlike Chitty; even his demeanor had turned conciliatory. Whatever happened in Dallas must have been the subject of the telegram.

"Well, counsel, we're anxious to get on with our next witness," Mr. Calloway replied. She was equally astonished at his words. He wrinkled his face at Chitty. "You haven't exactly been cooperative when we asked for some time."

"I regret that. The client, you know. Anyway, I'd personally be grateful if you agreed, but if you don't, I'll ask the judge. I think he'll understand."

Why didn't Mr. Calloway jump at the idea of delay? It was just what he wanted. After an extended silence, he said, "Harley, the judge said we've got to be finished by Friday. If we help Mr. Chitty out, do you think we can still do that?"

Miss Peach put a hand to her mouth so as not to betray further surprise. As far as she knew Dr. Wallace was their only other witness.

Harley didn't seem surprised though. "Maybe. If we rush it up tomorrow."

Mr. Calloway scratched his head in an overtly thoughtful way. "It's against my better judgment, but I'll agree, as long as you agree you'll do the same for us if we need it."

"Of course," Chitty said, smiling. "Do unto others, as they say."

As the lawyers headed for the judge's chambers, Mr. Calloway discreetly winked at her.

Chapter 16

"We call Dr. David Wallace."

As Wallace made his way to the stand the next morning, Harley watched the prosecutors. He expected them to exchange quizzical looks or maybe even make some dilatory objection, but they did neither. He scanned the spectator gallery. Schoolcraft wasn't even watching Wallace. He'd taken a seat behind Mr. Stanek and his son.

"State your full name, please," Harley said.

"David Richard Wallace."

"How old are you, sir?"

"I'll be seventy next year." Dr. Wallace's gray beard covered his necktie and neatly combed hair. He peered at Harley over round gold-rimmed spectacles perched on his nose. Papa and Harley had spent a good deal of time with him the previous night going over his testimony.

"Dr. Wallace, I'll be asking you some questions about Mr. Toby Topper in a moment, but first, I'd like the jury to hear about you." Harley stood beside his chair. "Can you describe for them your own history?"

Wallace matter-of-factly narrated his own story. Originally from North Carolina, he graduated from Wake Forest college and obtained a master's degree there as well. After that, he taught awhile and went to medical school in New York City where he obtained an additional degree from Philadelphia Medical College. He came to Texas in 1855 with his mother. He opened a medical practice at Independence but also taught Latin and Greek at Baylor University. When his good friend Rufus Burleson moved to Waco in 1861, he persuaded Wallace to come too. The war came along then, and he served as a surgeon in the army. After the war, he returned to Waco and was in practice with Dr. Sears until 1874.

"What did you do then?"

Wallace's manner was sober and confident. "I had become acquainted by then with Richard Coke, who was elected governor. He appointed me to be superintendent of the new state lunatic asylum in Austin. I was later reappointed by Governor Hubbard. In 1883, I was commissioned to supervise construction of a new state asylum in Terrell, where I served as superintendent until about three years ago. After that, I returned to Waco and have engaged in a consulting practice almost exclusively concerning nervous diseases, neuralgia, epilepsy, opium habit, and disturbances of the mind."

Harley eyed the jurors as Wallace answered. They looked receptive. "Let me change the subject now from you to Mr. Topper. Have you had an opportunity to conduct a professional examination of him?"

"I did a mental evaluation of him in the jail."

"What opinion did you reach as to his sanity?"

"Mr. Topper is suffering from a rare and curious defect of the mind which a preeminent British physician, Dr. Down, has described in the medical literature quite recently. Such a person is feebleminded but exhibits special faculties such as extraordinary memory in a narrow range. Paradoxically, he possesses both extraordinary disability and extraordinary ability."

The bell in the clock tower above them began to strike the time. Toby stopped rocking, bent double, and clamped his hands over his ears. Colonel Terry bayed from the courthouse steps outside, and Miss Peach rushed to Toby's side to comfort him. Poor fellow. He struggled to deal with the world around him. As the building shuddered with the ringing, a bird's feather dislodged from a perch somewhere high above and floated until it finally landed inside the bar.

After the bell pealed the final time, Harley resumed. "Would you please describe your examination of Mr. Topper for the gentlemen of the jury, Doctor?"

"I did an abbreviated physical examination and a mental evaluation. The most striking observations I made were of what he is displaying at this very moment"—all eyes fell on Toby—"these endless, repetitive movements."

"What were your observations about his mental state?"

Wallace stroked his whiskers and peered at the jury over his spectacles. "I was only able to inspire speech in him when I gave him a name from the city directory, and he responded correctly with the exact address shown in the directory, just as he did in court yesterday. It's truly remarkable, and I have personally never treated such a patient." He glanced toward Chitty and Wilson as if to preempt their questioning. "I tested him for insincerity by fabricating a name which did not actually appear in the directory, and he made no response other than continuing his rhythmic motions."

"Other than his extraordinary memory," Harley said, "what did you conclude about his mental ability?"

"He seems to be generally self-absorbed. To my most endearing and warm solicitations, he appeared indifferent. The eyes peer out as if upon an objectless world." He shook his head thoughtfully. "There's no engagement at all."

"So, your diagnosis is?"

Wallace's scholarly bearing grabbed the jury as if they were his students. "There were no signs of melancholia, delusions, psychosis, or moral insanity. No mania or hysteria. Mr. Topper is feebleminded, and I would place him in the classification of mental disease described by Dr. Down as idiot savant."

"Idiot savant." Harley let the words sink in. "Can you educate us about Dr. Down?"

"Certainly," Wallace said matter-of-factly. "Dr. J. Langdon Down is the renowned senior physician to the London Hospital and superintendent of Earlswood Asylum. Not long ago he delivered a series of lectures to the Medical Society of London on the mental afflictions of children and youth. The lectures were published in the February 1887 issue of the British Medical Journal. After seeing Mr. Topper's testimony in court yesterday, particularly his repetitive motions and unusual gift for memory, I reread the article. I have it here." He held the journal for the jury to see.

"What did you learn from it?"

Harley glanced at the prosecution table, expecting a hearsay objection, but they remained silent.

"Dr. Down described in his lectures some of the patients he had treated over a thirty-year span. For example, there was one who could recite Gibbon's *Rise and Fall of the Roman Empire*, from memory, backward or forward, after only one reading. Allow me to read some other particular passages if you will."

They still didn't object.

"Go ahead," Harley said.

"'One boy, about twelve years of age, could multiply any

three figures by three figures with perfect accuracy, and as quickly as I could write the six figures on paper; and yet, so low mentally was he that, although having been for two and a half years in the almost daily habit of seeing me and talking with me, he could not tell my name.' Let's see, here's another example: "'I have had one boy under my observation who, if he went to an opera, would carry away a recollection of all the airs, and would hum or sing them correctly.'"

Two jurors looked at each other.

"Here's another passage which I find pertinent." Wallace adjusted his spectacles and read from the journal. "'Another knows the home address of every resident who comes under his observation, and they are by no means few.'"

"Dr. Wallace, that is all truly astonishing." Harley paced back to Papa's favorite spot at the corner of the jury rail and the bar. From there, he could watch the juror's reactions out of the corner of his eye. "Do you have any explanation for such behavior?"

"Medical knowledge does not yet explain the origins or causes of this mental disease. It's a paradox of nature."

"A paradox of nature." Harley watched Toby rock. Most of the jurors did, too. "Are the opinions you've reached about Toby ones you're confident of?"

"Yes, though my diagnosis is incomplete. I should like to know more of Mr. Topper's medical and family history, including the possibility of consanguineous marriages, and particularly whether there is any family history of idiocy. I would like to know of the mother's physical health during pregnancy, including the use of alcohol or opium."

Harley returned to his seat. "Is this mental disease treatable?"

"It's certainly not curable. Mr. Topper needs to be confined to an institution where he can receive knowledgeable and compassionate care." He peered over his spectacles at the jury. "An asylum, gentlemen, not a prison."

None of the jurors reacted.

"Do you have an opinion about whether Mr. Topper has such a defect of reason from a disease of the mind that either he doesn't know what he is doing, or he doesn't know the difference between right and wrong?"

"In my opinion he is mentally deficient, is unaware of what transpires around him, and does not possess sufficient capacity of the mind to understand right and wrong."

Harley eyed Papa, who jotted a note and slid it over.

"Now, finally, Dr. Wallace, I have one final subject for you." He read aloud the question Papa had written. "In your opinion, is Mr. Topper capable of planning and carrying out a robbery and murder?"

"That is a cognitive process. It requires the perpetrator to engage in premeditation, to meticulously plan how best to achieve the desired goal. Those are cognitions well beyond Toby's skills. He doesn't reason as you and I do. He's incapable of calculating that he must kill two men in order to steal the money and that he would need to escape to avoid punishment."

Papa handed him another question. "But isn't he unusually intelligent to know all those addresses?"

"The only cognitive process he's capable of is memorization, and he's exceptional at that for reasons I cannot explain. He has the ability to remember my address is 1009 Austin Avenue but not of reasoning from that to the next level that my neighbors on the north side of the street have odd numbered addresses or houses across the street have even numbers. If he read their addresses in the directory he would remember them, but he comprehends no design in their numbering. Toby is incapable of planning a sequenced series of actions to achieve a desired purpose."

"You seem to be saying he's incapable of greed or malice?"

"Exactly."

"Could he have executed the robbery if someone else had planned it and put him up to it?"

"That's not possible either," Wallace said. "Making a delivery—riding a bicycle to a home and knocking on the door—is a simple, routine process that can be learned. Unlike a robbery, it requires little reaction to unanticipated events or improvisation. No, he isn't capable of even carrying out someone else's criminal enterprise."

Papa nodded discreetly.

"Nothing further."

"Mr. Chitty, you may cross-examine," Judge Goodrich said.

The prosecutor rocked back in his chair. "Dr. Wallace, you described Mr. Topper's alleged insanity as a paradox of nature, did you not?"

"I did."

"Meaning you don't know what caused it?"

"I do not."

Chitty eyed him incredulously. "Really? I'm quite surprised you have no opinion of the cause of his mental disease."

Wallace didn't reply.

Chitty pulled a large black book from his satchel. "Sir, isn't it your learned opinion and belief that the cause of insanity among men is this book?"

"I have no idea what you're referring to," Wallace replied. "What book is that?"

"The Good Book, sir." The prosecutor held it high for all to see. "Isn't it your belief that the teaching in our Holy Bible causes insanity?"

Chapter 17

The courtroom erupted in shocked murmurs.

"That's ridiculous," Harley blurted. What did his views on religion have to do with insanity?

"May I proceed without interruption, Your Honor?" Chitty asked.

"All right." The judge waved his hand. "Go ahead."

Chitty opened a newspaper. "Doctor, were you invited by the Texas Medical Association to address its meeting earlier this month?"

Wallace stared at him with a clenched jaw before answering. "I was. The association asked me to present my views on the increase of mental unsoundness in the latter half of this century."

Harley glanced at Papa. Somehow, Chitty had known in advance Wallace would testify and had investigated him. How did they find out? Miss Peach had been sure the jail guards had no idea who he was when they visited Toby.

"Did you present to the members of the association a paper you had written on that subject?" Chitty asked, referencing an article in the newspaper.

"I did."

"Did you say, sir, to that assembled gathering of distinguished physicians, that Christianity is the cause of increased insanity in this country?"

Wallace's eyes blazed. "I did not, sir. That's a misrepresentation of my words."

"Dr. Wallace, did you, with sarcasm dripping from your pen, write the following remarks and present them to the association?"—Chitty read from the newspaper—"'Are not we Christians, especially we of the United States, the people? Have we not the greatest and best government on the planet—the only decent one in fact? Our politicians tell us so, and they know. We have the only religion, or so our priests inform us. Their information is direct from the Deity, so there can be no mistake. We know it. True enough, no doubt, still the ugly fact glares out upon us from every part of our great country, that insanity is more common among us than elsewhere among men. And worse still, that it is alarmingly on the increase.'" Chitty gazed upon Dr. Wallace. "Did you write that, sir?"

Wallace gripped the witness rail. "You're taking my words out of their context."

"Did you write those words?"

"I did, yes. I did, but—"

Chitty leaned toward Wallace. "Did you also write that man-made systems of theology cause disastrous and deplorable results in the great middle class of America?"

Wallace's voice cracked. "I repeat—out of context."

"Did you say to the association meeting," Chitty charged, pointing an accusing finger at the witness, "you were against theology, and you believed it to be the curse of the country?"

"As I explained to them, I am against theology but not against the meek and lowly Jesus or his teachings."

Harley bit his lip. This had nothing to do with Toby. And how could Chitty know about this, but he and Papa didn't? This shouldn't have been a surprise to them. He glanced back at Miss

Peach, but her head was buried in her notes.

Chitty dropped the paper to his table and blinked innocently at Wallace. "So, doctor, you're suggesting I'm misinterpreting your words?"

"You most certainly are."

Chitty shrugged. "Well, sir, is it not true the imminent physicians, Dr. Clopton and Dr. Carhart, both addressed the group and stated they were offended by the idea Christianity was the cause of insanity?"

Wallace ripped his spectacles off. "And most of the members didn't agree with their absurd interpretation of my paper."

"So," Chitty said, lifting the newspaper again, "these two respected physicians were alone in taking your words that way?"

"Nearly so."

Harley turned to Papa, but he was intent on Wallace.

The newspaper crackled as Chitty referenced it again. "Is it true that after you spoke there came a vote upon whether to publish your paper in the Texas Medical Association's journal?"

"It has been published."

"Yes, sir, thirty-two members voted to publish, didn't they?"

Wallace fired back, "Enthusiastically so."

"And ten voted against publication?"

"They were defeated."

Chitty dropped the paper. "But well over fifty members abstained?"

Wallace didn't answer.

"Approval of publication is generally a routine and unanimous matter, is it not?"

"I've never paid attention."

Chitty next wielded a city directory. "There are twenty-six churches in Waco, not counting the eight colored churches." He dropped the maroon-colored book and hooked his thumbs in his vest pockets. "Of which, sir, are you a member?"

"None."

"Truly?" Chitty bent over the table and opened the directory to a marked page. "Not among the Baptists, the Catholics, the Christians, the Episcopalians, the Evangelicals, the Hebrews, the Lutherans, the Methodists, or even the Presbyterians?"

Dr. Wallace answered only with a scornful stare.

Chitty's gaze rose from the book to the witness. "According to the directory, there's a church for about every eight hundred residents of Waco, whether church-goers or not. Your absence is not for want of an empty pew, is it?"

Wallace didn't answer. The vein in his neck stood out as if it might burst. "Mr. Chitty, I trust the jury to give your baseless attack upon me the weight that it deserves."

"Ah," Chitty exclaimed, as if Wallace had touched upon some key point. "The jury." He looked from face to face at the men in the jury box. "Now that we've discussed your views on religion, let me ask you some questions as to how you feel about juries."

Harley cut a glance at Papa, who shrugged discreetly in reply. Over his shoulder Harley eyed Miss Peach. Ink stained her fingers. She looked from her copybook with a furrowed brow.

Chitty strode to the jury rail and leaned back against it. "Is it true that less than two years ago you testified to another jury in another murder case involving a woman you claimed to be insane?"

"Objection!" Harley shouted, jumping up.

"Goes to credibility," Chitty replied in a calm voice.

"Overruled," the judge said. "Answer the question, doctor."

More surprises. What was this about?

Wallace eyed Chitty without expression. "I've testified in a number of cases. To which do you refer?"

"Mary Newberry, in Johnson County," Chitty fired back.

"I did give evidence in that case."

Harley's gut clinched. He knew nothing about that case or Wallace's role in it. Chitty had dug deeply into the doctor's past.

"Actually, sir, you gave evidence quite reluctantly, didn't you?"

"I always prefer to be seeing patients rather than being in court," Wallace replied calmly, "if that's what you mean."

"Didn't you write an article about your experience for the *Texas Medical Journal,* the July 1893 issue to be exact"—Chitty held a paper-bound publication—"and didn't you complain in it that you were required to testify without remuneration?"

"Do you labor without pay, sir?" the doctor asked sarcastically.

Chitty stabbed his finger back at Wallace. "Did you make that complaint?"

"I was attached by the court and placed under a two hundred dollar bond to secure my testimony." Wallace gripped the witness rail. "And yes, I was not paid a penny for my professional work."

"I see."

Wallace persisted. "I'm sure the jurors expect pay when they work."

"You swore to that Johnson County jury the defendant was insane?"

"She most certainly was."

Chitty bent across the table, braced over extended arms, his eyes narrowed on Wallace's. "Mary Newberry dragged three children from their beds and slit their throats with a butcher knife, didn't she?"

"She was insane."

"They were her own grandchildren," Chitty almost screamed, "weren't they?"

"I repeat, she was insane."

Harley snuck a peek at the jurors, who were intent on the witness. Where was this leading?

Chitty didn't move, his glare still fixed on Wallace. "But didn't the jury conclude she was not insane?"

Wallace didn't move either, his eyes locked with his interrogator. "And the Court of Criminal Appeals overturned their verdict, sir. The jury was wrong."

Chitty eased back from his table and turned deliberately toward the jury. "In your opinion, Dr. Wallace, was that Johnson County jury . . . ignorant?"

"They were wrong."

"Did you not call them *ignorant* in your article about the case?"

"I don't recall writing that."

Chitty opened the booklet to a marked page. "Sir, did you not write 'It was very difficult to find twelve men sufficiently ignorant to serve on the jury?'"

"I'm sure I did. I meant ignorant of the facts of the case, of course. The murders were notorious in Johnson County."

Chitty's eyes widened. "So, you weren't calling the gentlemen of that jury ignorant?"

"I most certainly was not."

"All right. I'll come back to that later." He flipped to the next page. "In your article you complained about the prosecutor's conduct, didn't you?"

"I'm not sure what you're referring to."

"Allow me to read what you wrote—"

"I object to reading a hearsay article," Harley cried.

Chitty laughed. "I didn't object when they read an article from a medical journal. I'm entitled to do the same."

Now Harley realized the trap Chitty had laid by not objecting to Wallace's previous reading of the article. This lawyer plotted and planned like a general of the army.

"Overruled."

"Didn't you write 'When a medical man gives it as his opinion, based on all this evidence, reinforced by personal examination, that she was insane, the prosecuting attorney, fearing it would seem, the effect of this evidence with the jury, asked with a very grave look and significant tone of voice, 'Doctor, what is your religion?' Did he think because his witness belonged to no church and professed no creed, that he was less capable of telling the truth than if he repeated night and morning on his knees the whole Athanasian Creed and swore by the thirty-ninth article of faith?'" Chitty pointed his finger at Wallace. "Did you write that?"

"I did. And you have asked the same irrelevant question, I suspect for the same reason."

Chitty snarled back, "Well, let me read *your* next words. 'Or did he wish to prejudice an ignorant, superstitious jury?' Did you write that too?"

Wallace didn't answer.

"So you do believe the twelve gentlemen over there"—his hand swept over the jury box—"are ignorant and superstitious?"

"I don't know any of them. I have no reason to question their intelligence at all."

"Ignorant," Chitty relentlessly charged, "because they're not as smart as you?"

"I don't know them."

"Superstitious because they put their faith in the Lord God rather than the musings of some foreign doctor?"

Wallace didn't answer. Papa shifted in his chair.

"You called the verdict in Mary Newberry's case remarkable, didn't you?"

"The jury was wrong."

"Mary Newberry *confessed* to killing her three grandchildren, didn't she?"

Wallace slammed his hand on the rail. "Yes, like the crazy old women in Salem who confessed to witchcraft. I remind you sir, the Court of Criminal Appeals agreed with me the evidence established her insanity."

"And so, doctor, after the court overturned the jury's verdict, Mary Newberry went to the state asylum?"

"She was admitted to Terrell."

Chitty edged closer. "Where you had served as superintendent?"

"I did."

Chitty bent toward his quarry. "Your testimony was responsible for sending her there rather than prison as the jury decided, wasn't it sir?"

"There was other evidence."

Chitty almost shouted at the witness. "And when child-killer Mary Newberry got there, she hung herself, did she not?"

"She was a troubled soul."

He slammed his hand on the table. "And you say it was an ignorant and superstitious jury that convicted her of murder?"

"They were wrong."

Chitty's voice dropped, and he inched even closer to the witness stand. "Dr. Wallace, are you confident in your opinion about Mr. Topper?"

"I certainly am."

"Anyone who might have the temerity to disagree with you would be wrong?"

"I believe so."

"You're confident of that too?"

"I am."

Chitty faced the jury as he rattled off the next question. "Just like you're confident the jurors in Mary Newberry's case were wrong, the judge was wrong in making you testify without compensation, the prosecutor was wrong in questioning your religion, and Drs. Clopton and Carhart were wrong in disagreeing with your presentation to the Texas Medical Association?" He whirled back on Wallace, who was momentarily silent.

Papa slowly craned his head toward Harley. His look declared that Chitty had destroyed their witness and dismantled their case, but Harley could see that for himself.

"I don't know how to answer a question like that," Wallace replied. "Is it even a question?"

Chitty's voice cracked with emotion. "Everybody's wrong but you, doctor?"

Wallace glared back.

"I'll wager you think I'm wrong too?"

"The jury may judge for themselves."

"They will indeed." Chitty faced the jury one more time before he took his seat. "They will indeed."

Chapter 18

"Mr. Calloway, any questions?" the judge asked after Chitty concluded his cross-examination of Dr. Wallace.

"Yes, sir." Harley said a prayer in the silence that followed. He didn't know the answer to the question he had to ask. He carefully centered his weight on both feet and relaxed his shoulders. "Dr. Wallace, do you believe in God?"

"I most certainly do."

Harley let out a breath. "Would you please explain for the court the point in your paper to the medical association?"

"Certainly." Wallace turned to the judge. "We hear from the reports of lunatic hospitals that ten to thirteen percent of those insane can be attributed to religious causes. I do not believe true religion, before God the Father, ever was or ever will be the cause of insanity to any human mind. Religiosity and theology, on the other hand, doubtless have counted their victims by the thousands. Religion impels us to do unto others what we would have them do unto us. That altruism never did and never will, while the world stands, produce a single case of insanity. That unfortunate paper which I read before the medical association, to which certain bigots and zealots affected to take offense, meant just this and nothing more."

Harley blinked his thanks to Dr. Wallace. "That's all, Judge."

Papa scribbled a note and slid it in front of Harley. *Damage already done. Third juror in back is deacon in Baptist church.*

Harley's gaze panned across the jurors. Every one of them appeared to be God-fearing men. As he'd drawn it up before trial, Harley had thought the insanity case a strong one, its foundation laid with the testimony of Moon and Lazenby and its capstone firmly fixed by the learned opinions of Dr. Wallace, but after Chitty's surprising cross-examination, he feared the case had collapsed for want of support. The prosecutor had somehow learned Wallace would testify and done careful research on him. He made Wallace appear arrogant and wrong-headed.

But they had no more evidence and no time to gather any, so he rested Toby's case.

"The state of Texas calls Dr. Bernard Pepys," Chitty announced when the judge asked the State to proceed with its rebuttal case.

That they would call an expert at all was a complete surprise. Because Pepys wasn't from Waco, Harley knew nothing about him—nor did Papa, judging by the look on his face.

Harley jotted a note and passed it back to Wallace, who'd taken a seat next to Miss Peach. *Who is he?*

Wallace read the note, looked up, and shrugged.

In contrast to Wallace, the state's expert was a much younger man. Harley objected he wasn't qualified to opine on insanity, neither being an alienist by education nor a practitioner of mental health care by experience, but the judge overruled the objection.

"Dr. Pepys," Chitty said, "based upon your examination of Mr. Topper, do you have an opinion as to his mental condition?"

He twisted around in the witness chair to look at Toby, who rocked back and forth. "He's odd, but most certainly of sound mind and in fact quite intelligent."

"Why do you say that?"

"He responded to my questions appropriately. He displays a prodigious capacity for remembering information and reciting it upon request. He's singularly clever, I think. I gave him a Bible which I happened to have with me"—he glimpsed at the jury—"and I asked him to read the first chapter. He recited from memory the entirety of Genesis from one reading. It was precisely accurate, word for word. Truly remarkable. Could any of us do something like that?"

A juror on the front row shook his head.

"I could not," Chitty answered. "Thank you. Nothing further."

Harley had never cross-examined a medical man before, and in fact he'd only cross-examined fact witnesses twice, and neither of them were that important to the case on trial. He wished he'd had the same advantage as Chitty of knowing in advance this expert would testify so he could've prepared.

The judge peered at him. "Mr. Calloway?"

Harley rose. "How old are you, doctor?"

"Thirty-seven."

"So, you've been practicing medicine how long?"

"Over ten years."

"You're not an alienist by training or education?"

"As I said when Mr. Chitty asked me that earlier, my practice is general. I treat all manner of disease and injury. I do have experience treating patients with severe mental disorders, most caused by alcohol or opiates."

Should he ask how much experience? What if it was extensive? Perhaps it was better not to ask. "Have you ever treated an idiot savant?"

"Not that I know of." He turned toward the jury. "I suspect if that condition actually exists, of which I have doubts, then it is rare indeed."

"I saw you were in court while Dr. Wallace testified," Harley said, glancing back at his own expert. "Would you concede him more qualified to testify about that disorder?"

Pepys looked at Wallace. "His medical training was quite some time ago. Mine was the product of the latest advances in medical science." He broke into a smile. "You know what they say, counselor, you want a young doctor and an old lawyer."

The jurors chuckled.

Harley didn't. It was so much harder to hold the reins than to ride shotgun. It was as if he was blindly trying to navigate down an unknown alley with everyone watching him to see if he crashed into something. He glanced at Papa, but Papa's face was expressionless.

He had to keep going. "You practice in Dallas?"

"I do." Pepys added after a lull in questions. "As I said before."

"Doctor, are you familiar with Dr. Down over in England?"

"If he is supposed to be renowned as Dr. Wallace testified, then I'll say no one at the Massachusetts Medical College must have ever heard of him. My education was based upon the work of leading *American* physicians."

"You mentioned you examined Toby personally. When was that?"

"Earlier this morning."

"Where?"

"In the county jail."

"How did he appear to you physically?"

"Much as we see him today. As soon as I walked in, he began to rock and sway."

"How do you know he wasn't also rocking before you entered?"

Papa softly cleared his throat.

"The jail guard told me he only did that when visitors were around to see him."

The hearsay was out before he could object. It happened so quickly, yet Papa had seen it coming.

Papa whispered, "Lead him."

When Harley didn't immediately follow with a leading question, Pepys continued on his own. "The guard also said he was more talkative."

"Objection, hearsay!"

"He asked the question," Chitty answered.

"Overruled," the judge said.

Papa's blue eyes flashed a warning against further questions.

"That's all the questions I have, Your Honor." Harley said. "Pass the witness."

Chitty shot out of his chair. "You mean Topper is more communicative in private than he appears to be today in court?"

"Apparently."

That was preposterous. Harley's neck ached. He'd been ambushed by Chitty. Papa never would have let that happen.

Chitty leaned over to consult with Wilson and continued. "By the way, what church do you attend?"

"First Baptist Church, in Dallas."

In the second row of the jury box, the deacon flashed a smile at Pepys.

"That's all," Chitty said.

"Nothing further." Harley slumped back in his chair. Papa should have handled both experts. That was probably obvious to everybody.

Chapter 19

Just three days earlier Catfish had stood in the same place, ten feet from the jury, not having any idea what to say to the jury in defense of Toby Topper. Now in his closing argument, he felt little more confident, except he had an abiding belief that the boy was innocent. "If he doesn't have the mental power to premeditate a robbery and carry out his plan and doesn't even have the ability to follow somebody else's plan, then the only possible explanation is someone must have masqueraded as Toby."

He grabbed the top hat from the court reporter's desk, strode back to the defense table, and stood behind Toby as he rocked incessantly. "Toby's one of the most recognizable people in Waco. Nobody else wears a top hat like this and rides a bicycle."

While he advanced toward the jury, Catfish popped the hat onto his own head and doffed time and again. "Nobody else tips his hat incessantly. Mimic Toby and folks'll think you're Toby. Especially witnesses who didn't know him, like Mr. Prim. What better person to set up as a murderer than a man who can't defend himself?"

"No gentlemen, while Toby is plainly a simple-minded, he's not guilty of the crimes alleged."

Catfish believed what he'd said without the slightest

hesitation, but he also knew they'd produced no evidence at all as to who set Toby up. In his rebuttal argument, Chitty didn't let that escape the jury's attention.

***

Papa never appeared very concerned at times like that. Sweating a jury, he called it, but he never seemed to sweat. Feet propped on the defense table, White Owl billowing smoke, Papa read Strand Magazine, his favorite. "Harley, look at this." He held a page of engraved portraits. "Look like our Miss Peach?"

Harley examined the engravings of a British artist named Louisa Starr. The one depicting her at age twenty remarkably resembled Miss Peach. "Maybe."

They both glanced at her, sitting in the gallery speaking privately with Dr. Wallace.

How did Papa so calmly pass the time when so much was at stake? On the other hand, maybe his nonchalance today meant he was optimistic. Perhaps Harley's fears were unwarranted, and Papa felt good about their chances. He had a more experienced perspective after all.

"How do you think it went?" Harley asked.

"Never know with a jury, do you?"

"Right." Harley took off his jacket and slung it across the back of his chair. "Do you have an extra cigar?"

Papa's head jerked back before he pulled a White Owl from his satchel and lit it for Harley, who took one puff and broke into a coughing spasm.

Papa wasn't sharing how he felt about their chances. He must have thought they would lose.

After Dr. Wallace left, Miss Peach joined them. Harley put out his cigar; he didn't care for them anyway.

"How long do you think they'll be out?" she asked.

"No more than two shakes of a lamb's tail." Papa took the Waco newspaper from his satchel.

Harley's eyes met Miss Peach's. She did resemble that artist. He'd always been amazed at how much she said with only a look. As if her vocabulary needed any supplementation. He was grateful for her look because it expressed better than words that, win or lose, everything would be fine. She always seemed to know when he needed that.

Papa turned the page of his newspaper with a crackle. "Nothing but Cotton Palace in the news."

Harley watched him read. *I'm sorry Papa. I know I let you down. I'm not Catfish Calloway no matter how hard I try.*

Papa turned another page. His warm blue eyes flitted across the paper.

"I can't wait for it to start," Miss Peach said.

Wait for what? Harley tried to conceal a glance at her. Even in the courtroom, her face glowed. *I disappointed you too. I know how much you care about Toby.*

After she spoke, her eyes were on him, not Papa. She was saying by her kind expression that he did his best for Toby.

Harley tugged the folds in his vest taut. *My best wasn't good enough though, was it?* He should have researched Dr. Wallace's writings himself. He could have warned him how to handle it, or he could have asked the judge to exclude it from evidence as irrelevant. And he certainly should have been better prepared to cross-examine Pepys. Not only better prepared, but a more skilled questioner. Frankly, though he'd watched his father cross-examine scores of witnesses, he was, at best, an awkward questioner himself. Why hadn't he insisted Papa do it? He never would have made the kind of mistakes Harley had. And now

Toby would pay the price for Harley's incompetence. He should have stuck with researching the law and writing briefs, things he was better at. Papa was the trial lawyer in the family, not him. How foolish he'd been to think otherwise.

Miss Peach's look turned into a smile. "I thought you were marvelous today. The jurors would never trust Chitty or that horrid Wilson over you."

Harley gritted his teeth. It needed to be said. "Frankly, I'm not well-suited to jury trials. Papa, I think from now on, we should go back to the way we did it before. Me riding shotgun for you."

"That's silly." Papa put the newspaper down. "It was your first cross-examination of an expert witness. Nobody does anything perfectly the first time around."

But Toby shouldn't suffer because his lawyer was inexperienced. His cross wasn't just not perfect, it was positively calamitous. Harley dragged himself out of his chair. "Excuse me a moment." He headed for the restroom downstairs, avoiding Miss Peach's eyes. He had to quit moping like a disappointed schoolboy. Papa wouldn't do that. What's done was done.

Before he could get out, there was a loud knocking on the door from inside the jury room. He froze. The bailiff startled, hopped out of his chair, and hurried to the door.

It was a verdict.

Chapter 20

"Gentlemen of the jury," Judge Goodrich said, "have you reached a verdict on the question of whether Mr. Topper was insane at the time of the alleged murders?"

"We have," Mr. Bonner said.

The judge examined the jury's written verdict and looked up at Toby.

Catfish could see the result on his face. He helped Toby to rise. Once on his feet, he started rocking again.

The judge read the verdict. "Was the defendant, Toby Topper, sane or insane at the time of the shooting of Bill Hook and Lawrence Hay? Their answer is that he was sane."

"Good," muttered Old Man Stanek.

Toby continued rocking without alteration while Catfish and Harley held him tightly by both arms. The boy was surprisingly strong.

Judge Goodrich addressed the jury again. "Have you reached a verdict on the charges of murder?"

"Yes, sir."

Goodrich cleared his throat. "The jury has found the defendant guilty of first-degree murder of Bill Hook. Additionally, the jury has found the defendant guilty of first-degree murder of Lawrence Hay."

Toby rocked.

"Hang him!" Stanek shouted.

The judge's head shot up. "Now, Mr. Stanek, I need you to keep yourself, please."

While Stanek glared at Toby, his daughter wept.

Goodrich's manner turned solemn. "The jury has sentenced the defendant to death."

***

Every head in Bismark Hall turned as Catfish led Harley and Miss Peach to a back table. She had balked at going into a smoky saloon packed with a late-afternoon crowd of men, but he'd insisted. It was where they went after trials, and he wanted to hear their thoughts. They needed a way forward.

He dropped his cane on the tabletop, Latin side up. He'd been hopeful the jury would hear their side of it and find Toby innocent, or at least insane. He was plainly mad as a March hare and incapable of carrying out that robbery. Catfish lit a White Owl and blew smoke at the ceiling, where it merged into the gray cloud already hovering over their table. "We're not letting that boy hang."

Miss Peach put her handkerchief over her nose and eyes. Was she crying, or was it the smoke bothering her?

"His lack of reaction to the death sentence shows he can't comprehend what's happening to him," Harley said.

Catfish puffed his cigar.

The blond-haired German-born proprietor, Mr. Kophal, brought a bottle of Strathisla, Catfish's favorite Scotch whisky, and three glasses.

Miss Peach had ginger ale. "Are we going to appeal?"

"As soon as we can post a bond," Catfish answered.

Across the saloon a group of revelers broke out singing to accompany the player piano. "Daisy, Daisy, give me your answer do!"

Miss Peach raised her voice to be heard. "What are our chances?"

The singing spread around the saloon. "I'm half crazy, all for the love of you!"

"It's always a long shot." Catfish paused for the now boisterous chorus to finish.

"It won't be a stylish marriage, I can't afford a carriage." The self-appointed melodist-in-chief conducted the rowdy crowd by hoisting his mug high. A younger man in his cups at the next table crooned at Miss Peach. "But you'll look sweet ... on the seat ... of a bicycle built for two!"

Catfish blew smoke in his face, and the young drunk backed off, coughing. "Trouble is, some judges don't like granting new trials because they overturn a jury's verdict. They're elected officials, and the jurors are voters."

"I've got another idea." Harley pulled the code of criminal procedure from his briefcase. "We file an Article Seven Eighty-One plea."

Catfish rocked back, blowing smoke at the ceiling. "Remind me."

"A writ de lunatico. It's in chapter two." He quickly flipped through the pages. "Here it is. 'If it be made known to the Court at any time after conviction, or if the Court has good reason to believe that a defendant is insane, a Jury shall be impaneled to try the issue.'"

"Isn't that what just happened?" Miss Peach asked Harley.

"The judge ruled that we waived our challenge to Toby's competence to stand trial by requesting a trial setting and announcing ready. So we tried only the murder charges and our defense of insanity—his insanity at the time of the murders. Article Seven Eighty-One says if he's insane *after* conviction we can challenge imposition of punishment."

Miss Peach coughed, and Catfish put out his cigar.

"Makes sense." God bless Harley for knowing more law than Moses. "We'll have time to gather evidence. Harley, do you think we can keep Chitty from going into the facts of the killings in the writ hearing? That's what prejudiced this jury against Toby."

"It's irrelevant," Harley replied. "The issue in this hearing would only be his sanity after conviction, not at the time of the murders."

Catfish sipped his whisky. "Good work, son."

Harley stuffed the book back in his briefcase. "Though we have the burden of proof at the hearing to show he's insane, all we need to do to get a hearing is file an affidavit of a respectable person swearing he's presently insane."

"You can swear out that affidavit," Catfish said to Miss Peach.

"Yes, sir."

Harley poured another glass of whisky. "And then the judge must issue the writ ordering a jury trial. He has no discretion to refuse."

"What happens if the new jury finds him insane?" Miss Peach asked.

"The judge would suspend the death sentence until he regains his sanity." Harley sniffed his whisky. "Toby won't, of course, so he goes to an asylum for the rest of his life."

"Hmm," Catfish muttered. Better than prison anyway.

Miss Peach's eyes flitted between them, not watering anymore. "But we're still going to appeal the guilty verdict, right? So he can go free rather than to an asylum? You're not suggesting that writ instead of appealing?"

Catfish snatched his cane and spun it between his palms. "Not at all. We've got some good grounds, but an appeal takes time and there's no guarantee we'll get a new trial in the end. The lunacy writ gives us another way to save his neck, so we do both. Two bites at the apple."

"What do you want us to do, Papa?"

"Harley, you start the appeal and do the briefing. In the meantime, we'll get Miss Peach's affidavit on file and start the lunacy writ in motion. I intend to find out who set Toby up. That was what we lacked in the trial. It wasn't enough just to show Toby was incapable of committing the crimes; we needed evidence of who did."

Catfish excused himself to answer nature's call.

***

Not even a third shot of Strathisla while Papa was gone made the jury verdict any easier for Harley to take. He poured another when his father returned. "I'm sorry I didn't do better with Wallace and Pepys."

Papa shook his head. "We only jumped into the middle of this case three days ago. Didn't know anything and didn't have any time to find out. We were fighting a rear-guard action the whole trial."

"Regardless," Harley said, "I should have spent more time preparing Wallace."

"Wouldn't have mattered." Papa finished his whisky. "We had a turncoat."

Miss Peach leaner closer. "We had what?"

"Young Boswell sold us out. Saw him in a buggy with the walrus yesterday afternoon when I was coming back from Risher's Drug. I had something else on my mind and forgot about it, but I'm pretty sure they were ready for Wallace because Boswell warned them."

Harley was speechless. He downed another shot. What an ungrateful wretch. They probably wouldn't see him at the office again.

Miss Peach seemed just as shocked. "Wasn't that about the time they got that telegram and Mr. Chitty asked you for more time?"

"But he told us something had come up in Dallas," Harley said.

"Chitty isn't to be trusted or taken too lightly. When we go to court next time, we'll be ready for him. And, son, I want you to take the lead again on the experts."

"No, Pa—"

"Yes, you will, and you'll do fine. Trust me, son. Been there myself." Papa's warm blue eyes, his locks falling over his brow, his wisp of a smile were all the same as when Harley was a boy, when he cried after failing an examination in grade school because he didn't study, when Papa held him in his lap, when he said, "You'll do better next time, son."

Papa had been right back then. All Harley could do now was work even harder. At least brief-writing was something he was good at. He couldn't let everyone down again.

Miss Peach's shoe touched Harley's under the table. Her eyes said *All's well.* He withdrew his foot and twisted so Papa couldn't see his face. He blinked *Thank you* to her and turned back to Papa. "Do you think we should wait until we see if the Court of Criminal Appeals grants us a new trial before we spend time working up a new defense?"

"I'm confident you'll win the appeal for us, and when you do, I'll have proof of who set Toby up."

The door banged shut behind a group blown into the room by the needling late autumn wind and rain.

Chapter 21

Catfish was hopeful such a fine, sunny October day would shed new light on Toby's past. From his perch on a bench outside City Hall, he watched for Sergeant Quinn to emerge for his rounds. There were some nagging questions the officer could answer if he were willing, but Catfish knew better than to meet him in his office.

When Rome Walker came along, Catfish dropped his Stetson over Colonel Terry's head before the vigilant hound spotted that cantankerous old coot on the other side of Third Street. The colonel always growled at Rome Walker. Not sure whether it was because he was a Republican or because he was just a fractious example of the human species.

"How do, Mr. Walker," he said as Walker crossed the street. "How's the dairy business today?"

"See your cur-dog's taken to wearing hats," Walker grumbled. "Suits him."

At the sound of Walker's voice, a low muffled growl emanated from under the hat. Catfish mashed it down further as Walker disappeared into City Hall.

As he did, Lieutenant Palmer came busting out the doors in a rush. He glanced Catfish's way but didn't even grace him with a nod as he took off down Austin Avenue. That cross-examination in Cicero's case hardly warranted such lingering hostility, but Catfish was relieved Palmer was gone. He'd never let Quinn answer Catfish's questions.

Quinn exited the building minutes later.

Catfish relieved the colonel of his hat and waved it at Quinn. "How do, Sergeant, sit a spell?"

The copper took a seat beside him. "What can I do for you?"

Catfish wiped dog slaver from his hat lining and snugged it on his head. "Been fretting over Toby Topper's case. Can I visit with you about it?"

The officer glanced toward Lieutenant Palmer as he got farther away on Austin Avenue. "We really shouldn't be talking about that."

Quinn could rightly refuse to discuss the case since it was on appeal, but he was a good cop who cared about what was right, and Catfish hadn't detected in Quinn much affinity for either Lieutenant Palmer or the appointed special prosecutor. "Please. It's a matter of life and death to my client."

For a moment Quinn eyed Catfish as if debating with himself. "What do you want to know?"

Catfish had an abiding conviction that Toby was incapable of premeditating a robbery. But somebody did plan it and make it look like Toby was the robber. Maybe Quinn would answer his bigger questions if Catfish eased into them. "Been wondering, you folks ever find the rest of that money?"

Quinn snickered. "We've looked everywhere he might've hidden it, but no luck yet."

"Hard to imagine why a fella like Toby would have any use for all that money."

"I don't know."

"Makes me wonder if somebody else has it." Catfish poked at

a chunk of gravel with his cane, giving Quinn time to react, but he didn't. "You testified you got a tip about Toby's whereabouts. I was wondering who gave you that information?"

Quinn peered toward Palmer, who was disappearing into a bank.

"It's important," Catfish insisted.

Under the brim of his keystone hat, Quinn's brow wrinkled into deeply carved furrows. "Sorry, Mr. Calloway, he didn't give a name."

"Figured that," Catfish said. "Can you tell me anything at all about him?"

"I'm afraid I don't know anything."

Catfish's knees had been troubling him ever since the trial. He rubbed the ache out of his right one. "Well, sir, tell me this: I don't recall you testifying about how you learned the express wagon was left outside the cotton mill."

"The same man told us."

Mighty suspicious. Catfish stretched his leg, but the knee still throbbed. "Same fella, huh?"

"As I recall. It was a telephone call. I never met the man face to face."

Catfish raised his cane to greet a friend riding by in a buggy and asked Quinn, "Seem peculiar to you the tipster knew where the wagon was *and* where Toby was?" Catfish leaned back and looked up as if he was trying to find the explanation in the clouds. "How'd he manage that, I wonder? Did he follow Toby for some reason from the wagon to the shanty?"

"I didn't think about it."

"Or maybe they were in cahoots and he turned on Toby?"

"It's possible Toby had an accomplice."

He hoped Quinn would figure it out on his own. "Or maybe

the tipster did the crime himself and set it up to look like Toby did it?"

"All I know is, we found Mr. Topper with the money."

"Yes, sir, you sure did, didn't you?" Catfish tapped the sidewalk with the rubber tip of his cane. "Of course, that wasn't all of it. There was twenty-three thousand dollars Toby didn't have on him, right?"

"True."

"You testified you paid this tipster fella a reward put up by American Express. Where'd you send it?"

"Oh, if I recall, he contacted the company himself and arranged it all. We never saw the money."

Two spinsters strolled by. "Good afternoon, gentlemen," the older one said with a smile.

Catfish tipped his hat. "How do, ladies."

Quinn nodded to them.

"If I remember right, you testified you found several things at the shanty"—Catfish started counting off with the fingers of his left hand—"the stolen money and the pistol and the brown coat and the top hat?"

"Uh-huh."

"Anything else?"

"Not that I recall."

"Think hard, Sergeant. It's important. Was Toby sleeping on the floor? On a bed? Was there something around where he was sleeping maybe? Did he have food there? Water? Anything you can think of would help."

"Well, he was sleeping on the floor, but he had a dirty canvas spread out, and he was on that." He thought for a moment and brightened. "You know, there was some blood. I don't think I was asked about the blood in my testimony."

Of course the prosecutor didn't ask him about that. Catfish locked eyes with Quinn. "Where was the blood?"

Quinn shoved his hat back. "On the canvas, I think. Would have been about where his head was probably."

"Any blood on his head?"

"Not that I recall, but I didn't look."

Catfish's mind raced. Whoever did this knocked Toby out, left him with the incriminating evidence, and tipped the police. But he needed evidence. "Did you save the canvas?"

Quinn shook his head.

"Too bad." Catfish spun his cane between his palms, causing the handle to twirl. A glance down the street didn't show Palmer anywhere. "Do you remember anything else you found?"

"No, that's it."

"Anything in his pockets?"

Quinn's expression changed. "Well, now there was something in a pocket. A folded piece of paper. It had some numbers written on it, but they didn't mean anything."

"Numbers, huh?" Catfish stopped spinning his cane. Something else the prosecutor didn't ask him about in the trial. "Still have it?"

"It's probably still in the coat pocket where we found it."

Down the street, Lieutenant Palmer ambled from the bank onto the sidewalk and turned back toward City Hall. They didn't have much time.

"Mind if I see that paper?"

Catfish accompanied Quinn to a police storeroom at the top of the stairs where Quinn looked through some boxes.

"While you're looking, let me ask you this." Catfish dropped into a chair. His knees were throbbing from climbing the stairs. "Been wondering how it is Toby got by. Think he was living in that shanty?

Doesn't seem like a fella who could take care of himself."

"We did some checking. He lived at the Methodist orphanage."

That was consistent with what the young man at Risher's Drug had told Catfish.

Quinn pulled a large box off a shelf and placed it on a table. "I spoke with Rev. Vaughn. Topper had just gone to live there in July or August maybe, but the day before the robbery he'd run away, and they hadn't seen or heard from him since."

Run away? Maybe he'd been kidnapped.

Heavy footsteps echoed up the stairwell.

Quinn opened the box and pulled out a dirty brown coat. He searched both pockets and retrieved a scrap of paper. "Here it is."

Catfish held the paper to the light from the open door. There was pencil writing. *58–15–13.*

Something blotted the light. "Calloway, what are you doing here?" Lieutenant Palmer charged into the room.

"Lieutenant," Quinn said, whirling to face his boss. "Mr. Calloway was just looking at some of the evidence in the Topper case, sir."

"What evidence?" Palmer demanded.

Catfish held out the paper. "You find any of your finger smudges on this?"

Palmer's face exploded at the reminder of Catfish's cross-examination about the so-called fingerprint science. Palmer snatched the paper away and took a quick look.

Catfish struggled to his feet. "Mind if I copy it down?"

Palmer stuffed the paper in his coat pocket. "Good day, sir."

Catfish hobbled down the stairs, his knees now protesting every step, but he thought only of the missing bloody canvas and the numbers on that paper. He'd only had a second to memorize them. *58–15–13.*

Chapter 22

Catfish took the Fifth Street trolley about a mile and a half out to the north edge of town. There were a few houses scattered about and not much else but bucolic farmland and woods.

"Where you headed?" the conductor asked.

"Methodist Orphanage."

"Not much there. Big brick place on Herring. Never been inside myself."

Catfish pulled a calling card from his pocket. He'd written the numbers from Toby's note on the back as soon as he'd left the police office. *58-15-13.* Toby was obsessed with numbers but only street addresses as far as he knew. Didn't look like that—no street written. Maybe a talking phone number. Catfish hadn't ever used a talking phone without Miss Peach's help, so he never paid much attention to the numbers. He stuffed the note back in his pocket.

He alighted at Herring Avenue. On the north side of Herring stood the red brick two-story building. He picked up a stick by the road and tossed it into the pasture. Colonel Terry charged into the field, brought it back, dropped it at his feet, and waited for the next toss. "That's all now, Colonel."

After looking around the grounds, he went inside. The colonel found a shady spot on the front porch.

Reverend W. H. Vaughn and his wife met with Catfish in the parlor. Reverend and Mrs. Vaughn treated the inmates of the sixteen-room residence as their own children because, as she explained, practical religion cares for the helpless. Decent folks.

Rev. Vaughn spoke with a kindly tone the children must find comforting. "Toby came to us as a blessing in the late spring or summer. His name is actually Budge, but everyone called him Topper because of the curious top hat he wore constantly. I don't know the origin of his attachment to it. We kept it for him in our room because he seemed so obsessed with taking it on and off."

Mrs. Vaughn was a petite woman in her late forties. "It would just drive us to distraction."

Her husband was about the same age, but already graying. "We'd give it to him when he went outside."

"Did he go out much?"

Mrs. Vaughn glanced at her husband. "Every day. He came to us with an old bicycle. That was his other prize possession. He rode every single day, and at first I escorted him." She smiled. "I have my own bicycle, you know."

"So does my stenographer." Catfish remembered what the hack driver told him about seeing Toby riding with a woman. "You don't happen to wear a hat with flowers on it when you ride, do you?"

"Why, no I don't. The breeze would blow it right off." Her eyes turned mischievous. "I do wear bloomers though."

Catfish grinned. "So does my stenographer."

Reverend Vaughn continued. "One day he didn't return home, and the next day we learned he'd been arrested."

She wiped away a sudden tear. "He seemed to get along fine on his own and would always return before long. Until that last day."

Reverend Vaughn placed his hand over hers.

Catfish gave them a moment. "I know that must have been a shock. Tell me what you thought of him."

The grandfather clock chimed, and she waited until it finished. "He's such a sweet boy, but deeply touched in the head. I don't believe I ever heard him speak—well, maybe once or twice. But mostly he would sit in a chair in his room and rock back and forth lost in his own world. The Lord knows what inhabits his mind, but I never did."

Catfish felt the same. He pulled out the calling card with the number and showed it to them. "This wouldn't happen to be your talking-phone number, would it?"

"We don't have a telephone, if that's what you mean," Rev. Vaughn said.

Catfish stuffed the card back in his pocket. "Did you ever notice he had a particularly good memory for numbers?"

Mrs. Vaughn turned to her husband.

He folded his hands on his knee. "It was quite curious. One day—it was soon after he arrived here—I told him we were going to take a buggy ride to see some friends, and I looked up their address in the directory. I think maybe I read the name and address aloud after I found it. I left the directory open on the end table when I went upstairs to get my coat. I returned and found him reading it."

Mrs. Vaughn leaned forward. "We knew he could read, but he never showed any interest in the Bible. We tried to get him to read scripture, but he was indifferent to it. And there he was"—she wagged her head—"reading the city directory like it was the Holy Word."

Rev. Vaughn continued. "Anyway, we'd always let Toby drive the buggy when we went somewhere together. He seemed to enjoy riding around town and was perfectly adept at navigating the streets, by our directions of course." His eyes widened. "Well, that day I noticed he would slow down before I even told him we needed to make a turn. So, I tested him. I didn't say anything about turning onto Eighth Street, but he turned there anyway. I looked at Mrs. Vaughn, and she looked at me. Lord Almighty, before we knew it, he pulled up at their house without a word of direction from either of us."

"Praise the Lord," she said, swatting the air emphatically with her delicate hand. "I was flabbergasted."

Catfish scratched his head. "How in the world did he know the way?"

Rev. Vaughn's head jerked back. "I have no id—"

"Oh," she interjected, "I think I may know, Mr. Calloway. We have a city map framed in the hallway. We got it when we first moved here. One day I saw him staring at it. I had no idea why, but he must have remembered it."

"Dear," her husband said, shaking his head, "he couldn't remember the details of that map from only one time."

She shrugged. "Maybe he studied it when we were busy elsewhere."

"Toby appears to have an extraordinary memory for things like that," Catfish said. "How'd he come to make deliveries for Harry Risher's drugstore?"

"The Lord does work in miraculous ways, doesn't he? Do you happen to know Miss Kate Friend?"

"The editor of *The Artesia*?" Catfish asked. "That weekly newspaper?"

"Yes. Miss Kate brought Toby to us originally, and later I commented to her about his ability to find his way in town. She came up with the idea of getting him employment with the drugstore to make deliveries, and she arranged it all."

"We were grateful, of course," Reverend Vaughn said, "because it helped us with his expenses and kept Toby occupied."

Catfish had met Kate Friend briefly once. Miss Peach spoke of her often. She was quite a lady. Very interested in taking care of animals and an intellectual sort. School teacher, he recalled. Maybe she was the bicyclist in the hat. "Tell me about her involvement with Toby."

Rev. Vaughn answered. "She brought him here one day and asked us if we would take him in. I'd seen Toby riding his bicycle around town, but I'd never paid him any mind. Anyway, Miss Kate was quite concerned about him and made a generous donation to help support him."

Mrs. Vaughn touched her pale cheek. "She asked us to use the name Topper rather than Budge. I'm not sure why. It may have something to do with his parents."

Chitty had used the name Budge in the trial. Might be something to it. "Do you remember anything about the parents?"

"The details are lost to me," Reverend Vaughn said, "but there was something not quite right. You best ask Miss Kate to tell you about it."

***

Harley was exhausted and had little interest in going anywhere but home. He had his nose in law books researching insanity law so long that if he had to read another page, he would have gone mad himself. Thankfully, it had been fruitful. The opinion by the supreme court in *Guagando v. State* might just win the Topper appeal for them. Such success earned him a relaxing evening at home.

Harley's hope of relaxation ceased when Papa hobbled into the office. "Gather round."

Miss Peach had followed him in, and Papa winced as he dropped into his swivel chair and cranked it around to face them. His arthritis was giving him trouble again. "There's some daylight in Toby's case."

He reported what he'd learned about the bloody canvas, the odd numbers on the scrap of paper, and Toby's parents. Harley and Miss Peach agreed the numbers were probably three separate telephone numbers, and she offered to search the city directory or check with the telephone company until she could attach names to the numbers.

"Let me follow one path right now," Papa said. "Miss Peach, don't you know that *Artesia* lady editor?"

She startled. "Kate Friend? Why?"

"You know her talking-phone number?"

"They don't have a telephone. Just a moment." She opened the city directory. "*The Artesia* number is one twenty-one."

Papa frowned. "We can eliminate her from the talking-phone list then. Go see her as soon as you can, Miss Peach. She knows Toby. Find out everything you can about him, especially about Toby's folks."

She jotted a note. "I happen to be going to her home tonight in preparation for a Cotton Palace program we've been working on."

"Perfect. Harley, why don't you go with her? Be sure to ask her if she's ridden bicycles with Toby and if she wears a flowery hat while riding."

Harley glanced at Miss Peach as hopes of the relaxing evening at home faded. "Yes, sir. We can show her the numbers. What else are you thinking we'll learn?"

"I'm thinking Toby's father is in the thick of this robbery. There's apparently such a stain on his name that the charitable

Miss Friend tried to shield Toby from it and started calling him Topper instead of Budge. In three decades of defending criminal cases, I've seen villainy aplenty, but what father's infamy is so egregious, or the memory of it so vexing, it's better for his son to hide his true identity?"

Chapter 23

"Walk on!" Harley drove his buggy through the darkness toward their destination across the street from the Baptist Church. He focused his fatigued mind on the task ahead. "Before we get there, tell me about Miss Friend."

"Everyone calls her Miss Kate," Miss Peach said. "She's about my age or maybe a little closer to yours. She's from Alabama, I think, and lives with her mother, Mrs. Branson. Her deceased father was a doctor. Miss Kate teaches at the Fourth District School. She's been the editor of *The Artesia* since Mr. Goldstein started it a couple of years ago."

"I don't believe I've ever read it," Harley said.

"It's primarily a weekly society paper. Anyway, I first met her when I was in Baylor. She lectured on Shakespeare to our women's literary club, the Calliopean Society."

He yanked the reins. "Haw!"

After they turned onto Jefferson Street, Harley settled the horse back into a steady pace. "If Miss Kate isn't much older than you, how is it she was lecturing to your club?"

She spoke up to be heard over the horse's clopping. "Because she knows more about Shakespeare than anyone in the entire state of Texas. And maybe beyond."

"That's hard to imagine."

"You'll see for yourself."

"Huh?"

"That's what we're doing tonight, silly. I told you, Miss Kate has organized a program for the Cotton Palace. A group of us will do readings from a play, and she'll lecture on it. Have you read *The Taming of the Shrew?*"

"Uh-uh."

Peach loved to use the bard's figures of speech, but he'd always found Shakespeare hard to understand. Law abhors ambiguity, poetry adores it. He hoped she wouldn't expect him to discuss Shakespeare intelligently. "Gee!"

They turned onto Twelfth Street.

"Well, you'll hear some *Shrew* tonight." She laughed. "The play I mean."

Not wanting to disappoint her, he put on a happier face. "Oh, wonderful."

"Mr. Harley, you must—" She stopped suddenly, and her hand flew to the seat between them. "You know, I've worked for you for three years now. May I call you Harley?"

Was she joking or was this serious? He gazed off at the passing houses, a few already dark.

"Am I being too bold?" she asked when he didn't respond.

"No, of course not," he stammered. "Though I'm technically one of your employers, I don't see any particular impropriety." He lashed the horse into a faster pace on the long stretch toward Franklin Street. "Outside the office, anyway."

"Of course," she said. "And you may address me as . . . Peach."

She laughed playfully; he couldn't fight off her gaiety any longer and let slip a smile. Maybe this wouldn't be so bad.

"Anyway, Harley," she said with her brilliant smile, "tonight you must clap after my lines, of course."

Even in the dim lamplight of the buggy, her face radiated beneath her straw boater.

"Of course."

Finally, after a long, silent stretch down Franklin they came to Four-Fourteen Mary Street. He'd made it that far without being expected to opine on the meaning of Hamlet's soliloquy. Miss Kate's home wasn't far from his own boarding house. This must have been where he'd seen Peach walking with that other fellow after work. Did she joke with him too?

***

"Enter Lucentio and his man, Tranio," Miss Kate prompted from her stool in front of the line of players.

One of them was Professor Henry Hargrove of the Baylor English Department, the very man Harley had seen Peach walking with. Harley shifted impatiently as the young professor took his cue and spoke in a deep stage voice.

"Tranio, since for the great desire I had to see fair Padua, nursery of arts, I am arrived for fruitful Lombardy . . ."

Harley loosened his necktie a little. Did the others find it stuffy too?

" . . . and haply institute a course of learning and ingenious studies. Pisa, renowned for grave citizens. . . ."

Grave and dead. On and on the professor read, oblivious to Harley's repeated, involuntary yawning. He covered it awkwardly. Peach, sitting upright on her stool, her script on the music stand before her, gleamed with delight at Hargrove's dreary performance.

Lacking the mental energy to follow obscure Elizabethan dialog, no matter how learned the tiresome professor was, Harley resolved instead to focus on the lady who was the object of their visit. Papa would describe Kate Friend as fetching. She wore her hair short but adorned with a red bow, gold butterflies, and a clover pin with diamonds in a curious headdress that bobbed and bounced with the rhythms of the verse. Though shorter than Peach and not so attractive, she was a formidable woman. Even more so than Peach. It was her manner: very confident, yet still charming. And friendly. *Methinks the name suiteth the lady.* He thought he might voice that quip but decided against it. It likely wouldn't be the first such jest about her name.

The other professor, playing Tranio, discharged his lines in a high, squeaky voice from the opposite end of the line of players. "Mi perdonato, gentle master mine. . . ." He was Dr. Alonzo Dow Gregory. His character was as densely verbose as Hargrove's Lucentio, so Harley ignored the poetry and studied the curious little man. His wavy hair swept to each side in perfect symmetry, and his beard, likewise bifurcated, sprang down and out in two long, pointed cones of stiff, curly hair. The hairy projections were shaped like the new ice cream cones at the Corner Drug.

Finally, it became Peach's turn. "I pray you, sir, is it your will to make a stale of me amongst these mates?"

Harley broke into applause, startling everyone since there hadn't yet been any clapping. Peach's hand flew over her mouth, and her eyes cackled.

Miss Kate shot him a sideways glance, but Hortensio jumped in without pause. "Mates, maid! How mean you that? No mates for you, unless you were of gentler, milder mould."

Peach took her cue. "I' faith, sir, you shall never need to fear. Iwis it is not halfway to her heart; but if it were, doubt not her care should be to comb your noodle with a three-legg'd stool, and paint your face, and use you like a fool."

She winked at Harley. He dare not clap but furrowed his brow and mouthed, *Iwis?* Her eyes widened in glee at his perplexity.

The scene went on and on until it finally, definitively, mercifully ended. Lucentio delivered the last lines of Act One, Scene One, and Miss Kate uttered the closing exeunt. Harley started to rise, but it was obviously no longer over.

"My lord, you nod; you do not mind the play," Hargrove said in a new voice. Was he addressing Harley?

Dr. Gregory replied in the voice of Sly. "Yes, by Saint Anne do I. A good matter, surely; comes there any more of it?"

Harley's heart sank at the prospect of more.

"My lord, 'tis but begun," Peach said, now in the manly voice of the Page.

"'Tis a very excellent piece of work, madam lady would 'twere done!" Sly said.

Miss Kate broke into energetic clapping and proclaimed it well done. The players bowed.

"Bravo!" Harley added, gambling the play was over for the final time.

"Let us take a recess before we commence Scene Two," Miss Kate announced.

She'd promised they would speak of Toby Budge during the break. At last. Harley stood and stretched his legs.

She led them to her library, where they settled for a talk. So many books. How did she have time for anything but reading? "Toby's poor mother was my friend. I heard much of Toby from her. He was a more normal child when he was young. At least his later habits weren't yet manifest. He was quiet though. In fact, I hardly remember him ever speaking. As he grew older, the odd behaviors began and gradually worsened. By the time he was in his middle teens, Toby had almost totally ceased to communicate."

"The prosecutor thinks Toby is feigning insanity to hide his crime," Harley said.

Miss Kate smirked. "Nonsense. He's no player of antic disposition, I assure you. I lived with him."

"Had he any brain injuries?" Peach asked.

"None I know of or ever heard his mother speak of."

"Were there any others in the family who displayed the same behavior? Maybe a sibling?"

"He had no brothers or sisters."

Harley was anxious to get to the most important point. "What about his father?"

Miss Kate's face transformed into a frown. "The man was addicted to liquor. I hardly ever saw him. When Toby started becoming difficult to handle, he left."

"Left?" Harley asked.

"He abandoned his family. Nobody has seen him since. It was truly disgraceful. Poor Penny. She was left alone to take care of a boy impossible to care for."

"What happened to her?" Peach asked.

"She took opium to deal with it, apparently. At least the doctor said so after she died of an overdose. I suspect she might have been on it long before. It's all so terribly sad."

Peach jotted notes in her copybook. "Is that when he went to the orphanage?"

Miss Kate paused until Peach finished writing. "When Penny died my mother and I took Toby in. He was about nineteen maybe, and we couldn't handle him. It was so stressful for my mother in particular, and it broke my heart. Honestly, we didn't know what else to do. So, I took him to Reverend and Mrs. Vaughn at the Methodist orphanage, and thankfully they agreed to accept him. They were so kind. I was very grateful."

Harley wanted to know more about Toby's capabilities. "Were you aware of his unusual skill at recalling addresses?"

She dabbed the corner of her mouth with a handkerchief. "Mrs. Vaughn said he used to read the city directory. I always thought that unusual, but it held his interest apparently. One day I needed to know where someone lived, and I spoke the name aloud. Toby was sitting in the corner rocking, and suddenly he stated the person's address in perfectly understandable English. As you might imagine, I was astonished."

Harley recalled Toby's similar feat during the trial.

"It gave me an idea—this was not all that long after he went to the orphanage—I arranged for him to make deliveries for Risher's Drug Store. Harry's a dear friend. I accompanied Toby at first and taught him what to do. He had ridden a bicycle before his idiocy worsened, so perhaps that's why he knew how to ride. Anyway, he was able to do amazingly well, and Harry was quite pleased with him."

"So, you rode with him?" Peach asked. "Someone reported they saw him riding with a woman. Did you happen to wear a hat at the time?"

"I think I probably did."

"How did Toby manage if he didn't communicate?" Harley asked.

"Harry would write the address and give it to Toby so he wouldn't forget, but he didn't need it. Harry would say the name, and Toby repeated back the address without looking."

Harley and Peach exchanged glances. The numbers Papa learned about from Quinn clearly weren't an address. He told Miss Kate about the note in Toby's pocket, but she didn't know what it was.

"Harry would put the item in Toby's wicker basket, and he'd take off. I taught him to knock on the door, and the customer would take the item from his basket. Sometimes they would drop coins in a tip cup I affixed to his handlebars."

"That's amazing," Peach said. "I remember he delivered to my landlady once."

Miss Kate's expression changed. "I feel terrible. I didn't even know he'd been arrested and was so shocked to hear of the trial."

"Did you ever know him to be violent?"

"No, never," Miss Kate insisted. "Not once. He's troubled in the head, but not a bad boy at all. I've never seen him be unkind to anyone. Usually, it's just the opposite. He pays no heed to anyone around him."

"Can you explain his behavior with the top hat?"

When Miss Kate bent her head, the gold butterflies in her hair glinted in the lamplight. "That was his father's hat. I never saw Toby wear it until his father disappeared, and he began to wear it constantly. When he did, he stopped rocking, but he repeatedly doffed the hat as if in greeting."

"If his name is Budge, why did you ask the Vaughns to call him Topper?" Harley asked.

"I felt it best to disassociate him from the father who abandoned him and the mother who committed suicide."

Peach sighed. "So sad."

Harley finished his notes. "I think that concludes our questions. We might want you to testify, assuming we win the appeal and get him a new trial."

"Of course. I'm quite sure he didn't murder the express men."

"Oh?" Harley asked.

"The killer used a gun, right?"

Harley nodded.

"Well, it couldn't have been Toby then."

"Why?"

"Because he's terrified of loud noises."

Harley recalled Toby cowering at the sound of the courthouse bell.

Miss Kate gestured toward the railroad track on Mary Street. "As you probably noticed, there's a spur track that comes next door, almost right to our house. The Cotton Belt station is in the next block. The trains often blow their whistles. Toby would go into a state of panic. He'd rock back and forth even faster and cover his ears with his hands until it finished. Mr. Calloway, he's incapable of firing a gun."

"A gun isn't shrill like a train whistle."

"It's loud noises that bother him. One day a train was stopped in front of the house when we were sitting on the front porch. A trainman struck the coupling between cars with a sledgehammer, and it sent Toby into his state. It cracked as loudly as a gun." She eyed Harley first before she turned to Peach. "What did the killer do after he fired the gun?"

"He shot twice, killing both men, got onto the wagon, tossed the bodies off, and sped away."

Miss Kate folded her hands in her lap. "It wasn't Toby Budge. Maybe it was his father."

Chapter 24

Catfish limped through the front door of Risher's Drug Store in search of information about Toby's father and the strange set of numbers.

He found the young druggist at the far end of the long wooden counter filling prescriptions. "Mr. Calloway, how may I help you today?"

"My decrepit old knees are complaining about having to support my ancient carcass. Anything you recommend?"

"Have they been giving out on you when you climb stairs?"

Catfish chuckled. "On bad days, they do. On good days, they crack and pop like fireworks."

Risher turned to browse one of the shelves behind the counter. "I've got bee venom. I've got extract of rhubarb." He brought several bottles to the counter. "How about one of these?"

Catfish popped on his pince-nez and examined the first bottle. *Hamamelis Extract Witch Hazel.* "Hmm."

"Stanley's is popular," Risher said, pointing at the other bottle. "Just rub it into your knee joints every day."

Catfish picked it up for a closer look. *Clark Stanley's Snake Oil Liniment.* Doc had already given him a bottle of imported Chinese snake oil, which he'd never used. Chinese snakes were reportedly more benign than Texas rattlesnakes. He removed his spectacles. "Think I'll wait it out."

Risher replaced the bottles on his shelf. "Then try a nice chair in your parlor with your feet propped. It's probably more effective than snake oil anyway."

"Obliged," Catfish said with a nod. "By the way, your talking-phone number wouldn't happen to be fifty-eight or fifteen or thirteen, would it?"

Miss Peach hadn't had any luck with the numbers yet, but she was going to the talking-phone office that morning.

Risher gave him a business card. "Our number's one forty-eight."

Catfish pocketed the card. "One other matter, Harry, if you don't mind. About Toby Topper. Do you happen to know anything about his father or why Toby came to live at the orphanage?"

"Not really." Risher fiddled with some boxes under the display case on the counter. "Kate Friend introduced us. She felt sorry for him. I think she said his father had run off maybe." He scratched his head. "Seems like he'd worked at William Cameron's lumber company, but that's about all I remember."

"Do you recall where you sent Toby to make deliveries on his last day?"

"Oh, been too long."

"You don't have any records of that?"

Risher wiped the counter with a rag. "Sorry."

After lunch at Lemke's Union House, Catfish stopped in at Cameron's lumberyard. The Cameron foreman confirmed Kate Friend's belief that Budge had run from the responsibility of taking care of Toby. According to the foreman, he complained bitterly about how much trouble the boy was. He drank heavily to escape the responsibility and disappeared without even bothering to get his last week's pay. Two years later, nobody had seen him since. There'd been rumors he was somewhere in Dallas, but nothing definite.

After visits to Risher's and Cameron's, Catfish's knees were in open rebellion, and he was ready to concede defeat to them. Maybe he'd even resort to snake oil. Or whisky. But he had one more stop first before five o'clock that Friday afternoon. He'd promised Harley he'd stop by the district clerk's office and see if Chitty had yet filed a response to their writ de lunatico.

***

"Miss June, darlin', you're a picture of sunshine today," Catfish said.

The deputy district clerk's eyebrow arched. "Mr. Calloway, you must want something."

He'd known the occasionally delightful spinster since the creation. "No, no, I swear to complete sincerity. I gave up ulterior motives last year for Lent."

"Hmm." She dropped a stack of envelopes on the counter without the hint of a smile. "What is it?"

"If you'd be so kind as to get me the file in *State v. Toby Topper,* please ma'am, I'd be grateful."

"Hmm." She turned to leave and grumbled over her shoulder, "I'll have to go to the vault to get it."

Bless her heart, the vault was across the Sahara desert, beyond the River Jordan, over the Himalayas, all the way upstairs next to the district courtroom. *Godspeed, Miss June.*

As he waited for Moses to lead her back from the wilderness, he leaned on the counter to relieve his knees. He hoisted his satchel onto the countertop and lodged his cane next to it. The silver dollar Harley had mounted on the cane's handle glinted under the clerk's lamp. It was the first dollar Harley had earned as a lawyer, and he'd given the cane to his father as a thank-you for his legal education, both in school and out. On the shaft Harley had also carved their Latin creed. Good memories.

Martha used to chide him that he had a keepsake like the cane for every person he'd ever known and every experience he'd ever had. He'd reply they were just jiggers. Many were to remember cases or clients. The widow Farley's lace doily rested on his lamp stand at home. She was a rambunctious old gal, but the jury loved her. It got harder to remember a case he tried even a week afterwards when he tried so many. And besides, many of his jiggers were gifts, as the cane was. There were certain notions he feared forgetting more than he feared hoarding, and jiggers of some kind helped him remember. Truth be told, some of them—mostly from the war, like his old saber and a minié ball a Yankee shot at him—proved a more burdensome memory than a blessing, and he'd retired them from the office to the Growlery, his home library and sitting room.

He pulled the magic pencil from his vest pocket so he could record the filing date of their answer to the writ, but he broke into a smile—another jigger. Martha herself gave him that one and had it engraved with Harley's and Houston's names, but he didn't need jiggers to remember some people by.

His dear, thoughtful Martha. She'd been gone almost ten years now. He'd thought of her every single day since then and spoken to her most days. She had always been a good listener. Even after going home to her precious Lord, she'd been there for him. Helped him get through Houston's trial—Cicero's too, for that matter. He often thought about what they'd be doing if she hadn't passed. Probably sitting side by side in their rockers on the front porch like they used to. Probably talking about Harley, remembering Houston. *Oh, Martha, how I love to hear your sweet voice carried on the wind when I close my eyes and think of you. Darlin', I miss holding you close. I'm sure you know that, but—*

"Here 'tis."

The clerk dropped the file on the counter and went back to more important matters.

"Thanks, Miss June."

For a murder case, there weren't that many papers. He checked the judge's docket sheet to see if Chitty had filed a response. The docket sheet recorded all the important occurrences in the case in order by the date of the occurrence. There was no response yet, but the clerk had set the writ for hearing in July. There was a notation of the appointment of the special prosecutor at the railroad's request of the indictment, of the arraignment, and "not-guilty" plea of the joint motion for a trial setting. It still bothered him why Jaybird would agree to a trial date when he didn't even have a defense yet.

This case had gone to trial in less than a month after the robbery. Normally it could be as much as a year or more in a murder case, and this was a robbery and double murder. Then too, there was the complicating factor that the county attorney recused himself from the prosecution because he had a conflict of interest. That's why the judge appointed Chitty and the walrus as special prosecutors. Things had sure happened fast in this case.

He shifted his weight to the other leg, braced himself with his cane, and continued reading the docket sheet. The next entry was for the commencement of trial. Something was peculiar though, something missing. He told Harley so often a document was important for what it didn't say as much as for what it did say. He checked the docket sheet again to see if he missed it. No, there was no record of the appointment of Jaybird. Catfish had assumed the judge appointed Jaybird to defend Toby because he had no lawyer and couldn't afford one. The appointment of Chitty as special prosecutor was noted but not the appointment of defense counsel. Maybe Judge Goodrich just neglected to record it.

He cleared his throat. "Miss June, sorry to bother you again, but your docket sheet doesn't show when Mr. Jaye was appointed."

She peered up from her desk. "Wasn't appointed."

"Beg pardon?"

She raised her voice like he was deaf. "I said Judge Goodrich didn't appoint him. Only appointed the special prosecutor."

Catfish chewed on it—couldn't be true. "I didn't know that."

"I remember it distinctly. Mr. Jaye and Mr. Chitty came in together. They both wanted the earliest trial setting I could give them." She shrugged and went back to her work.

"I bet something like that never happened before."

She spoke without looking. "Now who would hire an old fool like Mr. Jaye to defend a murder case?"

Catfish dropped the docket sheet on the counter and stared out the window. His head pounded harder than his knees. Toby sure didn't hire Jaybird himself. Somebody else did. If the county wasn't paying him, who was? His sorry rascal of a father?

And why Jaybird of all people?

Why would anyone hire the worst lawyer in McLennan County to win a murder case?

Unless he wasn't hired to win.

Chapter 25

The clock gonged once. How odd. It was almost nine thirty on Monday morning, yet neither Mr. Calloway nor Harley had arrived at the office and that was so unlike them. Peach hadn't seen or heard from them since she said goodbye to Harley at closing time Friday afternoon. Mr. Calloway hadn't returned from his errands by then.

As she was typing a document something outside drew her attention. Harley's buggy pulled in front of the office, and he tied his horse to the post. He whisked into the reception room, hurrying right by her toward his office. "Good morning," he said with a smile as he passed.

She stopped typing. "Good morning."

Almost immediately he reappeared with his briefcase, still wearing his hat and coat. "I'm on my way to see Mr. Garlington."

She found the owners of the three telephone numbers, and one of them, number thirteen, was Garlington & Sons, a wholesale fruit business right across Fourth Street in the Willis Building. Coincidently, telephone number fifteen belonged to Williamson Drug, also across the street on the corner at Fourth and Austin. The third was some distance away, at Nineteenth and Morrow.

She looked out the front window toward the Willis building.

"Are you meeting Mr. Calloway over there?"

Harley checked the clock and sagged into the chair beside her desk. He stifled a grin. "He's laid up at home. His knees finally gave out Friday evening, and I took him home."

"Oh?" She frowned. Poor man. He'd been having trouble for several days, and it seemed to be getting worse. "Is there anything I can do for him?"

"He'll be fine. When I saw him Sunday, he was rubbing in snake oil. He mainly needs rest." He chuckled. "He's a little surly about it, but he's been at home all weekend with his feet propped."

"He must be roaring like a caged lion."

"A whole pride of them. He's beside himself to find answers about the Budges and those telephone numbers. I told him I'd call on Garlington."

She could visit the other two. "Can I help?"

Harley's eyes signaled there was something else, but he was still holding it back. "Papa wants you to contact Jaybird and ask him to meet us at Papa's house at one o'clock this afternoon."

"One o'clock," she repeated as she jotted it down. "Mr. Calloway's house."

When she looked up, he was struggling to keep a straight face. "Then I need you to stay by the telephone and wait for Papa to call."

"To call? You mean on the telephone?" Not Catfish Calloway. He had to be joking.

Harley broke into a huge grin. "He'll telephone you after he's called the other two numbers," he said with mock seriousness. "He may want you to follow up in person."

Peach's hand flew to her mouth. *No!* Mr. Calloway would sooner crawl twenty miles on his aching knees to see somebody than call him on the telephone. "I'm sorry, but I don't believe any of it."

He was now grinning like a Cheshire cat. "Peach . . . Miss Peach . . . first thing this morning I sent the telephone company over to Papa's house to put in a line."

Her jaw dropped entirely of its own doing. "Oh my!"

"I know it's hard to believe, but I've finally talked him into getting a telephone at his house."

"And he agreed? To a . . . talking phone?"

"It was the only way I could convince him to stay at home for a few days and rest his knees. He's going to telephone Williamson and Levinski and find out what they know."

***

Catfish stared at the confounded contraption on the table next to his chair. It was like the part of Doc's stethoscope he put on your chest, but it was mounted on a candlestick-holder and wired to an ear trumpet. He'd talked on one a couple of times but didn't understand or trust them. The man from the talking-phone company had said all he had to do was pick it up and tell the operator lady who he wanted to talk to or what number he wanted to call. But how was he supposed to know it was really the person he wanted to talk to if he couldn't see him?

When it rang, he jumped. Wasn't supposed to ring on its own. Colonel Terry stared at it too and started to growl.

"Hush up."

It rang again and stopped. Then it rang again. He picked it up and put the trumpet to his ear like he'd done before. Nobody said anything, so he hung it up. If the confounded thing would ring of its own accord, for no apparent reason, he wanted no part of it.

Not more than a minute later it rang again. He put it to his ear, like the talking-phone man showed him, but there still wasn't anybody there. He started to hang it up once more when a man's voice came on. "Pete, y'all there?"

"Pete? I'm not Pete," Catfish shouted into the mouthpiece. "Who're you?"

"I'm calling Pete. Who are you?"

"I'm Catfish Calloway. Who's Pete?"

"Pete Barnes."

Catfish pressed the mouthpiece close. "Well, I'm not Pete Barnes. Why you calling me?"

"I'm not. I told the operator I wanted to call number three hundred and ninety-seven."

Catfish eyed the receipt the talking-phone man left. It said three hundred and ninety-seven was supposed to be his number. "You got the wrong three hundred and ninety-seven, mister."

There was a loud click.

"You still there?" Catfish yelled.

He didn't say anything.

"Speak up man!"

Still didn't talk. Catfish slammed the trumpet on the candlestick-holder. "Colonel, the world's being taken over by machines."

It rang again. He stared at it. Heat rose in his neck. After two rings, a pause, then two more rings, he picked it up.

"Pete, that you?" the voice said.

"Mister, I ain't Pete. I don't know Pete. He's sure not here in my house. You quit bothering me, hear?"

"You ignorant old fool. I read about you in that detective book." It clicked again.

Detective book! Catfish grabbed his cane and struggled to his feet. "Come on. We're going to see Levinski."

Colonel Terry's tail wagged as if he knew something important.

As he headed toward the back door, the talking-phone rang again. Knees be damned, he charged over to it, grabbed the wire, and yanked it out of the wall. "No more rings!"

***

When Harley returned from Garlington's, Papa was at the office talking with Peach with his feet propped on the chair beside her desk.

"What'd you find out?" Papa asked Harley before he could say a word.

"Nothing." Harley dropped his hat on the hook. "Nobody'd ever heard of Budge."

"Toby ever make any deliveries there?"

"No, sir. A fellow named Thompson remembered him riding around town, but it was pretty clear nobody had any connection to him or the robbery. They didn't even remember it happening."

"You believe 'em?"

"I do. I talked to Williamson too. No luck there either."

Papa started rubbing his left knee. It must have really hurt.

Harley was anxious to learn how Papa's new telephone line had worked. According to Williamson he hadn't called them. "Did you telephone Levinski?"

Peach covered her mouth.

Papa didn't answer immediately. He extended and retracted his leg several times, wincing as he did. "Never got ahold of him. So, let's pay him a personal visit." His boot clunked to the floor, and he grabbed his cane.

Harley glanced at Peach, whose look betrayed she knew something.

"You sure you're up to it?" Harley asked.

Papa hobbled toward the door as his dog hopped up, wagging his tail. "Colonel, get."

***

Catfish waited in an armchair in the bay window while Sarah Levinski fetched her husband from the back. He gazed out toward Nineteenth Street where the colonel waited in the buggy.

He'd known Jake for several years because he repaired his old Waltham watch. Had a shop on Austin Avenue three doors from Williamson Drug Store. Just around the corner of the same block from Garlington & Sons. What did any of them have to do with Toby? Maybe Jake would give the answer.

"Why, Mr. Calloway, how nice to see you," Jake said, entering the parlor.

"How do." Catfish stayed seated. "Pardon me for not standing, but the arthritis has got a grip on my knees today. Folks, this is my son, Harley."

They greeted him and sat on the couch.

Polish-born Jacob Levinski had a thick accent. "You need watch work, my friend?"

"Here on law business today."

Jake's eyes narrowed. "I'm not in trouble?"

Catfish smiled. "It's about Toby Topper. You know him?"

"I don't think so. Do you, Sarah?"

She shrugged.

"He used to make deliveries for Risher's Drug Store before he was arrested for robbery and murder. We're defending him and were wondering if he ever made a delivery here. Young man on a bicycle?"

"Uh-uh," Jake said.

Nor did they know anybody named Budge, nor anything about the robbery. They didn't recall ever speaking about it on the talking phone with anyone.

After they left, as Harley's buggy rattled along the gravel street back toward their office, Catfish twirled his cane between his palms. It was downright peculiar. It was inexplicable why Jake's talking-phone number would be in Toby's coat pocket at the time of the robbery. Maybe the real robber put it there, but why? Or was it already there when he stole Toby's coat? "Three talking-phone numbers, three unconnected people, and none of 'em have any apparent link to Toby or the robbery."

"I can't figure it," Harley said.

"It's peculiar two of the numbers are for businesses in the same city block, and the third number is associated with a business also in that block." He stopped twirling the cane. "All in spitting distance of our office."

"There must be something to it. It can't just be a coincidence."

"Maybe. Toby's not the talking kind. He does know plenty of numbers though."

"So?"

"While we meet Jaybird, let's send her back to see if Toby knows talking-phone numbers like he knows street numbers."

Chapter 26

Colonel Terry heaved himself up from his place in the bay window of Catfish's house, lumbered over to the stranger, and sniffed him. Catfish checked Jaybird's breath when he first arrived, and there was no odor of alcohol even up close. It was only half past one but still prime drinking time for a drinker. Jaybird winced when the colonel windmilled near him, and brushed off his trouser legs. The colonel returned to his perch, circled it three times, and collapsed into immediate slumber.

"What did you want to discuss with me, gentlemen?"

Catfish pointed to a document Harley held. "Here's our appeal brief in Toby's case, if you wouldn't mind signing it on the last page."

Harley handed Jaybird the thick document, stapled into a blueback cover. "We plan to send it to Austin immediately."

Catfish opened a box of White Owls and took one while Harley gave Jaybird a pen. The brief was a masterpiece of legal reasoning backed by an impressive array of case law. Catfish had never in his whole career been able to craft a brief of that quality. Not his strong suit. "And Harley, be sure to give Mr. Jaye a copy for his file."

After Jaybird scratched his name on the original, he flipped through his copy too hastily to read anything. Peculiar fella. The edges of his white collar were grimy, and the cuffs tattered. Without alcohol to mask it, mustiness emanated from him.

Jaybird dropped the brief into his lap. "I shall devour every word of it at the first opportunity."

Harley placed the original in his briefcase. "It's set for oral argument in April."

"Ah." Jaybird's eyes popped wide. "You don't expect me to participate in that, do you? The . . . that is to say, the argument? I'm not—"

Catfish caught a whiff of fear to go with Jaybird's mustiness. "Harley'll do that for us. He's our law man."

"Excellent." Jaybird expelled a stale breath and smiled at Harley. "Very wise choice."

"Cigar?" Catfish passed the White Owl box.

"No, thank you. I don't smoke." His eyes darted from Catfish to Harley and back. "Is there something else you wanted?"

Catfish lit his cigar. "You know, Mr. Jaye, now you mention it, there is one other thing I've been curious about."

"What is it?"

"I was wondering who it was exactly that hired you to represent Toby?"

"Oh? Well. It was Mr. Topper."

Catfish's pulse quickened. "Toby's father?"

Jaybird nodded.

Catfish put on a surprised face and eyed Harley. "Didn't we hear his father ran off sometime back?"

"Several years ago," Harley said. "He vanished."

"Peculiar." Catfish stroked his whiskers and gazed out the bay window toward Washington Street as if he was trying to make sense of it. When Jaybird began to shift in his chair, Catfish addressed him. "Did he come to your office in person?"

Jaybird's face was pale but for the web of tiny veins that converged on his bulbous red nose. "I never spoke with the gentleman."

"Then how'd he go about hiring you?"

"I received a letter and the fee by mail."

Catfish tapped ashes into a spittoon. He didn't rush. Didn't want to spook Jaybird. "By mail?"

"Uh-huh."

"Cash money?"

"Indeed."

"And he wrote a letter?" Harley asked.

"It was quite brief. He wrote he was Toby's father and desired me to represent the young man in the case. The envelope contained some treasury notes." Jaybird's eyes flitted back and forth between Catfish and Harley. "It was more than my usual fee for criminal matters, so I was delighted, of course. Anybody would be, you know."

"Of course." He probably celebrated the entire fee away before the day was out. Catfish blew a smoke ring. "How long after Toby was arrested did he contact you?"

"Oh my, let's see. It was less than a week, I think. I remember dining at Delmonico's on the Sunday after I received the fee. Remarkable oysters, you know." Jaybird smacked his lips. "Anyway, I met Toby at the jail on Monday, I think."

Catfish tried to make sense of this chain of events: The killing was early Wednesday morning. Police got a tip that afternoon. They arrested Toby that evening. The post office was closed on Sunday. Jaybird must have picked up the letter Friday or Saturday, so it was mailed Thursday or Friday. Only one or two days after the killing, at most. Mighty quick to hear Toby's arrested, find a lawyer, and mail money to him. If his father was in town and cared enough to hire a lawyer, why didn't he just go see Jaybird in person? If he was out of town, how'd he hear about it that quickly and get money to Waco?

"Mind me asking how much his daddy paid you?"

"Not at all." Jaybird beamed like he was worth every penny. "It was five hundred dollars."

Trying not to appear too eager, Catfish took another draw on his cigar. "What denominations of notes did he send?"

Jaybird sighed. "I don't receive many hundred-dollar bills, you know, but there were five of them."

As he suspected.

Harley too, apparently. He jotted a note. "Do you still have his letter?"

"Oh, no." His eyes darted from Catfish to Harley and back. "No reason to keep it, you know."

Harley set his pen down. "Where did the envelope come from? Did it have a post mark?"

"I didn't pay much attention to that, really." He shifted in his chair again. "Did I do something wrong?"

Catfish puffed the White Owl. "No, no, not at all. Still got the envelope?"

His eyes popped wide again. "Should I have saved it?"

"Just wondering."

Harley looked from his notes. "Did he sign his name?"

"Perhaps. I don't recall now."

Catfish blew a smoke ring across the room at Martha's old Singer sewing machine table. She'd never approve of him keeping a whisky decanter on it. Jaybird had been eyeing it. "Mr. Jaye, a minute ago you called him Topper. Is that the name he used?"

"I believe so."

"Not Budge?"

"I never heard that name before Mr. Chitty used it in court."

Catfish tapped out his cigar. So, a day or two after Toby's arrest, Mr. Budge had appeared out of nowhere following an absence of years, calling himself Topper for some peculiar reason, hired the worst lawyer in the county to represent the feebleminded son he'd abandoned years before, paid Jaybird five hundred dollars in the same denominations as the stolen money, and didn't even attend the trial before disappearing again.

"Mighty peculiar, Mr. Jaye." Catfish drummed his fingers near the wrecked talking phone on the lamp table. Harley's eyes followed the wire from the contraption to the wall where it used to be connected. Catfish ignored the scolding look that followed. "We'll let you know how the appeal goes. By the way, can we contact you by talking phone?"

"Telephone?" He chuckled. "Oh, I can't afford one of those."

"I can't either," Catfish said, winking at Harley. "Last thing, Mr. Jaye, and I'll let you go. Do you happen to know a fella named Jacob or Jake Levinski?"

"I don't believe I do." Jaybird got up to leave. "Why?"

"No particular reason. Thanks for stopping by."

Harley escorted Jaybird to the door.

Catfish hiked his pants legs and kneaded Chinese snake oil into his throbbing knees. Miracle snakes. Wished he had one.

When Harley dropped into a chair, his lips were pursed. "Why'd you rip the new telephone out of the wall?"

Catfish guffawed. "Dang thing didn't work right. Some surly fella looking for somebody named Pete was on it every time it rang. And it wouldn't stop ringing."

"He must have called the wrong number."

Catfish waved the receipt at Harley. "Same number they gave me. He told me so."

Harley's face turned from peevishness to something approaching mirth. "Did you buy a party line?"

"A what?"

"A party line. It's shared with others."

"I bought the cheapest they offered because I've no intention of ever using it again. Which is why"—he stabbed a finger at the severed wire—"I terminated my agreement with 'em."

The situation hardly warranted the grin on Harley's face. "All right, Papa. You'll probably be back on your feet in no time anyway."

Catfish wiped his hands and stuffed the stopper back in the snake oil bottle. "Already feeling like a thoroughbred."

Harley turned serious again. "Do you think Toby's father set him up?"

"Seems to me any father who'd abandon a mental-cripple son is the kind of father who'd blame the boy for his own misdeeds. He'd think of it as payback for the trouble Toby caused him. I don't know why he'd call himself Topper though."

"Maybe Toby inherited the name along with the hat."

"Maybe." Catfish chewed on the cigar stub. "I want you to turn over every stone until you locate Budge."

"Any ideas where to start?"

"Kate Friend. Find out if she knows of any kin Budge or his wife has anywhere."

Chapter 27

"Toby, I brought a treat for you." Peach slid the basket across the table and pulled back the cloth cover for him to see the still-warm muffins. She smiled and watched his eyes, which darted toward the basket. "Try one."

Toby stopped rocking, grabbed a muffin, and gobbled it. He ate another and began rocking again. He didn't look at her once, even sideways.

She'd gone to the jail to find out if Toby knew the three telephone numbers, but she had more in mind. Dr. Wallace had suggested she try to maintain a relationship with Toby, however one-sided it might seem. The doctor thought it might be calming. When she asked him what she should do when visiting, he suggested merely being there would help. The sound of her voice was probably soothing to him because the only voices Toby usually heard were prisoners and jail guards. Her voice might even remind him of his mother.

"It's a chilly day today." She bent to watch for a reaction and smiled, but there was nothing. "Can you believe it's November already?"

He rocked slowly, never taking his eyes from the tabletop.

The door to the visiting room creaked open, and the jail guard's grinning face appeared. "You all right in here, missy?"

"I'm fine, thank you."

"Just holler if you want me to come save you." He laughed and shut the door.

She took a deep breath, wondering if he was the guard who told Dr. Pepys that Toby only rocked when visitors came. "Has that man been mean to you, Toby?"

He rocked indifferently.

She so desperately wanted to get through to him somehow. "Mr. Calloway sends his regards."

Toby rocked.

"And Mr. Harley, too."

Toby rocked.

"They wanted me to ask you if this number meant anything to you?" She leaned forward and spoke the number slowly and distinctly. "Fifty-eight."

No reaction.

Maybe he knew it by its constituent digits. "Five-Eight."

Nothing.

"Thirteen. . . . One-Three."

Still nothing.

"Fifteen . . . One-Five."

Toby just rocked.

"Williamson Drug Store."

"Four-Oh-One Austin."

That was correct. It didn't mean there was any significance to it, though, because that business was listed in the directory he'd memorized.

"Jacob Levinski."

"Four-Oh-Seven Austin. Residence. Forty-eight, eight, seven."

It took a moment for what he'd said to sink in. Peach repeated the name and got the same answer exactly. *Oh my!* Four-Oh-Seven

Austin was Levinski's watch shop address, but Toby obviously understood the numbers forty-eight, eight, and seven as his residence address. How, though, without a street name? Levinski's home was at the corner of North Nineteenth and Morrow Avenue, but that couldn't be the street number because it wasn't forty-eight blocks north of Austin Avenue. It was probably only six or seven. She must tell Mr. Calloway the numbers fifty-eight, fifteen, and thirteen from Toby's note probably represented a single location, as he originally speculated.

"They were also wondering if your father has visited you recently?"

No reaction at all.

"Do you remember your father? Mr. Budge?"

Nothing.

Ordinary conversation wasn't going to strike a spark in that poor boy. She glanced at her handbag where her book poked out. That night was the weekly gathering of Shakespeare devotees at Miss Kate's. They'd been studying the sonnets in addition to the Cotton Palace production.

She opened the book to Sonnet Eighteen. "Listen to this, Toby. It's a poem by William Shakespeare. Have you heard of him?"

Toby rocked.

"This is one of my favorites, and it's quite lovely." She tilted her head to catch his attention but couldn't. She read with the melodic voice the bard inspired in her. "'Shall I compare thee to a summer's day? Thou art more lovely and more temperate. Rough winds do shake the darling buds of May, and summer's lease hath all too short a date.'"

Toby slowed.

"'Sometime too hot the eye of heaven shines, and often is his gold complexion dimmed; and every fair from fair sometime declines, by chance or nature's changing course untrimmed.'"

Now motionless, Toby stared at the tabletop.

His reaction spurred more emotion in her voice. "'But thy eternal summer shall not fade nor lose possession of that fair thou ow'st, nor shall Death brag thou wand'rest in his shade, when in eternal lines to time thou grow'st.'"

She peeked from the book. He watched her out of the corner of his eyes, head bowed only slightly, his body utterly still. She recited the couplet by heart, locking on to his sideways gaze. "'So long as men can breathe or eyes can see, so long lives this, and this gives life to thee.'"

He neither rocked, nor spoke, nor blinked an eye.

She turned the book around and slid it slowly across the table toward him so as to arouse yet not unsettle the muse. His eyes fastened on the page. Something there arrested him. Maybe it was curiosity, perhaps awe. Could the beauty of the verse have captured him? Or was it the opposite—could the passion of poetry have freed him from his passionless world? Did he feel as she felt about that verse? Did he feel?

She watched for some sign.

But after a moment he began to rock, though more slowly than usual.

She retrieved the book. Perhaps reading it again would stimulate more. "'Shall I compare thee to a summer's day? Thou—'"

Toby broke in as if on cue, reciting from memory. "'Thou art more lovely and more temperate.'" His voice was clear, his phrasing a precise iambic pentameter. "'Rough winds do shake the darling buds of May, and summer's lease hath all too short a date.'" His head dipped one beat.

Yes!

"'Sometime too hot the eye of heaven shines, and often is his gold complexion dimmed; and every fair from fair sometimes declines, by chance or nature's changing course untrimmed.'" Toby dipped another beat.

She beamed, her eyes cheering him on.

He soared into the last quatrain. "'But thy eternal summer shall not fade nor lose possession of that fair thou ow'st, nor shall Death brag thou wand'rest in his shade, when in eternal lines to time thou grow'st.'"

"Yes!" She clapped.

Toby's eyes gleamed. "'So long as men can breathe or eyes can see . . .'"

She added her voice to his, "'. . . so long lives this, and this gives life to thee.'"

She reached across and squeezed his hands. "Wonderful!"

There was a vibrant spirit there, a soul that, for a moment, broke free from its unseen bonds. She couldn't wait to share it with Harley. She watched the poor boy rock back and forth, to all other outward appearances his features like any other boy. But this boy was twice trapped by some strange disorder of the mind as well as by the physical bondage of a false accusation. They had to free him of both. There was urgency in winning his case because she now understood how much he did care about freedom. He just couldn't express it.

But in an instant, the gleam had passed. Toby rocked, staring with empty eyes once more.

Peach sagged back in her chair. Yet it had been there, hadn't it? There had been a light glowing warm within him, if only briefly lit.

She breathlessly searched the book for Sonnet Twenty-Nine.

***

Peach knew what he was going to say before words ever formed on his lips.

Dr. Wallace squinted at her over his spectacles. "My dear, I'm afraid Toby neither comprehends nor feels. What you suggest isn't possible."

Except for the whopping of the ceiling fan overhead, and the snoring of Colonel Terry by the door, silence pervaded the law office. Mr. Calloway and Harley were there too, but they didn't come to her support. As Peach shifted in her chair, her cheeks warmed. She had to make them all understand. They had to drop the insanity writ or Toby would be confined to an asylum for the rest of his life and that was nothing but a prison without bars.

The doctor wasn't at all shy about his opinions. He probably never brooked disagreement on a diagnosis. "As I've explained before, he's incapable of such emotion as you or I might experience. He reacts to external stimuli in a narrow range. He was able to repeat words he heard you say and words he read himself, but the words had no meaning at all to him."

She had come back from her last meeting with Toby convinced not just of his innocence, but that there was so much more to Toby than a prodigious memory. She wouldn't be so easily talked out of that. "Respectfully, sir, I had a different sense."

"My dear, I know how sincerely you desire to believe there's a human heart beating inside Toby Topper, but I can assure you his heart only serves its biological function. He doesn't feel. You are quite mistaken."

Now Mr. Calloway couldn't remain silent. "Couldn't she have stirred something in him, doctor, even if just memories of his mother?"

She waited for Wallace to agree, but he didn't, so she

persisted. "I saw something in his eyes that wasn't there before. Aren't the eyes the light of the body?"

"Well, there's no darkness there at least," Wallace finally answered. "That's the most important thing. While he's incapable of love, he's also incapable of malice."

Miss Peach squared her shoulders. "Gentlemen, I know I'm no physician. I know I'm a mere stenographer, but I watched him. I believe he does have emotions."

All eyes fixed on her.

"Go ahead," Mr. Calloway said.

Harley watched her intently. Somehow, he was encouraging her.

"I think he feels, but his feelings are trapped deep within him by his disease of the mind."

Dr. Wallace stroked his whiskers. "Why do you believe that?"

At least they were listening. She told them about the joy Toby showed when she gave him encouragement, about the gleam in his eye when he recited, about her sense that excitement grew in him as their interaction continued.

Dr. Wallace recorded the specifics in his notes. "Fascinating. It's possible one reason for his extraordinary memorization is because praise from others reinforces that skill."

"I feel certain it did," she said.

"But as I said before, his ability lies in a very narrow range. He appears to have only the one quite simple skill of memorization. It's nothing more."

She pursed her lips to hold her tongue.

Mr. Calloway touched her arm. "Darlin,' you put poetry in his heart if nothing else is there. Let's be thankful for that."

Peach flushed. *Please don't patronize me, Mr. Calloway!*

Dr. Wallace drummed the table. "Dr. Down wrote of

feebleminded patients with extraordinary skills of music and mathematics. I suspect the meter of verse might have a similar attraction. But it's neither an emotional affinity nor a cognitive one."

"But he understood iambic pentameter," she insisted.

Dr. Wallace shrugged. "He might have recited a verse in iambic pentameter from memory, but I doubt he understood it."

"He did though!" Why could they not see? "In a matter of minutes, he learned three sonnets perfectly." She reached out and touched the doctor's arm. "You must understand, Dr. Wallace, in Sonnet 116, he said 'fix-ed.'"

He shot a confused look at Mr. Calloway and back at her. "I'm not following."

"Don't you see? I didn't read that sonnet to him. He read it silently and recited it aloud from memory. Flawlessly. He said 'fix-ed' in two syllables to make an iamb. He understood iambic pentameter."

Wallace's fingers tapped the tabletop again.

"He did," she pleaded, her cheeks flushing again. "How could he do that if he didn't understand the metrical foot? If he didn't feel the emotion of the poem?"

"I doubt he comprehended what he was doing. It was merely rote. My dear, he's fully capable of memorizing a verse and delivering it with precision, but not of understanding it. He could never compose a line of iambic pentameter."

Her face felt hectic red. "You're wrong!"

"Whoa, Miss Peach!" Mr. Calloway's hand shot up. "He's just trying to help."

Her chair scraped the floor as she pushed away from the table. She rushed out and slammed the door. She dropped into her desk chair and buried her face in her hands.

The door opened and Harley followed.

Peach dabbed her eyes. Was she not explaining it well enough? Or did they just not care? "No one understands him."

"I do." Harley took a seat close by and rested his forearm on her desk.

"You don't act like it."

"Zipporah, please—"

"Don't call me that," she snapped.

"Listen. I know how you feel."

She shook her head slowly side to side with her eyes closed before she cast them on Harley. "All three of you speak of Toby as if he were a laboratory specimen. A curiosity, a freak of nature. Like he has no soul. Harley, what are you representing him for, if not to free his soul?"

"Calm down." He patted her hand. "We're all on the same side of this."

She pulled away. "Don't lecture me."

He didn't reply.

She buried her face in her hands again. Harley had such a gentle heart. Why couldn't he understand? Toby was trapped inside a body that failed him, and now he was inside a cold iron cage. What mortal would not feel madness creep upon him, would not seem mad to others? She shut her eyes tightly, took a deep breath and let it out slowly.

Harley's tone softened. "Remember what you told me when you thought Papa was too close personally to Cicero Sweet's family? That it impaired his professional judgment? You were right about that."

"This is different."

"How?"

"Harley, I don't have any personal relationship with Toby

Topper. He's our client only. But shouldn't we always care about our clients?"

"Of course, we should. But it's a fine line between caring and caring too much." He got up to go back to the meeting with Wallace. "Peach, I give you my word, I'll do everything humanly possible to free Toby, but I can't do anything about his disease. I'll work night and day to win that appeal, and we'll set him free. You must trust us."

A tear streamed down her cheek. *I do.* If they could only do more.

Chapter 28

What a thrilling place. Peach tugged Harley's arm. "Come on. Let's look around."

Thousands of chattering people were packed inside the great exhibition hall for the opening of the Cotton Palace. A breathtaking frieze on the inside wall depicted chariot races from the popular novel *Ben Hur*. The entire interior was decorated with cotton, mosses, and ferns. It was as big an event in Waco as any she could remember. Everyone compared it to the World's Fair in Chicago of the previous year.

When Harley had invited her to accompany him to the grand opening her heart had leapt. She'd felt so badly about how she had acted toward him. He'd only been trying to comfort her, and she'd been rude to him. She hoped to make amends.

"Oh my," she said, "there's Hamp Boswell."

The young man was standing at an exhibit unpacking a box onto the table.

Harley started toward him. "I have a thing or two to say to that rascal."

"Harley, please don't!"

Before he even got close to the exhibit, Boswell spotted Harley, hurriedly finished what he was doing, and scampered off in the opposite direction, disappearing into the crowd.

"He doesn't seem very sociable," Harley said with none too subtle sarcasm.

It was only then she realized Boswell had been at the bookseller's booth, Hill Brothers. How ironic since he never seemed very interested in reading. Harley went to the table where the young man had unloaded a stack of books. They appeared to be dime novels, and Harley picked one up before she got a good look at it.

"Damn!" Harley flipped through it without looking up.

"What is it?"

He didn't answer.

The book in his hand was a thin paper-wrapped book with a title in large red letters: *The Adventures of Thaddeus Schoolcraft, Railroad Detective.*

His hand was shaking, and she couldn't read the rest, so she picked up another from the table. The subtitle was *The Waco Train Station Murder.* The author was Miriam Gartrell Giselle.

Harley looked up. "It's a fictionalized tale of Schoolcraft's exploits based loosely on my brother Houston's case." Harley held up the cover and pointed to something below the Beadle's banner. "This is labeled No. 1. It appears to be a serial."

How dare they peddle such an awful book at the Cotton Palace? And why was Boswell delivering them?

Harley bought all the copies. "We can't let Papa see this."

He went directly to a trash barrel and dropped them all inside. Without saying a thing, he started walking briskly down the aisle.

She concentrated on forgetting both Boswell and the novel. There was a crowd of people craning their necks to see a gigantic eagle constructed of various grains suspended from the ceiling as if in flight.

Another familiar face appeared in the crowd. Peach turned away quickly.

Harley turned with her. "What's the matter?"

"It's that horrible man." She glanced over her shoulder at the crowd beneath the eagle.

Harley looked too. "What horrible man?"

He had his back to them, but it was clearly him. He was gawking at the bird. She put up a hand to shield her face and hurried down the aisle away from the eagle.

Harley caught up with her. "Who was it?"

She kept walking. "The jail guard."

"Peach, what are you talking about?"

She stopped and peered over his shoulder at the crowd by the eagle. He was gone. "I just saw that brute I encountered when interviewing Toby. That horrid deputy who flirted with me." She spied the crowd again, finally satisfied she'd avoided him. "Oh, he's dreadful."

He spun around and craned to see. "Are you afraid of him for some reason?"

She shuddered. "I don't like him ogling me." She dragged Harley along the aisle to another exhibit that had drawn a crowd. "Oh look, it's Mrs. Slaydon's collection."

They stopped at some curiosities on display.

"Harley, look at that." She pointed to a set of glittering glass prisms. The prominent exhibiter was married to the owner of the big woolen mill located a couple of blocks away. They apparently traveled the world, judging by the display of her collected souvenirs. "Look, they're from a chandelier at Fontainebleau Palace."

Harley grinned. "Did she steal them?"

She slapped his hand. "Oh, hush."

He ducked his head to hide his grin and drifted away from the display, wandering the aisle. "The woolen trade must be booming."

"Speaking of Slaydon's," she said, catching up, "have you heard whatever happened to Mr. DeGroote?"

Now that caught his interest. Sterling DeGroote had been a manager at Slaydon's mill, but he was also the secret owner of Miss Jessie's bawdy house where the killing of a prostitute occurred seven months earlier. That case had consumed the lives of all three of them at Calloway & Calloway until it ended in the July trial in which their client, Cicero Sweet, was convicted and sentenced to prison. At least Mr. Calloway's jury argument saved him from hanging. DeGroote and his son, Peter, both played despicable roles in that affair. They lied, they concealed important information, and in the end, Peter's testimony had convicted Cicero. She hoped they both got what they deserved.

Harley must have felt the same. "I understand DeGroote lost his job after Mr. Slaydon heard he owned a brothel. He moved his family somewhere else. I heard maybe it was Dallas."

"He probably fled in disgrace."

"Exactly. Papa was so angry with him. They'd been friends before."

Well, that chapter was closed now. She gestured with delight toward a flower stand. "Harley, buy me a rose."

Just as he was helping her pin it on her jacket, she spotted the jail guard coming along the aisle toward them. She grabbed Harley's arm, spun him around, and hustled him down a crossing aisle.

Just then, the crowd turned toward the far end of the large hall as the parade of dignitaries arrived amid the clamor of a festive march. The Iowa State Band, dressed in special white cotton uniforms, led the parade. She'd read about their performance at the World's Fair. Behind them marched a platoon of the Waco police, followed by the carriages of dignitaries.

She pointed toward one of them. "Is that Governor Hogg?"

"I believe so."

Governor Jim Hogg, seated beside his wife, waved and smiled like any good politician. His three sons and daughter, twelve-year-old Miss Ima, sat across from their parents.

"That poor child must endure endless jokes about her name." Peach watched the girl. Miss Ima Hogg, indeed. What parent would name a child that?

"Hers might be a misnomer, but her father's isn't," Harley said.

She chuckled. Governor Hogg was a man of prodigious girth.

Following the Hoggs came the directors of the Cotton Palace, the Lady Managers, including Miss Kate—she spotted Peach and waved—the city council, the Baylor cadets, and the Waco Union Band. Peach dragged Harley closer to the stage where the ceremony would take place. Bodies were packed so tightly in front of the stage she could hardly breathe as they waited for the dignitaries to make their way behind the curtained stage.

Trumpets blared as the curtains opened. The governor and his entourage were flanked by the Cotton Palace royalty: Colonel Parrott, in a royal ermine robe, as *King Cotton,* and Miss Hattie Trice, in an elegant gown, as *Texas,* his queen. Governor Hogg made brief remarks opening the exhibition, and the crowd dispersed to visit the exhibits.

Harley checked his watch. "Thirsty?"

They stopped at a cider stand near the stage. Harley purchased glasses of cider, and they sat at a small table. The venue was decorated like a garden patio, with potted plants and trestles with hanging moss.

Before long Kate Friend stopped at their table. "Peach, what do you think of everything?"

"It's wondrous. It's simply spectacular."

Kate joined them. "I'm glad you think so."

Harley leaned closer to be heard over the buzz of the crowd. "I was actually going to call on you pretty soon anyway."

"Oh?"

"I wanted to ask you about Toby Topper again, if you don't mind."

"Of course not, Mr. Calloway."

"My father wanted to know if you know anything about Toby's father hiring Mr. Jaye to represent Toby?"

Miss Kate touched her cheek. "Why no, I don't. I'm quite surprised by that."

"We're not sure it's true," Peach said.

"Do you know of any of his father's kin," Harley asked, "or maybe his mother's? We're trying to locate the father."

"There's a cousin of Penny's who lives in Dallas. I got a letter from her recently. She asked me if any of Penny's personal effects were still around. She was looking for the family Bible. I'd be happy to provide you with her address."

"I'll stop by and get it," Peach said.

After she left, Peach looked at Harley. There was something she had been wondering for some time. "I have to confess, Harley, I'm not sure why it's important who hired Mr. Jaye."

He leaned closer. "Jaybird's notoriously inept. He's drunk whenever he goes to court. He shouldn't be representing anybody in any kind of case, but certainly not a murder case. As Papa says, if Jaybird defends, the client loses."

"So is the point that he was hired by somebody who didn't really know him?"

Harley shook his head. "Just the opposite. We suspect the person who hired him knew him very well, or at least his reputation."

She leaned closer.

"Papa thinks somebody hired Jaybird so Toby would be convicted."

What a despicable thing to do to that poor boy. "Who would want to do that?"

"Papa says it's the person who set Toby up."

"No, surely—"

Over Harley's shoulder, the jail guard came into view again—his back to them, thankfully. He was milling about in the crowd not twenty feet away. He was such a large man, with all that short, curly brown hair. Maybe he wouldn't see her.

She shielded her face and peeked at him over Harley's shoulder and through the mossy white trestle. "It's him."

Harley glanced back at him. "Peach, you're overreacting. A deputy sheriff won't bother you."

She snuck another peek as the man turned, and she saw his face more clearly.

She gasped and clutched Harley's hand.

Chapter 29

"Don't look," Peach whispered.

Harley began to turn, but she gripped his hand tightly.

"No!" She bent her head over the table, propping her forehead on her extended fingertips. "He's moving."

Harley snuck a peek to his right, but she squeezed his hand again. Out of the corner of her eye, she watched a small clutch of people amble up the aisle near them.

Once they'd passed, her eyes darted to Harley. "That's not the jail guard."

"Then why are you acting this way?"

She peered around the trestle. An elegantly dressed black-haired lady traipsed along to the man's right. He looked so much like the deputy.

"It's Big Joe."

"Jessie Rose's strong-arm?"

"And she's with him."

Big Joe was the thug who protected Miss Jessie's prostitutes, and the lady—the harlot—to his side was the madam herself, though today she was neither garbed nor painted in her customary tacky manner. It was just four months ago that Peach and Harley first had the misfortune of encountering them when Mr. Calloway's client, Cicero Sweet, killed a prostitute in Miss

Jessie's bawdy house. Joe and Miss Jessie both lied to conceal the identity of Sterling DeGroote, the real owner of the bawdy house, and of his son, who was at the heart of the whole the sordid incident.

They were both dreadful people, but she especially feared Big Joe. Mr. Calloway had sent her to the bawdy house to spy on them during his investigation of the case. Disguised as a department store clerk, she'd found herself face to face with Big Joe—close enough she could smell him. It was a foulness she'd never forget. Nor would she forget the way his good eye leered at her, the other eye drooping horrifically. That was the face she saw today.

Haley scooted his stool around the table beside her and embraced her shoulders. "Are you sure it's Joe?"

Surprised but pleased by his sudden closeness, she leaned into him. "There's no mistaking that eye."

Harley's gaze followed them down the aisle as they browsed the exhibits. "Why did you think he was the jail guard?"

"They look so much alike." His ogling was terrifyingly like Joe's. In fact, the two men were similar enough, except for the droopy eye, they could be brothers.

Harley squeezed her shoulder.

When the horrid man's face came into view the last time, she remembered the bruise on Toby's head. And that Joe had threatened violence against Mr. Calloway. Big Joe and the jail guard were so alike in appearance, so alike in behavior, so alike in her reaction to them, that an alarm sounded within her. "We've got to get Toby out of that jail."

Chapter 30

Harley watched his father prop his right leg on a wooden crate. He said his left knee had revived thanks to those wonderous Chinese snakes, but the right one still griped when he walked. He eased his foot to the floor. His spectacles were perched on the tip of his nose because he was reviewing the indictment in a new case. They were recently hired in a new case, and it was more on Papa's mind than anything else. The arraignment would be that afternoon.

At the sound of the front door opening, Peach went to the reception room. After a moment she returned, perusing something she took from an envelope. She eyed Harley momentarily but skirted the big worktable to Papa's side of the office. "I think you need to read this, sir. Billy just delivered it."

"What is it?"

She handed the single sheet to Papa. "A telegram from Mrs. Hodge."

Papa slipped off his spectacles. "Who?"

"She's the cousin of Toby's mother. In Dallas." Peach dropped the envelope on the table in front of Harley. "After Miss Kate told us about her, I sent a telegram asking if she knew where Mr. Budge was."

Papa replaced his spectacles and began reading the telegram.

Harley didn't see anything important on the envelope, but maybe the telegram would contain the key to finding Budge. "What's it say?"

Papa tossed the telegram on the table. "Budge died long before the robbery."

That was like a kick to Harley's gut. "No!"

Papa nodded. "Not what I expected."

Harley read it himself. *In answer to yours regarding Toby's father. Died of Tuberculosis last year. In pauper's grave now. Sorry.*

"I didn't expect that either," Harley said.

Peach retrieved the telegram and envelope. "Where does this leave us?"

"There's your query." Papa mouthed a White Owl but didn't light it. "I was sure he was involved." He spat the tip of the cigar into the spittoon. "Somebody kidnapped Toby, knocked him out, took his hat, his coat, and his bicycle, and pretended to be him. After the robbery that somebody tipped the police about where Toby was and where they'd find the express wagon. Sergeant Quinn found Toby knocked out with his head on a bloody canvas. Though he had a pistol and some of the money, it was a small part of the loot. That somebody is likely the one who hired Jaybird to lose the murder case, and then he sat back and waited for events to run their course."

Harley rocked back in his chair. If they won the appeal, they were no better off now than when the first trial began. Other than the insanity plea the first jury rejected, their only other possible defense evaporated in front of them like a Panhandle mirage. "What now?"

Papa glanced at the calendar. "Let's see—it's December now, short of four months till the argument in the Court of Criminal

Appeals. We've got time to figure it out."

How could he so calmly take news like this? Toby's life was in their hands. Harley's hands. And he didn't even know where to start. "Yes, sir."

Chapter 31

Harley was late. The Christmas party was to begin at five Friday evening, but he never even left court until after that. He'd been in a hearing in the Fifty-Fourth District Court, which convened in the basement of the Provident building because there wasn't sufficient space for a second district court in the courthouse. The hearing was in *Barnes v. Pitcairn,* a small breach of contract claim, but the client was demanding, the other side was unreasonable, and the court was impatient. He'd already invested more of his time in the case than the paltry fee would warrant and spent the whole afternoon in a contentious scrap with the opposing lawyer over what should have been a minor legal issue. To top it off, though he won the hearing, his client was still unhappy, got mad at Harley for not doing more for him, and stormed out. Toby Topper didn't even do that when he was sentenced to hang. Of course, he was insane.

The bailiff was already locking up. "Harley boy, why you in such a doggone rush?"

"I'm late for a Christmas party with some of Miss Peach's friends." It was four days before Christmas, but between the recent disappointing revelation in Toby's case and the frustrating afternoon in Barnes' case, Harley was no longer in the spirit of the season.

The bailiff grinned. "Little red-haired Miss Peach, eh?"

Harley's face warmed despite the cold air. He yanked his overcoat and hat from the rack by the door. "Well, the party's at Miss Kate's, actually."

"You know, that Peach, she's a mighty fine-looking gal." He winked at Harley as if there was some secret shared between them.

"She's a proficient typist." He lamely tried to sound indifferent.

The bailiff leaned against the door jamb. "Well, I hear you're courting her."

His face warmed. Who would be saying something like that? "I am *not* courting her. She's our stenographer."

"Well, I'm just saying what I heard."

"You heard wrong." Harley tore through the doorway. "It's strictly business between us."

"If you say so. Tell Mr. Catfish Merry Christmas."

"Right."

He took off, taking the stairs from the basement to the first floor two at a time. When he threw the door open, he was hit with a blast of cold air. Five twenty p.m. and dark already. He completely lost track of time. When he went into the building for the hearing in the early afternoon, the sun was shining through the clouds, but in the meantime a norther blew in. Where did his day go?

He should never have agreed to go to a party with Peach. Employers didn't socialize with their female employees; it would be unprofessional. Going to the Cotton Palace with her was a mistake. The previous visit to Miss Kate's for the evening of Shakespeare was strictly business.

At least he was meeting her there rather than picking her up at her boarding house. There would be other people at the party too, but he wouldn't stay long. He'd pay his respects to Miss Kate and her mother, greet the others, and make his excuses to Peach.

To Miss Peach.

He was heading down the sidewalk toward Mary Street, past the Blake building and the Baptist Church with its festive decorations, when he realized he still had his briefcase. He should've gone to the office first and dropped it off. It was only two blocks from the Provident building. He stopped, started to turn back, and decided against it. He wouldn't be there long anyway. Miss Kate would understand.

At the intersection with Mary Street, he spotted Mr. Moon coming toward him from across the street.

"The good Lord bless you this Christmas time, Mr. Harley."

"And you too, Mr. Moon."

"I just been at Miss Kate's to leave off a cake from my Maudie, and I seen Miss Peach there. The ladies, they invited me to stay and have some punch," Mr. Moon said, grinning. "Miss Peach say y'all stepping out tonight."

Son of a gun! She had no right to tell people something like that. "I'm afraid she misunderstood. We're both attending Miss Kate's social event, that's all."

"Oh, I sees. Sure enough. Didn't mean to upset." He started walking away.

"That's all right." Harley managed a cheerful smile. "Merry Christmas to you and Mrs. Moon."

Stepping out—how could she have thought that? He wasn't courting Peach.

Miss Peach.

Maybe he should go home and forget about the party. He started to turn around but didn't. He promised he'd attend, and he would, but he never promised to enjoy it.

***

Peach's gaze darted to the clock. Again. Where on earth was Harley?

At half past five, he blew in, icy as the December air. She tried to catch his eye, but the hostess reached him first. Peach stood off to the side, watching.

"Mr. Calloway," Miss Kate said, "thank you so much for coming."

"It's my pleasure."

His usually affable face was twisted into the most awful frown. Miss Kate took his hat, coat, and briefcase. He must have come straight from court since he brought his briefcase. He waited there, surveying the entry hall but skipping right past her.

She approached him and dipped her head. "Merry Christmas, Harley."

"Oh, Miss Peach." His face flushed. "Good evening."

That was an odd greeting. "Are you all right?"

"Of course." His frown returned. "Why would you think otherwise?"

"I'm not sure," she said, searching his face for some explanation. "Just an impression."

He gave her a blank look, nodded at Professor Hargrove, who was emerging from the parlor with a cup of tea, and went toward the dining room.

"Did your hearing go well?" she asked, following in his wake.

"Fine," he said, but his attention flitted around the room. "Excuse me, Miss Peach, I see there's punch, and I'm a bit dry."

"Of course. I'd be happy to pour you a cup."

"Oh, don't bother. I can get it."

Something was wrong. She persisted. "Miss Kate is about to do a reading from Dickens."

"I can't stay long." He turned his back on her and went into the parlor.

He must have lost the hearing. Then why did he say it went fine? She let out a sigh. Like his father, he would explain when he was ready. She followed him into the parlor where the punch bowl nestled among sprigs of holly. Their eyes didn't meet. She went to one end of the table and poured herself a cup of tea while he moved to the other. He ladled punch into a glass but didn't look at her.

"The Shrewsbury cakes are delicious," she said. They were piled on a platter between them.

"That's nice." He picked up a plate and reached for one, but stopped and put the plate back. He sipped the punch instead.

"Do you like it?" she asked.

"Very nice."

"There's also a pound cake in the dining room. Mrs. Moon made it."

"Oh." He took another drink of punch and checked his watch.

She sipped her tea. "It's awfully chilly tonight, isn't it?"

"It is." He finished his punch. "I'm afraid it's time for me to go." He placed his cup on a tray and headed out of the room.

Why wouldn't he tell her what was wrong? "Don't rush off so soon, Harley. You just got here."

He paused without looking back at her and spoke in a lower voice over his shoulder. "It might be better if you addressed me as Mr. Calloway in public."

Suddenly chilled, she inched closer to the parlor stove. "Of course. I'm so sorry."

"Good evening," he said, heading into the entry hall.

Peach glanced at the grandfather clock. He'd stayed less than five minutes.

On a tea table across the room was the gift she'd made for

him. She had been quite pleased with it—a white linen handkerchief with the initials, *HAC.* She wasn't skilled at embroidery, but Miss Kate's mother had helped her. She'd labored over it since Thanksgiving, starting over three times before she finally felt satisfied with her work. Maybe she would give it to her brother instead.

She strolled into the entry hall. To her surprise, Harley had stopped to converse with Miss Kate. She hid her confusion by sipping tea. Even its trusted sweetness turned bitter.

She passed behind Harley toward the dining room as the professor emerged.

"Oh, Dr. Hargrove," she said as loudly as she could with delicacy, "how nice to see you on such a cold unwelcoming evening."

Chapter 32

Catfish knew exactly how this would turn out. Harley was already surly as a barn cat when Elihu Stoker arrived at the office. He should've warned Harley. "How do, Mr. Stoker."

"I'm in dire straits."

Stoker was a decent fella but always worried about some impending catastrophe. He had a farm west of town. His closest neighbor was the fractious dairy farmer at whom Colonel Terry always growled. Rome Walker tormented Stoker over the most minor matters for the sheer joy of seeing a man fret. Stoker always took it seriously and assumed the worst. Largely because of Rome Walker, Stoker had been Catfish's client for years. Charged him a quarter every time. The new year of 1895 would likely be no different.

"Mr. Stoker, you remember my law partner, Harley."

"Your boy, isn't he?"

"That too. I asked Harley to look into your trouble with Rome Walker." Stoker had caught Walker fishing a waterhole on Stoker's side of the river. When he ordered Walker off his land, the disagreeable trespasser said he now owned that riverbank by adverse possession because he'd been fishing it for years. Stoker was terrified he'd lose his river access.

Stoker eyed Harley as if he wanted to see his law license. "I'll be John Brown! How long you been a lawyer?"

"Almost five years," Harley answered.

Stoker turned away from Harley dismissively. "Catfish, I want to sue him before he steals my land."

Catfish beckoned the old farmer to sit. "Listen to this first. Harley, tell him what you found."

"Good afternoon, Mr. Stoker," Harley said, sitting across the table from him. He waited for Stoker to reply but proceeded when he didn't. "The law of adverse possession requires that he have actual possession of the land openly and notoriously under a claim of right that is hostile to your ownership, and that he be in such possession for a period of at least ten years."

Stoker stared blankly at Harley. "You telling me Rome Walker owns my land?"

"I didn't say that at all." Harley seemed instantly frustrated. "It wasn't open and notorious if you didn't even know he was doing it."

"Well, John Brown!" Stoker whipped around to face Catfish. "Catfish, we better sue him."

"Well, sir, Harley says—"

"Catfish, you're my lawyer, and I want to sue him."

A quarter's worth of good legal advice was never quite enough for Elihu Stoker. Catfish reached for the hefty gilt-spined edition of *Gammel's Laws of Texas* he positioned on his desk before Stoker arrived for his appointment. "Let me show you what Harley found, Mr. Stoker." He thumbed through a few hundred pages, settled on one at random, and positioned his pince-nez spectacles on his nose as if he needed them. "Let's see, here it is."

Stoker sat upright. A furrow parted Harley's brow.

Catfish nodded and removed his specs. "According to the Corpus Juris Texanimus, in a situation like yours, no lawsuit is necessary or even permitted, whether the possession be per stirpes, per minas, per proxima amici, or per incuriam. And that's it, tantum et tale." He shook his head and reverently shut the massive leather tome.

"It says that?"

"It does."

"In a situation like mine."

Catfish nodded. "Ipsissima verba."

"I'll be John Brown," Stoker sighed. "So, what does it mean?"

"You can't sue."

"I can't sue."

"It's lex scripta."

Stoker was silent for a long minute. He rose from his chair, fished around in his pocket, and dropped a quarter on the table before departing without a word.

Catfish followed him to the door. "If you want to run it by another lawyer you might try J. Birdsong Jaye."

When Catfish returned, Harley hadn't moved. "Papa, I've never heard such nonsense from you."

"It was trickum legis, no more."

"It was gibberish."

"Not to Elihu Stoker. He craves Law Latin like a hypochondriac needs a placebo."

Miss Peach rushed in, grinning broadly. "Mr. Harley, did you charge him a quarter?"

Harley slammed his chair against his desk. "I didn't give him a wooden nickel's worth of help."

She just stood there.

"I apparently know less about advising clients than I know about cross-examining doctors," Harley said as he brushed past Miss Peach and fled the office.

Colonel Terry hopped from his roost by the door, ready to go too.

For a heartbeat or two, Miss Peach stood there like she was nailed to the floor, her shoulders tensing. "Did I say the wrong thing?"

"Not at all," Catfish said.

"He's been so aloof recently, like I've offended him somehow."

Catfish thought he noticed mounting fretfulness in Harley, particularly since they learned about Budge. Now it was weighing on him so much it affected how he acted, even toward people for whom he cared. And Harley didn't realize how sweet on him Miss Peach was. She looked for meaning in every sideways look he gave her. "Doesn't have anything to do with you, darlin'."

"What's wrong then?"

"Harley's feeling like he can't do anything right," he said, tapping ash into the spittoon. "He isn't quite used to the ups and downs of practicing law, and you can't make too much of either one. Hard lesson for a young man to learn."

"Is Toby's case still bothering him?"

"Look over there." He pointed to a piece of cardboard on Harley's desk, where he'd written on it in large block letters: *AUDI ALTERAM PARTEM*. Like his old man, Harley kept jiggers. "The curse of the Calloways."

"Or the calling." Her shoulders relaxed and a wry little smile worked its way across her face.

Such a bright young lady. He smiled back. "That too."

She took a chair opposite him, propping her chin on her hand. "I was afraid he was angry with me for some reason."

"Far from it. Sometimes Calloway men have trouble seeing what's right in front of 'em."

"What's that?"

"You."

She blushed. "Is it so obvious?"

"Only to those who see."

"Will Harley ever see?"

The colonel ambled over and plopped down.

"Colonel Terry, you see, don't you, fella?" Catfish rubbed his ears. "Right now, Harley needs us to lift him up while he's stuck in a down."

"I can do that, Mr. Calloway." She straightened herself. "I'm not giving up on Harley any time soon."

"I know you aren't."

He liked her spirit. Sometimes she reminded him of Martha but more often of his mother. His folks had come to Texas from Tennessee and from North Carolina before that, and Mother had been the most determined woman he'd ever known. Sometimes it seemed like pigheadedness, but he finally realized it was just her abiding resolve to improve their lot in life. Daddy, on the other hand, had very little resolve. As long as he could hunt and fish and drink, Daddy was happy. But it was Mother who dreamed bigger for the family, who made sure her children all got an education, who held the family together when Daddy got drunk in Tennessee and killed a revenuer, who'd led them to Texas, planted roots, and started their lives over. It was Mother who kept the farm going when Catfish's younger brothers were killed in the war and when Daddy left her to find gold out west. It was Mother who defended Daddy's side of things no matter what sorry thing he did.

Mother's hair had been red too. She was a Murry.

"For Harley," he said, "it just takes time."

She smiled. "Patience is a virtue?"

"That's what my mother always said."

Chapter 33

The KATY locomotive's whistle shrieked three times as it rattled across the bridge over the San Gabriel River approaching Taylor, where they'd change lines to the I. & G.N. into Austin. Harley pressed against the window. The river had raged over its banks from recent Spring rains that left massive oaks stranded in a vast sea of water. Papa sat across from him, also watching the country speed by.

It had been over six months since Toby's trial. The next day, April second, would be a big day: oral argument in the Court of Criminal Appeals. Arguing law to judges came easier to Harley than trying a case to a jury, yet his stomach was no more settled. What if there was an appellate opinion on point he hadn't found in his research? Would he freeze if a judge asked him a question he couldn't answer? On one hand he was grateful for Papa's support and help, but on the other, Papa would see every mistake he made. And if he made more mistakes, Toby would hang.

He had to focus on his preparation. Readiness calmed all fears, Papa had always said.

He turned to the next page in his research notes only to discover something he hadn't seen before—a leaf of octavo-size linen notepaper tucked between pages. A neatly sketched plump peach adorned the top of the cream-colored page with handwriting below. He'd seen her doodle daisies and birds, but never a peach. He couldn't suppress a chuckle.

"What is it, son?"

Harley held the drawing for Papa to see.

He laughed. "Miss Peach draw that?"

"Apparently." Harley scanned the text below. "She's written some lines from Shakespeare she must have thought I could use in my argument."

"Don't tell me." Papa studied the ceiling of the passenger car. "Have I not hideous death—"

"Within my view." Harley read Peach's writing aloud. "What in the world should make me now deceive, since I must lose the use of all deceit? Why should I then be false, since it is true that I must die here and live hence by truth?"

Papa squinted. "Shakespeare's saying a dying man isn't going to the pearly gates and face St. Peter with a lie on his lips, right?"

"Right. But more importantly, when the man knows he's dying he also knows he has nothing to gain by lying. So he must be telling the truth. It's the dying declaration exception to the hearsay rule."

Papa snorted. "Depends on the man."

As soon as the trial judge had allowed testimony that the express agent cried 'Topper' as he lay dying, Harley knew he had a point for appeal. He had a good argument the judge committed harmful error because the speaker was the only person who got a close look at the shooter's face. The jury likely credited his word. "Shakespeare says he's truly honest only if he knows for certain his death is imminent. That's the point. If he thinks he might live, he could still benefit from a lie. So, the Code of Criminal Procedure requires the prosecution to lay a predicate he was conscious of his approaching death and believed he had absolutely no hope of recovery. They didn't prove that."

"Shakespeare must've been half lawyer to know that." Papa mused. "Have I not hideous death within my view."

"At least he knew some law."

Papa cleared his throat. "You know, son, Miss Peach sure knows a thing or two herself. She wrote me a note about those lines when you were making this same argument to Judge Goodrich."

Harley's face warmed. "She and Miss Kate and some others read Shakespeare together every week."

"That explains all this poetry we're hearing from her lately." Papa gazed out at the passing countryside. "Mighty bright girl."

Harley knew exactly where this was headed, and he didn't want to talk about it. He caught himself thinking about Peach even before he found the drawing, but he had to keep focused on his work.

"I think my stronger point is on our objection to Toby's competence to stand trial."

Papa shrugged.

He knew his father agreed the insanity point was better, but Papa strongly believed Toby didn't do it and was itching for a new trial on the murder charge. The news Mr. Budge was dead at the time was a setback, but Papa was still convinced of Toby's innocence. He just couldn't figure out who the real robber was.

There was movement to Harley's right. A man had stopped in the aisle beside him.

Thaddeus Schoolcraft wore his usual wry smile. "Good afternoon, gentlemen." He tipped his bowler.

"Schoolcraft, what are you doing here?" Papa asked contemptuously. He was generally loath to be rude to anybody, but Schoolcraft was the exception.

"Actually, I'm traveling to Austin for the same reason as you. I'm with Mr. Chitty and Mr. Wilson." He pointed his cane toward the next car.

"Really? What's your interest?"

Schoolcraft steadied himself as the train rumbled over a crossing. "The KATY has an interest in seeing our good customers get justice, and American Express is a very good customer. I'm going to watch you make your appeal, gentlemen."

"We're honored," Papa said, now with overt sarcasm. "Maybe you can autograph some of your dime novels for the judges."

Where had Papa seen that book? Harley was surprised he hadn't said something.

Schoolcraft laughed as he steadied himself when the train went into a curve. Locomotive smoke billowed over their car. "So, you've seen it?"

"Heard it was hot."

Harley needed to intervene before things escalated. "Is Mr. Chitty or Mr. Wilson arguing for the state?"

"Neither actually. The Attorney General will argue for us."

"Crane?" Papa asked.

Schoolcraft smiled. "Himself."

Martin McNulty Crane, the former senator and lieutenant governor, had been the Attorney General of the State of Texas for only a matter of months.

Papa folded his arms. "Figured you needed reinforcements, huh?"

The train lurched as the brakes started to engage. Schoolcraft grabbed the back of a seat. "Speaking of reinforcements, my new assistant has accompanied me on this trip."

Harley eyed Papa. Did Schoolcraft really think they cared?

The detective grinned and touched his cane to the brim of his bowler. He started back up the aisle and paused before he got too far, raising his voice over the screeching brakes. "I'm sure you'll enjoy seeing him again."

Chapter 34

That evening, Catfish descended from their room at the Driskill Hotel to the mezzanine in search of the gentleman's smoking room to meet an old friend. While Harley was preparing to argue their case, he would catch up with the inestimable entrepreneur, George Washington Littlefield.

He'd first met him at school in Independence, but George didn't stay at Baylor University long. They crossed paths again in the war. Since then, George got as rich as Croesus in real estate and cattle until he discovered all the money ended up in somebody else's bank. That's when he became a banker too.

And now, apparently, he'd bought the Driskill. It had been a grand hotel to begin with, but George decided it needed fixing up. Everywhere Catfish looked there was fresh paint, new rugs, marble sculptures of this god or that goddess. He was even putting electric lights in all the rooms.

Catfish clapped his friend on the shoulder. "George, I admired you when I heard you'd turned banker, but I'm surprised to see you in the hotel business."

A bellman swerved around them as George flung his own arm wide to brush him past. "I prefer running cattle to running bellboys and chambermaids, but there's money here."

"And your bank's here, too, apparently."

George pulled out a money clip and peeled off a ten dollar note issued by his own bank. He signed his autograph under the name, American National Bank, and gave it to Catfish. "Down there on the first floor. You need anything, Catfish, just show the teller this. I liked this hotel so much I bought it."

They strolled into the smoking room, and Catfish followed his host to a pair of surprisingly comfortable cow-horn armchairs. "So do you call yourself a banker or a rancher or an innkeeper?"

An attentive servant brought them whiskey and cigars before they could even get settled.

"Cowmen call me a banker, and bankers call me a cowman," George said. "Suits me either way."

Catfish sipped his whiskey. "How's Old Nath? He still with you?"

"See for yourself." He beckoned the colored man who stood immaculately dressed inside the door, a carnation tucked into his lapel. Catfish hadn't noticed him as they passed. He'd been George's personal servant since the war.

"Evening, Mr. Calloway, sir. It's mighty nice to see you again."

Catfish nodded at the old gentleman. "How do, Nath."

"He'll be happy to take you and Harley to the capitol in the morning for your hearing." George turned to Nath. "Use the Brougham. Anything they need, be sure they get it."

"Yes, sir, I sure will," Nath said, going back to the doorway.

That was when Catfish noticed a table of gentlemen near the outside wall. A blue haze hung like a cloud over the entire room, but smoke couldn't obscure the man with the horseshoe mustache. Deep in conversation with Chitty and the walrus, Schoolcraft bent over a table littered with drinks and smoking ash trays. There was someone else Catfish didn't know at the table with them but two more men he did recognize stopped to talk.

He eased back in his chair and lit his cigar. "Looks like my adversaries are courting powerful friends."

George turned as newly elected Governor Culberson spoke with Chitty. Attorney General Crane, at his elbow, began introducing the governor to the others as the unknown man offered cigars to the two newcomers.

"Who's the fella passing out cigars?"

Littlefield strained to see. "Don't know his name, but he's some kind of a clerk."

"For who?"

"You don't want to know."

Catfish's head swiveled back to his friend. He had a sinking feeling. "Who?"

George took a swig. "The Court of Criminal Appeals."

Catfish grunted and tapped his cigar over a tray on the table, but the ceiling fan caught the ashes.

George brushed them off the Jaguar skin upholstery of his chair. "My friend, the Driskill's where men do deals."

"Business deals or politics?"

"Generally," George said, "they're the same."

"You think there's railroad money passing over there?" Catfish crammed his cigar into the tray. "I'm fixing to make my presence known before any judges come in too."

"Too late." George pointed at a table on the other side of the room. "Justice Davidson."

"I feel the dyspepsia coming on. Night, George." Catfish drained his drink.

The governor and the attorney general had moved on to

another table before Catfish reached Chitty's. He squeezed behind the walrus with barely a pause for pleasantry. "Evening, gents."

Their heads popped up from their huddle, and Schoolcraft broke into a grin. "Why, Mr. Calloway, won't you join us?"

The clerk stuffed something into his pocket.

Catfish slid past them and didn't even look back. "Another day maybe."

He slipped out the door of the parlor as quickly as he could, and someone else brushed past on the way in. He didn't recognize the young man at first, but he stopped and turned around.

The young man stopped too. "Hello, Mr. Calloway," said Hampton Boswell.

"Hamp. What are you doing here?"

"I'm meeting some gentlemen." Boswell scanned the room, and they both saw Schoolcraft waving him over. "Excuse me."

As he sauntered into the smoking room toward Schoolcraft's table, a copy of the dime novel poked out under his arm.

Schoolcraft's new assistant—and former spy.

Chapter 35

It was important she did her bit to help Toby, however she could, on the same day Mr. Calloway and Harley were arguing his case in Austin. Peach waited beside the head jailer's desk, the book of sonnets in her lap.

The jailer had said she'd have to visit Toby in his cell because the visiting room was occupied. She'd never been inside the cellblock before; they'd always met clients in the more private visiting room. She waited for the guard who'd escort her to his cell, hoping the crude deputy who resembled Big Joe wasn't the one on duty. The door from the cellblock finally clanged open, and the deputy appeared. The crude one. As soon as he saw her, he broke into that awful grin, and she jerked her gaze back to the head jailer.

He glanced up from his paperwork. "Deputy Buckram, take this lady back to see Topper."

Her hand flew to her mouth. *Oh my!* Was this man really Big Joe Buckram's brother?

"Good morning, missy." Deputy Buckram winked at her. "Follow me."

She trailed behind him, but not too closely, into the long hallway. A single dangling light bulb flickered at the end of the hall, barely showing the way. The stench of vomit and urine hung like a fog between the cells on both sides. Arms dangled through the iron bars from the shadows. Buckram's boots drummed a slow pace on the wooden floor. She threw a handkerchief to her nose and followed.

"Hey, girlie, come to see me?" A toothless drunk slobbered between the bars to her right.

He aroused a swarm of whistles and catcalls as the cells came alive with miserable creatures.

She hurried closer behind Buckram, careful not to stray too near either side.

"It's a whore, boys."

"Put her in my cell, Buckram!"

The deputy marched on as if they didn't exist. Her throat tightened. It was so much farther to the end than she thought.

A bare arm grabbed at her from the left. "I been with her. She's poxy."

"I don't mind," yelled somebody from the darkness across the hall. "Give her to me."

Finally, the deputy turned a corner, and she scampered close behind until they reached the end of a shorter hall.

Deputy Buckram stepped aside. "Here go, missy."

With relief at finally reaching a friend, she rushed to poor Toby's cell only to find another prisoner inside it leaning against the bars to her right. To her left Toby rocked back and forth on a bench, head down.

"Toby," she cried through the still locked door.

He didn't respond.

Deputy Buckram rattled his blackjack across the bars. Toby's head popped up, and sunlight from the small window illuminated his face.

Peach gasped. "No!"

Chapter 36

As Harley rose beside him to speak, Catfish soaked in the simple majesty of this courtroom, its carved fixtures, its corniced doorways, its louver-shuttered windows, its brass chandeliers, its cream-white columns lifting the deeply molded ceiling as close to God's infinite wisdom as any earthly design might achieve. In this place mortal men solemnly decreed justice or injustice, life or death, for those convicted of crimes against their fellow man.

"May it please the court." Harley spoke from the right end of the single long counsel table beneath the judges' bench. "Harley Austin Calloway and William J. Calloway for the appellant, Toby Topper."

Justice Henderson held up his hand. "Just a minute, counsel. I'm confused by the record. Is your client's name Topper or is it Budge?"

Catfish vaguely remembered Henderson from college. They'd been in Baylor together before the war, but Henderson came back afterwards and graduated from the law department.

"He was born Toby Budge," Harley replied, "but has been known as Toby Topper for some time now."

"Very well. You may proceed with your argument, Mr. Calloway."

While Harley introduced his first argument, Catfish

compared the three gray-haired, black-robed justices to their portraits which hung on the wall behind them. All three were of Catfish's vintage. Justice Henderson, who'd only been on the court since November, was a former district attorney. Justice Hurt, the presiding judge since the court was created, had also been a district attorney, and Justice Davidson came to the court from the attorney general's office. Three former prosecutors. Hurt, at least, had also been a defense lawyer.

"Your Honors, the *Guagando* case, which we cited in our brief, is most on point to our competence challenge."

Catfish couldn't help but watch him. Harley was good. Smart young man. Smarter than he'd been at that age. Catfish had argued to the Court of Criminal Appeals a few times, but he always felt more comfortable in front of a jury. Harley, on the other hand, was already showing how much more he knew about the law of insanity than the justices.

"Like the case at bar, the trial court in *Guagando* refused to conduct a competence hearing and instead proceeded directly to trial on the murder charge."

The Attorney General grabbed a book from the stack in front of him and started flipping pages.

Harley held a volume of the Texas Reporter under his arm. "Like this case, the defendant in *Guagando* made his request for a competence hearing after the case was called for trial, after the arraignment, after his not-guilty plea, and after the jury was selected and impaneled. The trial judge said they could try insanity later if the defendant was convicted, denied the request for a separate sanity hearing, and proceeded with the murder trial, which resulted in a conviction. Only after that did the court finally hear the insanity evidence."

"Which also happened in the case at bar?" Justice Henderson

shrugged. "Your trial judge did submit the insanity question to the jury, right?"

Harley didn't flinch. "He did, but as a result of refusing to hear the competence challenge *before* the murder trial, Mr. Topper couldn't assist us in his defense, and the jury found him guilty of murder."

Catfish caught himself nodding enthusiastically and jerked his head down before the justices noticed.

Justice Henderson persisted. "I understand you have a hearing on a writ de lunatico set for trial in July anyway. Why does it matter whether he got his competence hearing before or after the conviction as long as he gets one at some point?"

Justice Hurt wrote furiously while Harley spoke. The other two justices listened.

Harley opened the case reporter to read. "As the opinion in *Guagando* states, the question presented to the trial court was this: 'Is the accused mentally competent to make a rational defense?'"

At the other end of the long counsel table from Catfish, the walrus shoved another open book in front of the Attorney General. The turncoat Boswell sat back, legs crossed. He'd finally gotten a place at the table. They could have him.

"Your Honors"—Harley's voice had such authority to it— "the Supreme Court reversed *Guagando's* conviction on the basis of Article Forty-One of the Code of Criminal Procedure, holding this: 'The right to have this fact determined before proceeding with the trial for murder is given to a defendant on whose behalf such a plea is presented.'"

Catfish wanted to applaud. That case was right on point.

Chitty stared at the high ceiling.

Justice Hurt glanced from his notes. "Was there expert testimony in *Guagando v. State*?"

"Indeed, Your Honor. Of the four physicians who testified, two testified he was sane, one opined he was insane, and the fourth faulted the examination all the physicians made of him and said, and I quote him, 'The examination, so far as testing the insanity of defendant, was not worth a fig.' The Supreme Court found the evidence sufficient to warrant a new trial."

"Not worth a fig," Justice Henderson chortled to his colleagues.

The justices propounded a few more questions, which Harley answered easily. Such a bright boy.

"Let me address the hearsay point now, Your Honors."

Harley turned the page of his notes. Catfish strained to see the sketch of a ripe little peach at the top of the page. That sweet girl was such a gift to—

The bailiff tapped him on the shoulder. Catfish rocked back, and the bailiff pointed at the open door in the back of the courtroom. Old Nath stood out in the hall.

Harley was unloading both barrels of Shakespeare on the justices as Catfish quietly headed for the door. A spectator in the gallery caught his eye. When had Old Man Stanek come in? The man stared balefully at Catfish, his burly arms crossed over his overalls. Neither was his daughter or his son with him. That man was determined to see his notion of justice administered to Toby.

Outside the courtroom, Catfish approached Nath. "You need to see me?"

"I'm so sorry to trouble you, Mr. Calloway, sir, but you got this telegram, and it's marked urgent."

"Thank you." Catfish unfolded the telegram from Miss Peach and paled at the first sentence. *Toby beaten in jail.*

Chapter 37

Catfish glared at the impertinent jailer. He hadn't hopped on the next train and rushed back to Waco that afternoon to suffer a jailhouse nabob's display of self-importance. He was there to protect his client and wouldn't brook resistance. "Are you refusing to talk to me about how my client got bludgeoned in your cell, deputy?"

His highness busied himself straitening papers without deigning even a glance. "I'm not at liberty to discuss county business, mister. You'll have to talk to the sheriff tomorrow."

It was almost midnight, and patience was no longer a virtue. Catfish turned to Miss Peach and took a blueback document from her. He flipped a page or two and eyed the man. "I don't imagine Sheriff Burke would appreciate getting hauled in front of the judge in the wee hours on a writ of habeas corpus to answer questions you could easily answer right now. Do you think he would?"

The jailer scowled at him and finally eased back. "No need for that. Have a seat."

Catfish yanked the chair out of the way and bent over the desk. "How'd this happen?"

The jailer lit a cigarette. "It must have been another prisoner. Smoke?"

"Who?" Catfish demanded, bracing himself on the desk.

The jailer brushed his trousers and propped his boots on the desk. "You must know how criminals are, Mr. Calloway. Nobody fessed up to it."

Catfish rose to his full height. "Who was in the cell with him?"

"All of 'em." He slid the prisoner register across the desk. "We were washing down the cells and put all of 'em together in the holding cell until we were done."

Catfish pinched on his spectacles and studied the names, but none stood out. "None of these fellas saw him bloodied up?"

"They said he banged his own head against the wall swaying back and forth like he does."

He handed the list to Miss Peach, but she didn't know any either. She gave him the medical report.

Catfish glanced at it. "According to Dr. Black, two black eyes, contusion on his forehead, bruise on back of his head, bruised ribs. You're saying he did all that to himself?"

"That's what the prisoners said. Maybe they're all lying, of course. They're criminals."

"Who found him?"

The jailer wheeled his chair around and yelled down the hallway. "Buckram, come on in here."

Miss Peach retreated toward the front door.

A burly deputy came in and stood beside the jailer's desk, his feet spread wide, and his big hands braced on his hips. Catfish studied the man's face and glanced at Miss Peach. She was right. He looked just like Big Joe, except the deputy didn't have a droopy eye like Joe did.

"Buckram found him." The jailer addressed the deputy. "This here's the crazy boy's lawyer. Got some questions for you."

"What you wanna know?"

Catfish leveled his gaze on Buckram. "Tell me about when you found him."

"He was all curled up on the floor. Got blood all over our cell."

Catfish snorted. Our cell. He scanned the doctor's report again. It mentioned a large knot on the back of his head. "He was conscious, huh?"

"Sure was."

He was lying. "Other prisoners around him?"

"No, they was all backed way off. Said they didn't have nothing to do with it."

Catfish turned on the jailer. "I want to talk to 'em."

"Suit yourself."

The deputy led them to the cellblock where Catfish stood in the hallway and loudly asked who saw what happened to Toby Topper. Nobody answered. Catfish checked on Toby, found him quietly rocking by himself in a cell, and went back to the head jailer's office.

"We took him to Doc Black right away," the jailer explained. "Says he'll be all right after he heals a little."

Catfish slapped the papers he was holding against the edge of the desk. "Lucky he didn't get beaten to death as closely as your man Buckram watched them."

Buckram bristled. "They's all criminals, mister. I ain't responsible for what they does to each other."

"We've got him in a cell by himself now," the jailer said. "That's all we can do."

If he cared about protecting Toby, he'd fire Buckram. Catfish made a show of taking the blueback legal document from Miss Peach and reading through it again. He was careful not to let them see its actual title, a deed of trust on a piece of property owned by another client. "You're not gonna let this happen again?"

"We're doing all we can."

Catfish stood beside Miss Peach. "I wouldn't want to be the one who had to explain to Judge Goodrich why one of his prisoners got hurt while the case was on appeal."

"He's gonna hang anyway," Buckram sneered.

"Not if I can help it." Catfish started for the door but turned back. "By the way, you related to Big Joe Buckram?"

"He's my brother." He shot a stream of tobacco into the spittoon and wiped spittle from his chin. "What of it?"

"Just wondering. Met him before."

Buckram laughed. "You must be a customer at the whorehouse."

Catfish ignored him, and they got out of there. Next door, the clock in the courthouse tower struck twelve, sending Colonel Terry into a fit of baying. The night was dark as pitch.

Catfish had been to that sporting house, all right, but not as a customer. He recalled another dark night on Washington Street when Big Joe had threatened him with a blackjack. He slipped his arm through Miss Peach's. As for the Buckram boys, she was right: They were nobody to trifle with.

"Do you think it was the deputy who beat Toby?" she asked.

"Not much doubt."

"Why would he do that?"

"Seen plenty of swine like them. Some hurt other folks out of pure-d meanness. Others have a reason."

"Did he have a reason?"

"Likely didn't have anything better to do."

Chapter 38

Three weeks after the appellate argument, back in the smoky Bismark Saloon, Mr. Calloway raised a glass of Strathisla to his son. "To victory!"

Peach applauded. Though it wasn't over yet, this was Harley's first real taste of winning in an important capital case, and all his anxiety, his restlessness, his aloofness, even his rudeness, all of it had its root in this. The win was twice sweet: once for Harley, but even more for Toby. Now, for the first time, there was hope he might go free someday after a retrial. She lifted her glass too, even though it was only ginger ale. "To Harley!"

She had witnessed his transformation earlier that day when the news arrived by post from the Court of Criminal Appeals. Harley ripped open the envelope and skipped to the end of the opinion to see the outcome: The court unanimously reversed Toby's conviction and remanded the case for a new trial. He belted out a rebel yell, startling the slumbering Colonel Terry, and proceeded to march around the big office worktable reading aloud the remainder of the opinion. The court had held Judge Goodrich's decision to deny Toby a hearing on his competence to stand trial violated Rule Forty-One of the Code of Criminal Procedure, as Harley had urged. There would be another sanity hearing. More importantly for Toby, because Judge Goodrich had admitted inadmissible hearsay into evidence, the appeals court had also ordered a new trial on the murder charges—again, as Harley requested. The court's reasoning was almost verbatim from his pen. She had beamed with pride at him.

Hours later in the boisterous saloon, their celebration continued unabated. The younger Calloway's lovely black locks tumbled over his forehead as the elder's white ones did when he tossed his head. Harley sloshed more whisky into his glass and raised it again. "To Peach and Shakespeare!"

The sentiment rendered her instantly light-headed. Personally, this was thrice sweet a victory because Justice Henderson had even quoted Shakespeare in his opinion.

Mr. Calloway's blue eyes glistened even in the dim light. "Peach and Shakespeare!"

She wanted to hug them both. She raised her voice to be heard over the hubbub of the saloon. "But it was Harley who made them hear."

Mr. Calloway broke into a wider grin. "Audi alteram partem!"

It was undoubtedly a rare thing that Bismark patrons heard any Latin. Three vulgar fellows at the next table must have gotten the gist of it though. "Part 'em, boys!" one shouted with a slur. The thick smoke burned her eyes.

Mr. Calloway had always preached the only way to lessen the misery of losing was to love winning more, and Harley had taken those sermons to heart. He should have eased off at this point but refilled his glass instead. He pulled them closer to be heard over the crowd. "This time around, I'll prepare Dr. Wallace better."

"The clerk told me the competence hearing's been reset to April thirtieth," Mr. Calloway said. "The last day of the spring term of court. She set the murder case for trial in July."

It hit Peach then that if the jury found him insane, there'd be no murder trial, and poor Toby would go to an asylum for the rest of his life. He didn't deserve that either. "How do you feel about our chances?"

Mr. Calloway leaned over the table. "What?"

"What are our chances of winning the competence hearing?"

"First jury found Toby sane," Mr. Calloway said. "I wonder if we don't have a better chance to prove somebody else is the killer."

She turned to Harley.

A frown swept across his face. "Wait a minute!" he answered loudly. "After all we've done to get a new sanity hearing, we're just going to give up on it?"

Mr. Calloway put a finger to his lips.

Harley glanced around at the other tables and lowered his voice. "Papa, that's not like you. Toby's clearly not sane. If we can get him a fairer sanity hearing, he won't have to risk another trial on the murder charges."

"True," Mr. Calloway said, eying Peach.

She wasn't going to give up either. "Kate Friend doesn't believe he could even fire a gun, at least not twice."

Harley downed another shot of whisky. "I'm hoping we won't even have to make that argument."

Peach gently squeezed Harley's arm. "But, if we think Toby didn't do it, why are we still going to prove he's insane?"

Harley's face was fully red. "Two bites at the apple." His words took on a slight slur.

Peach cleared her throat and folded her arms on the table. She didn't mind if others heard her or not. "If he didn't commit any crime, why should he have to be locked in a lunatic asylum for the rest of his life?"

"We have to take two bites."

She blew out a breath. "Well, I don't think it would be right to put him in an asylum if he didn't do anything wrong."

Mr. Calloway dropped some money on the table and stood. "Thankfully, we don't have to settle this tonight."

She had been ready to depart for some time.

"Papa, wait." Harley clapped his hand over Peach's forearm. "We haven't had a toast from Peach yet. What about it, my love?"

My love? Peach pulled away from him. There's nothing falser than vows made in drink. "I think we should go."

Mr. Calloway grabbed Harley's arm.

She wasn't a lawyer, and it wasn't her place, but somehow, she had to convince a more sober Harley to drop the competence challenge.

Chapter 39

"I have little memory of it, but I sense I made a fool of myself last night," Harley said across the drugstore table from her. "I wanted to say how sorry I am."

The tension in Peach's shoulders immediately dissipated. The warmth had returned to him. His coal-black hair was neatly combed, his eyes were bright, his manner was polite. His words needn't say anything more because his tone imparted everything. If she could have only thrown her arms around him.

He'd come to the office late the morning after the Bismark Hall celebration and right away had asked her to go with him next door to the Corner Drug. They'd first walked to the post office and gotten the mail and had taken a table in the back of the drugstore, away from other patrons. The shiny metal counters of the brightly lit soda fountain, the hissing of carbonization, the whistling of the soda jerk, the fresh air from the open front door, and the gaiety of the customers of all ages, were all such a welcome change from the saloon. It was more to her liking, and Harley would have known that.

She sipped her tea. "You needn't apologize."

He extended his hands in supplication. "I put myself upon the country."

Harley sometimes resorted to legal expressions like that to

help him deal with difficult personal situations. Yes, he was himself again.

She smiled to mirror his warmth. "It was the whisky."

"That was part of it. But you didn't deserve to be the brunt of my reaction to Papa's suggestion we abandon the insanity defense."

"Maybe there are good reasons to do it."

Harley stirred milk into his coffee. "I feel like we have a shot at winning another competence hearing. I know more now than I did then."

She agreed, but that missed the point. He hadn't changed his mind, but maybe he would at least listen to reason.

He slurped the steaming coffee. "I do hear what you're saying about Toby not deserving an asylum, but what choice do we have? If we can't prove somebody else did it, then it's too risky to drop the competence challenge."

"Couldn't we make the competence challenge afterwards if he's convicted again? That's what we planned to do before."

"There's a bigger risk in doing that this time. Since we appealed on the very point his competence to stand trial must be determined before the trial, I don't think we can in good faith wait until afterwards again. Judge Goodrich would be furious, and if we had to go back to the Court of Criminal Appeals they would be too."

It was hard to argue with that. She sipped her tea while pondering her rebuttal. Her eyes fell on a postcard in the stack of mail she dropped on the table. It had a typewritten address but no return address and was for *Mr. Callaway*. His name was misspelled, but that was a common mistake. She wondered which Calloway it was for and flipped it over.

Harley didn't wait for her to answer. "I really think—"

She gasped.

"What is it?"

She shoved the typewritten card across the table. *stop protecting killer or you regret—idiot must hang.*

Chapter 40

Catfish tossed the note down. "This is a threat, and it proves we're right. Whoever murdered the express agents is anxious for Toby to get the official blame and have the police close the case. He's on edge after we won the appeal. It was one thing when he just had to outsmart Jaybird, but now he knows we're in his way. We have to smoke him out."

"How?" Harley asked.

That's the part Catfish wasn't sure about. He paced the office, puffing on a White Owl, and occasionally stopping by the door to pet the colonel. The ruling of the appellate court had prodded the killer to poke out of his hiding place. The idea of a new trial ate at him and he reacted. There had to be a way to stoke the pressure and provoke him to show more of himself.

Miss Peach's face popped up as he paced toward her. "Mr. Calloway, if Toby didn't do it, do we still have to prove he's insane?"

Catfish stopped and tapped ashes into the spittoon. She was worried about Toby. If he didn't commit any crime, why should he be locked in a lunatic asylum for the rest of his life? Dang good question. He'd been thinking the same thing. He dropped into a chair, rocked back, and propped his boots on the table.

What was going on inside the killer's head? He'd probably

feel safer if they focused on Toby's sanity and not on who actually killed the express agents. Wouldn't much matter to him if Toby went to an asylum instead of a prison if everybody thought he committed the murders. Maybe Miss Peach was right. "What do you think we should do?"

She didn't hesitate. "Concentrate on proving who did it and hold off on insanity."

She shot a glance at Harley.

He never wanted to relinquish a good defense he fought so hard to secure, but he didn't appear resistant. "The threat changes things."

"Good." Catfish pulled his watch and wound it slowly as he worked through his new idea. "Here's what we do. Miss Peach, take a letter for me, darlin'."

She flipped open her stenographic pad, blotted her pen, and waited.

Catfish stared at the tin ceiling, puffing on his cigar. "Dear Judge Goodrich. This is to advise the court that, on behalf of our client, Mr. Toby Topper"—he tapped out his cigar as Miss Peach coughed—"we withdraw our previous challenge to his sanity to stand trial. We ask the clerk to remove the sanity hearing from the docket. We intend to announce ready for trial in the July term and will not assert an insanity defense to the murder charges. For the court's information, we intend to go to the jury on our 'Not-Guilty' plea. We intend to prove the identity of the real murderer at trial." He eyed Harley and Miss Peach. "Yours very truly, et cetera, et cetera."

The other two exchanged glances.

"How does that smoke out the killer?" Harley asked.

"Miss Peach," Catfish said, "how long will it take you to typewrite extra copies of that letter? I want one for Chitty, one for Jaybird, and one for the newspaper."

"Newspaper?" Harley asked.

Catfish winked at him.

Miss Peach shrugged. "With carbon paper, I type them all at the same time."

She brought that confounded carbonated paper into their office when she started working for them three years ago. The more copies you needed, the fainter they got. "No, now I think about it, I want it handwritten to the judge and handwritten copies for all three of the others."

Her eyes popped wide. "That will take a little longer."

"Fine." They had three months. He chewed the cigar for a few moments. "You know, I changed my mind. Think I'll write 'em out longhand myself."

Harley and Miss Peach both looked stunned, as he anticipated.

"That's not really necessary, Mr. Calloway. I'll be happy to write them all if that's what you want."

"No, thanks anyway though." He couldn't help but enjoy this moment. "You might not know it, but I have excellent penmanship and good penmanship is a mark of character."

Harley smiled. Catfish had probably said the same thing about a thousand times to the boys growing up.

He looked at Miss Peach, who'd never received that pearl of wisdom. "Good penmanship shows you're careful, you're concerned about being right, and you don't care how long it takes to get it right." He reached into his trial box and fetched his Wirt pen. "However long it takes."

Both Harley and Miss Peach looked surprised. As expected. Harley once asked him why he bought a new-fangled fountain pen. Catfish showed him the magazine advertisement in which

Mark Twain said he used a Wirt. Didn't have to dip the thing. Mighty clever.

Harley squinted. "So, you want the judge to know you're of good character?"

"I want folks to know I won't rest until I prove who the killer is."

When the word got out that their defense strategy had changed from insanity to innocence, the killer would squirm. He'd realize they weren't intimidated by that threat and knew what was going on. He'd have to do something. Step out in the light of day.

Because he'd know Catfish Calloway was personally coming after him and wouldn't stop.

Chapter 41

There was no way on God's green earth Thaddeus Schoolcraft would help. Harley knew that, but Papa insisted he try anyway. They hadn't anticipated Hamp Boswell would be there too.

"Thank you for agreeing to meet with me, sir," Harley said to the detective. Schoolcraft's second floor office was only a block away, across the street from the Pacific Hotel at Fourth and Franklin. "I was hoping you might answer some questions."

"Concerning?"

"I know, because of your relationship with American Express, you're probably not inclined to help Toby Topper, but—"

"My inclination is to do whatever is necessary to bring a killer to justice." Schoolcraft rocked forward in his chair. A towering rolltop desk, with papers jutting from every cubby, loomed behind him. "I feel pity for the boy, but imbecility doesn't excuse wicked deeds."

Harley curbed his impulse to spar. "But what if he didn't do it?"

Boswell leaned against the wall with his arms crossed as if he knew the conversation would be short. The room was dimly lit because the blinds on the windows were closed.

"Sir," Harley said, ignoring Boswell, "if the real killer is still at large, then the railroad and the express company are still at risk of further crimes by him. I'd be surprised if punishing the wrong man was really in your company's interest."

Two desk lamps flanked the detective and illuminated the expressive face surrounding his horseshoe mustache. He meant to convey impatience. "What I'd be surprised at is if you and your father really believed Topper's innocent."

"We do, sir. Dr. Wallace says he's incapable of premeditating a robbery and murder. He says Toby doesn't have the mental ability to think that through."

"Nonsense," Schoolcraft said contemptuously. "Your father claimed your brother wasn't capable of murder either."

Harley tensed. He couldn't let Schoolcraft provoke him. It had been open hostility between Papa and Schoolcraft ever since the trial of Harley's brother. Papa always blamed Schoolcraft for what happened to Houston because the detective was instrumental in securing his conviction for murder. The dime novel tore open those old wounds.

But Papa wanted information only Schoolcraft had. The local American Express office had said they were never involved personally in dealing with the informant other than to transfer the reward money to Schoolcraft, who handled it all himself. American Express relied on the railroad's detective because it didn't have its own detective close enough to help. So Schoolcraft was the only one who had contact with the informant, and Papa believed that informant had to be the killer. He thought Schoolcraft might be more willing to reason with Harley than himself.

Harley had to try, so he bit his lip at the mention of his brother. "Hear me out, sir, please. Dr. Wallace says flight from a murder scene is an act of human reasoning that's beyond Toby. He doesn't have the mental capacity to figure out that if he doesn't flee, he'd be caught and punished."

Boswell snickered and took a chair. "He's smart enough to remember everybody's address."

It was all Harley could do to refrain from slapping the impertinent Judas, but that wouldn't help accomplish his mission. "Doesn't it require more thinking ability than that to understand you'd need to shoot the express agents to take their money, that the authorities would be upset about that shooting and want to punish you, and therefore you'd need to flee the scene to avoid apprehension? You saw Toby, Mr. Schoolcraft. Do you really believe he can think that through?"

He smirked. "So, he has a twin brother who three eyewitnesses saw rob the express wagon?"

Here was his chance. Even if Schoolcraft wouldn't help, Papa had thought telling him this would help spread the word they were getting closer to finding the real killer. "No, we know somebody else set Toby up to cover his own actions."

Schoolcraft erupted into laughter and Boswell joined. "Someone pretended to be Topper? That's even more far-fetched. I read in the newspaper you're abandoning your insanity claim. Your father is getting desperate."

"Wait." Harley extended his hand as Schoolcraft made to rise. "Think about it for a minute. Who better to blame for the crime than someone who acts in such an odd way in public that people recognize him instantly by his actions? All it takes is mimicking those actions to make people think it's Toby. Remember what Sam Prim testified? He said he didn't see the killer's face, but he saw him tipping a top hat and it looked the same as when Toby did that in court."

"You're reaching here, counselor."

Harley scooted his chair closer to Schoolcraft's desk. "Bob

Lazenby's eyesight was not good enough to see the shooter's face, and the boy who was fishing had his back turned. Nobody identified Toby's face as the face of the robber. Anybody could wear his hat and coat and ride his bicycle, and as long as he tipped the hat like Toby did, eyewitnesses would think it was Toby."

Schoolcraft eyed the clock on his desk.

"What if we're right? Would you rest easy knowing you'd hung an innocent boy, idiot or not?"

"You lawyers are all the same. Have you forgotten Cicero Sweet? Your father always claims his client's innocent."

Harley had eventually realized Cicero wasn't innocent, but Toby was different. "Papa believes every man deserves a fair chance to present his side of it. Help us see if there's proof of Toby's innocence. If there's not, then the next jury is likely to reach the same result the first one did."

Schoolcraft's face exclaimed *I'm ready for you to leave.* "Why are you wasting your time trying to convince me?"

Harley couldn't give up yet. "Papa's wondering about the tipster, and you're the only one who spoke with him. Whoever called in the information about the location of the abandoned express wagon also told the police where Toby was. How'd he know both locations?"

"How does that help you?"

At least he was listening now. It was unexpected, but maybe he was softening. "We think the real murderer put you on to Toby. He kidnapped him, took his bicycle, his coat, and his top hat to the scene, and mimicked Toby. Then he tipped you about where to find Toby and the evidence."

Schoolcraft lit a cigarette. "Even more far-fetched."

"It's absurd," Boswell added.

Harley swatted smoke away from his face. "Did you know the

police also found blood where Toby was sleeping in that shanty? Ask Sergeant Quinn if you don't believe me. What if he wasn't sleeping but had been knocked out? Would that cause you to question if he was guilty?"

"He wags his head constantly." Boswell said. "He probably banged it on something."

"Tell us what you remember about the tipster. What do you have to lose?"

Schoolcraft rose from his chair and crossed to the window overlooking Fourth Street. He yanked the venetian blinds open, and streaks of sunlight slashed across the room. He stuffed his hands into his pockets and appeared to be watching something outside. Light reflected off the side of his face. His bowler hung on a hook beside him, and his blackthorn cane rested in an umbrella stand. "I never met the man," he finally said without turning.

Harley was breathless. "Yes, sir?"

Schoolcraft didn't respond.

Boswell jumped up. "You should leave."

Harley ignored him. "But did you pay him, sir? Who was it?"

Schoolcraft turned and leaned against the windowsill, crunching the blinds. "He telephoned in to arrange the payment."

"What name did he give?"

"He wouldn't give a name."

Of course, he wouldn't. "Where'd you send the money?"

"He told me to leave it under a rock on the east bank of the Brazos near the suspension bridge."

Son of a gun! Just what a killer would do. He couldn't believe Schoolcraft was actually helping them. "Before or after the police caught Toby?"

"After."

Boswell plopped back down with a frown on his face.

Harley had to keep the detective talking. "Did you watch to see who picked it up?"

"I didn't care. It was after the police captured the killer. The evidence was so clear Topper did it that I had no reason to doubt the informant. His information was corroborated when Quinn found some of the money on Topper."

There had to be something else that would help. "But didn't you wonder about why the man was being so secretive?"

His answer came slowly. "Maybe I should have."

Boswell's eyes narrowed in disbelief at his boss' reaction, but it appeared Schoolcraft genuinely wanted to find the truth.

Harley was hopeful. "Anything you can remember about talking to him would help. Please, sir, think."

Schoolcraft turned his back and stared out the window again. Silhouetted against the bright light, he finally spoke. "He had some kind of an accent. European, I think."

"That's helpful." Harley tried to think of immigrants in the area. Jacob Levinski maybe?

Schoolcraft turned again, his face shadowed by the bright light behind. "When Mr. Stanek made his outburst in court, I thought for a moment his accent sounded familiar. I'm not sure, but it could have been him."

Chapter 42

He didn't look much like a killer. Catfish dragged a stool on the front porch a few feet from Old Man Stanek's rocking chair. "We'd like to visit with you about how Toby Topper came to be accused of murdering your son-in-law."

The old man halted rocking, and his eyes narrowed. "What you want? Killer in jail, yes?"

Harley had remained on the rock walkway leading to the farmhouse. He propped a foot on the porch steps. "We think the wrong man's in jail, sir."

Stanek's jaw clinched, but he didn't make eye contact with Harley. "Right man."

His chair screeched and the porch slats moaned in reply when he started rocking again. As if he were alone, Stanek gazed past Catfish at a horse nosing the ground in a distant pasture. Hard fella. Wasn't the chatting sort.

Catfish wasn't in a hurry. Chickens pecked at the dirt under a giant oak tree near the house. Its shade spread over the front yard weeds. Neat mortar-free limestone walls enclosed feedlots for pigs and cows, and a stone barn anchored a large recently plowed field that climbed a rise in the mostly flat countryside. The farm was twenty miles north of Waco near the small Czech immigrant community of West.

His burly son, Andel, leaned against a cedar post supporting the porch roof. His daughter must have been in the house, but Stanek didn't invite them inside and didn't call for her to join them.

"I know you want justice for your family." Catfish doffed his hat and brushed dust from the crown. "But punishing the wrong man isn't justice for your daughter."

Stanek clinched the arms of his rocker. He must have been in his seventies. Unruly gray hair and a bushy beard edged his ruddy moon face. His eyes were dark, cold. "What you want here?"

"We've been told you gave information to the police."

"Information?" He glanced at Andel. "What information they want?"

Andel shrugged. Like his father, the young man had a bushy beard jutting from his square jaw.

"About Mr. Topper."

"I know nothing of idiot, Topper."

Catfish tried not to sound accusatory. "The railroad detective told us you did."

Stanek began to fume. "I don't know railroad detective."

Catfish nodded. "I wasn't sure."

There weren't any wires coming into the house, so they didn't have a talking phone. Too far out in the country for that. He handed the calling card with the number on it to Stanek. "This number mean anything to you?"

The old man glanced at the card and immediately handed it to his son. Andel examined it front and back. "Uh-uh."

Catfish took it back and kicked a broken branch off the porch. They weren't making much progress. Maybe it'd be better to push him harder and see how he reacted. "We think you tipped the police where to find Mr. Topper and the express wagon."

Old Man Stanek spat back, "Why you think that?"

Catfish fixed his eyes squarely on Stanek, silently, until the old man finally returned the look. "Did you collect reward money for turning Toby in?"

Stanek gawped at him but said nothing.

Andel eased over beside his father. "They don't mean anything, Poppy."

Old Man Stanek's jaw pulsated, and he stopped rocking. His eyes didn't leave Catfish.

Harley retreated from the front step. "Sir—"

Andel waved his hand toward Harley. "It's best if you leave."

Catfish pressed forward, bracing his forearms on his knees. "You get any reward money?"

The old man's eyes got big as saucers, and his head twitched uncontrollably. "You think Jakub Stanek take money for Duša's broken heart?"

"Mr. Stanek—"

"Get off my farm!" The old man stumbled out of his chair, waving a fist at Catfish. "Get!"

"Poppy, please!" Andel tried to restrain him. "Mr. Calloway, you better leave."

Harley drove them back to Waco. The wind had come up, and bluebonnets quilting the surrounding pastures bent back northward. The buggy horse kicked up more dust from the road.

Catfish tied a neckerchief over his nose, tugged his Stetson, and clamped his eyes shut. Old Man Stanek might have been hiding something or might have just been emotional over their loss. He had a temper, but the robbery wasn't a crime of passion. It was premeditated. And neither of the Stanek men seemed like killers. It would have been like Schoolcraft to send Catfish off on a wild goose chase out of spite.

The buggy rolled along the road toward the Brazos, and the towers of the suspension bridge rose gradually on the horizon. As they clattered over the bridge, past the spot where somebody masquerading as Toby gunned down two express agents, Catfish tried to imagine the face. And the voice. He slipped the threatening note from his pocket: *stop protecting killer or <u>you</u> regret—idiot must hang.* He read it aloud trying to mimic Stanek's accent. Even over the clopping of the horse and the rattling of the bridge planks, one word stood out. Just like in the threatening note, Stanek had said the word *idiot*.

Was Schoolcraft telling the truth?

Chapter 43

It was his last chance to find out something important about Stanek. Harley leaned on the post office counter after striking up a conversation with the West postmaster. "Do you happen to know the Staneks?"

"The Staneks from north of town or the ones to the south?" He spun his stool around to face Harley. "They're different families, you know."

"The ones I'm talking about live south of here, toward Waco."

Papa had been equivocal about whether he really thought the Staneks killed one of their own, but it was his way to leave no stone unturned. He wanted Harley to find out if there was any bad blood between the Stanek family and Bill Hook. Czech immigrants were a tight knit group, but Hook wasn't one of them. Maybe Duša married him against her family's wishes. Harley had gone back to the area the following day to speak with Stanek's neighbors, who were mostly Czech themselves. They were all suspicious of Harley and refused to talk. He'd traveled a great distance to discover little that was new.

Then he met James Berkley, the postmaster, and he wasn't a Czech.

"Sure, I know 'em." He dumped a bag of letters on the

counter and began sorting as he spoke. "Jakub Stanek's a widower. He's got a son named Andel and a daughter. Andel's a real nice fellow. Don't talk much. Miss Duša moved back in with 'em after her man got killed. The Staneks get letters from Bohemia. Of course, most of them Czech folks do, you know. Anyway, Mr. Stanek would come in about once a week, but I haven't seen him as much lately." He looked at Harley over his stack of letters. "You Stanek kin?"

"No, sir," Harley answered. "Was there any trouble you know of between Miss Duša's husband and the Staneks?"

He laughed. "There's trouble between Jakub Stanek and just about everybody. He's a cantankerous old cuss."

"Yes, sir?"

"One day this other customer picked up a package from the old country by mistake." He neatly stacked each pile of letters on the counter. "It was addressed to Jakub Stanek, but this other fellow thought it was for him. His name was Jacob Stanzic. He lives here in town. The handwriting was hard to read, you know?" Berkley broke out laughing. "You should have seen Jakub Stanek's face when he found out Stanzic took his package. He started cussing in Czech and stormed out of here and marched right to Mr. Stanzic's house and blistered him up one side and down the other."

So, the old man did have a temper. "Did he get along with Duša's husband?"

"As far as I know, as well as he got along with anybody." Berkley held a letter to a lamp and examined it from both sides. "Czechs! Most of 'em can't spell ordinary English."

"Do you know of any reason Mr. Stanek or Andel might want Bill Hook dead?"

Berkley's eyes darted to Harley. "You mean Stanek killed Bill Hook?"

Harley shrugged. "I'm trying to find out what happened."

"Who are you, anyway?" Berkley asked, alighting from his stool. He adjusted his sleeve garters and braced his hands on his hips. "I don't generally talk to other folks about people's private affairs."

"I'm a lawyer from Waco. I represent the boy accused of killing Bill Hook."

"Oh." He eyed Harley a moment and grabbed another bulging sack from the floor and dropped it on the counter. "Law business, huh?"

"Yes, sir."

He dumped letters from the sack on the counter and started placing them on the stacks he'd already made. After he was done, he took each stack and shoved the letters one by one into pigeonholes behind the counter. "There's nothing I know of. As far as I know, by seeing with my own eyes, Jakub Stanek was fine with his son-in-law. Oh, maybe he didn't like the way Bill treated Miss Duša sometimes, but I don't think he'd want him dead."

Harley folded his arms on the counter and tried to appear interested but not too interested. "How'd he treat her?"

"Well, I don't know this myself, mind you, but folks talk." He looked back over his shoulder at Harley, letters in hand. "They say Duša's man drank too much. Folks say one time Miss Duša come home to live with her parents for a spell, and she had a black eye."

That might be a motive. "Did you see that yourself?"

Berkley went back to his pigeonholes. "Oh no, that's what folks say. They talk, you know."

"When did that happen?"

"Been a while back now. Maybe a year ago?"

That timing would be about right. "How long did she stay at home?"

"Never saw her myself. Just what folks say."

Those talkative folks might know something more about it than Berkley. "Who could I speak with about that?"

Berkley finished sorting letters and brushed his apron. "Oh my, well, I don't know as I recollect who it was exactly that was talking about all that business. Anything else I can do for you?"

Harley thanked him and left.

It was after sunset when he finally returned to town. He left his horse and buggy at the stable and, exhausted from his travels, trudged along the alley behind the U.S. Courthouse toward his boarding house. It had been raining earlier, and no one else was in sight when he crossed Fourth Street to the alley between the Blake building and the Artesian Steam Laundry. Mud sucked at his shoes as he neared the steps at the back door of his boarding house. He fumbled in the darkness for the doorknob and stepped onto something soft. He jumped back and stooped to see what was on the top step.

It was a dead crow, black as the night.

Chapter 44

Peach didn't like bicycling home in the dark—the night was especially dark—but she had no choice, and the air was fresh after a nice spring rain. May showers always cooled the evenings.

It had been a lovely evening at Miss Kate's, though Macbeth had gone on entirely too long. Dr. Gregory insisted on finishing Act IV. He took the second witch's part and screwed his high voice into the most tortured witch's chant imaginable, but she had to admit his performance of the final part of the scene was masterful. "By the pricking of my thumbs, something wicked this way comes."

As she pedaled along Franklin Avenue past the boarding house where Harley lived—it would have been faster to cut directly over to Columbus Avenue—she glanced over her shoulder at the second-floor window where the light was on. He was probably reading. He was like his father in his love for books, though he preferred Sir Walter Scott to Twain or Dickens. She thought about stopping for an unannounced visit. She could try to reenact Dr. Gregory's bewitching performance. Harley would laugh—or more likely he'd yawn because it was so terribly late.

Her thoughts scattered at the sound of a horse's whinny behind her, and she glanced over her shoulder. The sidelights of a carriage bounced up and down quite some distance back.

She pedaled on, but try as she might, she couldn't put Mr. Harley Austin Calloway out of her mind. He could be so frustrating sometimes. He liked her—she was sure of that—but was it more? It certainly was for her, and she thought of him whenever her mind wandered. When the front door of the law office opened in the mornings, and Harley would smile and say good morning, she would find herself shorter of breath every time.

She rode under the glow of the streetlight at the corner of Eighth Street. The carriage horse still clopped behind her even after she turned onto Eighth toward Columbus.

Harley had a slight touch of his father's wit, and she couldn't help but smile when he tried to exercise it. He tried so hard sometimes, bless his heart. But witty or not, he was very smart. Most young men she knew spoke to her only of silly, unimportant matters as if she was incapable of conversing about a serious topic. Harley was different.

She delighted in talking with him about their work. The cases were fascinating, and she adored being a part of them. Harley genuinely valued her opinions and sought her advice about many things. She especially loved helping them get ready for trial. If she couldn't advocate for a client in court herself, she would do everything she possibly could to assist those who could. Mr. Hampton Boswell might not think it much of a contribution, but Harley and Mr. Calloway certainly did, and they were the ones who mattered.

She turned the corner and gazed behind her. No carriage. She let out a breath.

Did Harley feel the same sense of gravity as she about their shared work? She hoped so because she surely felt they had a purpose—*audi alteram partem,* as Mr. Calloway constantly reminded them, making people hear the other side—and it was so important. She and Harley had even spoken of it once, if only briefly. But they didn't need to say it aloud. She had been so relieved when Harley finally let go of the insanity defense. She couldn't bear Toby being locked in an asylum for the rest of his life.

She pedaled across Austin Avenue. City Hall was so wonderfully lit to her right, but it must have been late, though, because no one was out on Austin. She casually glanced back. The carriage was there again. How odd they hadn't passed her or turned away.

There was this about Harley, and it was the problem: Every time she felt they were getting closer—when her cheeks warmed and her breathing quickened, when she yearned to take his hand boldly, when her heart seemed about to burst—he would say something so utterly mundane and back away as if they were mere acquaintances. It was so maddening. It had taken her weeks to get over his snub at the Christmas party. He hadn't meant anything by it, of course. He was under pressure. She'd given the handkerchief she'd embroidered for him to Mr. Moon. The *HAC* initials stood for Honorable American Citizen, she'd told him. It wasn't really a lie.

She turned left on Columbus, her destination now only two blocks away. The carriage was still behind her though closer now. What a coincidence of routes.

Maybe she should just tell Harley how she felt. That would fix his wagon. She tossed her head. *Mr. Harley Austin Calloway, you listen to me because you need to understand this: I love you.* She smiled to herself. He'd have to declare his intentions then.

Her musings crashed when a man's voice shouted, "Giddy-up!"

The clopping of the carriage horse grew louder, and she glanced back over her shoulder. It was even closer; the horse was trotting. The carriage rattled and creaked, louder, and louder. She twisted back and gasped in air. What was happening? There was Judge Clark's house ahead. Should she pull up to his door? No, she was almost home. As she pedaled harder toward home, the gravel crackled under her tires.

Another backward glance. Another gulp of air. She pedaled faster, clutching the handlebars so tightly her knuckles blanched white, her thumbs pricked with pain. The carriage was in the middle of the street over her left shoulder. The horse's eye gleamed white. She bent to the effort, pedaling as hard as she could, her billowing bloomers pressed against her legs. Her hat blew off. She gained distance from the carriage for a brief moment, but she tired and the gap between them closed. The clopping pounded in her ears. The horse raced past her to the left.

She eased off pedaling to let it pass, but instead the carriage also slowed until the driver's seat was alongside her. She sensed the mass of the vehicle and turned to see who drove it.

In the darkness, a large dark shape swooped toward her.

"No!" she screamed.

Chapter 45

Oddly, the door was still locked. Harley had arrived a little after eight in the morning and noticed through the window the lights were off inside. Miss Peach was always there by then and had already opened the office. He unlocked it and pushed the door open. A piece of paper fluttered to the floor inside the door. He picked it up and went in. He hung his hat and coat on the rack, dropped his briefcase on the floor, and read the note.

idiot die peech live
not tell police

Harley staggered back against the desk and reread the note. The dead crow flashed through his mind.

He rushed into their office. The lights were off, the ceiling fan was still. Just as they left it the evening before. He hurried back to the reception room. Peach's bicycle wasn't where she usually put it in the mornings. He threw open the front door and skipped the curb into the street. He craned his neck to the north along Fourth Street in the direction of the boarding house where she lived, but there was no sign of her. He glanced the other direction, but there was no Peach there either.

He'd left the buggy on the curb, horse still hitched, because he'd planned to visit a client outside of town. He jumped in and lashed the horse into a gallop toward Mrs. Sparks's boarding house. He raced across Fourth Street and tore around the corner in front of the Williamson Drug Store. He swerved around a trolley and cut back in front of it, rushing past a bank and across Fifth Street. He glanced at his watch and whipped the horse again. Past Sixth Street, the bakery, the Y.M.C.A., the toy store, the Sedwick building. She was probably at home, feeling unwell. He lashed the horse again. The buggy cornered Thirteenth Street on one wheel, staggered, righted, and he raced past Columbus five more endless blocks.

He found Mrs. Sparks clearing the breakfast table.

"Is Peach still here?" he asked breathlessly.

"I'm not sure," Mrs. Sparks said. "I haven't seen her since she left home for work yesterday morning."

They went to her room. Pink satin pillows topped a perfectly made bed. They checked out back where she kept her bicycle, but it wasn't there.

There was tightness inside him, his breath somehow constrained. Harley thanked Mrs. Sparks and rushed to his buggy. Peach had told him yesterday it was the evening for their Shakespeare meeting. She'd asked him to go, but he'd declined. Maybe she stayed last night at Miss Kate's for some reason. He lashed the horse into a trot again and turned up Columbus.

About a block on the other side of Judge Clark's house there was a bicycle lying beside the road. He yanked the reins to a halt, jumped out, and ran to it. It was Peach's. He searched the area frantically. On a lawn next to the curb, he found her hat.

"Peach!" he yelled.

A man was sitting nearby on his front porch.

Harley shouted at him. "Have you seen Zipporah Peach?"

"Who?"

"A young lady in her twenties, ginger hair."

"Haven't seen anybody like that."

Harley hurried from house to house, but no one had seen her. No one knew how the bicycle had gotten there either. He checked the bicycle again, thinking a tire might be flat and she'd walked somewhere, but the tires were fine. Could she have fallen off and hurt herself? Surely, she would have knocked on a door for help.

He searched his mind for some explanation short of someone harming her. People like her didn't disappear. Maybe she told him she was going somewhere after Miss Kate's, and he wasn't paying attention when she told him. Or maybe the sudden shower caused her to seek shelter at a nearby house. But she wouldn't just go off and leave her bicycle there when the rain stopped. Try as he might, he couldn't escape the realization that the note explained her disappearance.

idiot die peach live.

The dead crow pounded his brain.

He threw the bicycle and the hat into his buggy and took off for Miss Kate's.

"Peach left here late," Miss Kate said. "As far as I know, she was going home."

Harley bit his lip. "She apparently didn't."

"Have you contacted the police?"

He couldn't take the chance.

not tell police.

He thanked her and left for the office. Thank God, Papa was there.

Papa had found the note on Peach's desk. "Any signs of violence, son?"

No, it couldn't be that. Nobody would want to hurt Peach. Harley shook his head.

"Let's get the police," Papa said.

"The note said not to." He told Papa about the crow.

"Looks to me like somebody's kidnapped her."

"Why?"

"They're trying to scare us. To force us to let Toby hang."

Harley snatched the note where Papa had laid it on the table. "It must be Stanek. The note reads like it was written by a Czech."

He shoved the note back at Papa, but he didn't respond.

They couldn't just do nothing. "Let's go to the Staneks before it's too late."

His father started pacing.

"Papa . . ."

"Slow down, son. Don't jump to obvious conclusions."

"This is no time for slow." His voice cracked with the emotions he struggled to control. "If we don't go to the Stanek place now, they'll kill her."

Papa stopped pacing and stood in front of him, hands bracing his shoulders. "This is a threat, no more. The killer wants us to let Toby take the blame. I don't think it really has anything to do with Miss Peach."

Harley broke away from his grip, almost shouting back at him. "How can you say that? It's Peach they kidnapped."

"I know how you feel, son. It's my fault for not taking that first threat more seriously. But look, I'm not so sure it's Stanek."

"If it's not, who could it be?"

Papa tweaked his mustache. "Somebody crafty enough to plan the robbery in advance, plotting it so Toby gets the blame. Then he kidnaps Toby, takes his hat, coat, and bicycle to commit the robbery. He tips the police afterwards where to find Toby after he's knocked him out and left him in the shanty. He hires the most inept lawyer in town to defend Toby and waits for the court to punish the obvious killer. Somebody smart enough to do all that wouldn't tell us not to contact the police but leave her hat and bicycle on the street for anyone to find."

"Who else could it be? Chitty?"

"No, he may be unscrupulous, but he's not a criminal. He makes too much money off the KATY to risk his career doing something like this. He has no reason to."

"Schoolcraft then?"

"He's smarter than this."

"Or Big Joe?"

"Too stupid."

"So, the only likely one is Stanek. We've got to go after him before he hurts Peach."

Papa held up his hand. "We've got to stay calm and figure this out, son. Whoever it is, he's not going to do anything hastily."

"I don't know why you think that." Harley sprang up, rushed across the room, and pulled Papa's old Schofield from a desk drawer. He broke open the cylinder. Empty. He rummaged the desk for the box of ammunition until he found it. One by one, his hands shaking, he began to load bullets into the cylinder. "I'm going to the Stanek place."

Papa didn't move. "Old Man Stanek doesn't have a type-writing machine. He couldn't have written that threat."

One of the cartridges tumbled to the floor. Harley fumbled in the box for another and stuffed it into the cylinder. "How do you know that? Maybe his son does. Or his daughter-in-law."

"If he took the time to typewrite that note, why didn't he take the time to make it sound less stilted?"

"Because he doesn't know how not to."

"He'd never be that foolish. We know about him. We just visited him. He knew we suspected him of something." He grabbed the note. "If Stanek wrote this, do you think he'd believe we wouldn't know it was him?"

"He's angry, Papa, and not thinking straight. Vengeance does that to people."

"Not this time."

Harley took the last cartridge from the ammunition box and dropped it into the pistol. "Why?"

Papa leaned over the table, his arms outstretched for support. "Would he think we wouldn't storm out there and confront him, like you're about to do?"

Harley slammed the pistol breach shut, spun the cylinder with his palm, and stuffed the gun under his belt. "I don't know what he's thinking and don't care, but I'm going, whether you come or not."

Harley flung the door wide open, sending the umbrella stand clattering.

Chapter 46

As Harley's buggy topped the bluebonnet-covered hill, black smoke drifted downwind from the Stanek place in the valley below—or what was left of it. He whipped the horse into a gallop, and Papa white-knuckled the sides of the jouncing carriage.

They careened down the hill and along the dirt lane to the farmstead. Stanek's carriage was abandoned in a pasture by the lane, the horse uneasily grazing still in its harness. When Harley yanked his horse to a halt, clucking chickens scattered.

The only other sounds were of the gusting wind and the faint crackling of the few still flaming timbers. The barn and a couple of sheds appeared undamaged, but the rest was not. The front yard was scorched bare where two days ago weeds had flourished. The grand oak formerly shading the yard, now a skeleton stripped of its limbs, its branches, and its leaves, stood solemn watch. Smoke drifted in sporadic puffs and columns from piles of unrecognizable debris. Embers glowed in beds of ash. Two blackened limestone chimneys towered over the smoldering rubble.

Harley flew off the buggy at the edge of the ruins. An unseen wall of heat blasted his face and hands, stopping him in his tracks. Musky, fetid air emanated from beyond, where the house stood vividly in his memory. Occasional gusts of breeze tossed ash and soot whirling aloft and breathed life into glowing orange scars on charred timbers.

"Peach!" he shouted, scanning the scene for any sign of her. "Peach!"

Papa had gone to his right, beyond the porch debris. How could he be so calm? How could he move so—

Papa stiffened and twisted back to Harley. The hairs on the back of Harley's neck rose as one.

"What was she wearing yesterday?" Papa asked.

Harley surged forward, stumbling as soot hit his face and flooded his eyes with tears. "Bloomers, I think. She was riding her bicycle straight to Miss Kate's after work."

Papa's gaze was locked downward.

He wiped his eyes and peered into the smoldering ruins, forearm shielding against the wall of heat. "What is it?"

Papa blocked his view. "What color bloomers?"

"White, with pink stripes." Harley's legs felt suddenly weak. "What do you see?"

Papa's eyes met his. "Don't go any closer, son."

Chapter 47

"Mrs. Sparks, does that cloth look like it came from Miss Peach's pantaloons?"

Miss Peach's landlady sniffled into her handkerchief before she answered the Justice of the Peace. "Her bloomers. That's what she wears when she rides her bicycle." She caught herself. "She used to anyways."

Catfish couldn't focus on her words; the coroner's inquest was a blur. But he'd held the burned cloth in his own hands. It appeared to have once been white with a pink stripe, and it was now yellowed and brown around the edges. Those edges were burned, not cut. An unburned edge appeared to be a hem. He'd remembered those bloomers too.

The coroner addressed his six-man jury. "Since the deputy found this cloth next to the smaller of the two corpses, I think it reasonable for you to conclude that body belonged to Miss Zipporah Peach."

A surge of tears flooded over Catfish.

He'd watched from the buggy as they recovered two bodies, one large and one small; both had been burned beyond recognition. He'd prayed it wasn't Peach, but he'd known better. Even so, it was shocking to hear it pronounced the following day in an official inquest. He was thankful Harley wasn't there too.

Miss Kate had agreed to stay with him at the office during the inquest. Harley had resisted at first but finally given in.

Mrs. Sparks was saying something about her bicycle, but he'd missed the beginning of it.

Miss Peach used to ride all the time. When her folks had sent her that box camera, Harley took her photograph while she pretended to ride. Catfish pulled it from his pocket. She was bent over the handlebars as if she were flying down the street, but her blouse didn't billow, and her beautiful hair was black and white. Her face was frozen in playful joy, but there was no color in it. *I'm so sorry.* He buckled forward on the bench and buried his head in his hands. *Darlin', I'm so sorry.*

When he next realized somebody was speaking from the witness stand it was no longer Mrs. Sparks. Instead, a hack driver was testifying about seeing Miss Peach riding her bicycle late the night she disappeared. He remembered her bloomers.

When Thaddeus Schoolcraft took the stand and lectured the jury about his own findings, Catfish lacked the will to scorn him as he deserved. Disdain required spirit, and he had none left.

The detective lifted the scrap of burned canvas they'd also found in the debris of the fire. "The letters *AMER* are still visible. I'm quite certain it spelled American Express. This appears to be what's left of the stolen express bag."

The Justice of the Peace surmised one of the Staneks murdered the express men and later the other male. The killer must have been Andel, he speculated. He and his sister, Duša, must have fled with the money. "All three Staneks must have been involved in the robbery and argued afterwards about division of the money," the Justice of the Peace suggested. "The children decided to cut the old man out and started the fire to cover it all up."

Catfish raised his head from his hands. He'd seen Old Man Stanek and Andel together. He'd seen how they treated each other. They weren't capable of doing what the JP described.

After the hearing Schoolcraft approached Catfish, for the first time with neither rancor nor derision on his face. "Please accept my condolences about your stenographer, Mr. Calloway. I know you probably don't believe me, but I'm truly very sorry."

Catfish's world was turning upside down. Miss Peach was dead, and Thaddeus Schoolcraft had turned human.

As he walked Austin Avenue toward the office his mind warred with the coroner's findings. Why did those two fragments of cloth survive? The bodies burned beyond all recognition, but the cloth scraps didn't? Wasn't it lucky one of them just happened to show the name, American Express, and the other identified the victim? Too convenient. While the case wasn't over in his own mind—he had so many questions—and his mind raced through them, his heart barely beat at all.

Not sure any of it mattered to him anymore. Nothing else mattered much. There was another hole in his heart. And a young man who needed his father. They'd finally come to peace after the death of Martha and of Houston, but how could they recover from a third loss? How could Harley?

Life was so tenuous—scarlet fever's chance touch, the noose's sudden jerk, a desperado's senseless act. Where was God's hand?

At the office, Harley was downing a bottle of cheap rye whiskey and by noon, it was mostly gone. Now, he was slumped over his desk. His tie was loose, his vest unbuttoned, his hair mussed, his eyes red. Catfish recognized the signs all too well. He'd experienced that despair himself. Twice. Hopelessness ate at you from the inside. You couldn't eat, couldn't sleep, wouldn't talk. Didn't care about anything or anyone. Such misery left nothing of your soul when it finally ran its course. Harley would be in its grip all night and for days to come if Catfish didn't do something. Harley needed purpose. They both did.

***

By late afternoon, a small crowd of mostly colored people had gathered outside their law office. They wore their best Sunday-go-to-meeting clothes. In front of the group, Mr. and Mrs. Moon held baskets of food. Others brought flowers.

Catfish threw open the door. "Come in, please."

"Oh no, sir, Mr. Catfish, we don't want to be no bother. We just brung some things for you and Mr. Harley. We won't come in, though."

"Of course, you will." Catfish held the door and motioned them inside.

"Mr. Catfish," Mrs. Maudie Moon said in her high, powerful voice. "We just want you to know how sorry we are. We're gonna miss that child."

A young girl, hiding behind her grandmother's skirt, burst into tears.

"It's all right, honey." Maudie, a large woman with a black pillbox hat and white gloves, hoisted her with little effort. "She's with the Lord. Hush now."

"Won't you come in and have a seat?" Catfish pointed the way toward their inner office. "I can offer you coffee."

Ben removed his tattered brown hat. "We can't be staying. If I could just offer up a prayer, Mr. Catfish?"

"Please do."

"Oh, Lord, we don't always understands what it is you has in mind for us, but we got the faith."

"Amen!" whispered his sister, Irene.

"We pray you take good care of Mr. Catfish and Mr. Harley 'cause they lost somebody dear, and they hurting. We know you got Miss Peach with you, Lord…"

"Amen!"

"And you'll hold her close too," Ben concluded as Harley dabbed his eyes.

"Come here to me, Mr. Harley, don't you worry. She's in a better place." Maudie wrapped her arms around him and started humming a hymn.

***

That evening Catfish and Harley had supper at Catfish's home. By that time, church folks had brought mounds of food. They ate little. Mr. Wolfe had delivered dozens of flowers.

For so long there was only silence between them.

"Papa, I cared for her." Harley's eyes glistened in the lamp light. Harley's look was so much like when his mother passed. And when Houston died.

And like then, Catfish couldn't find a way to ease the pain. He couldn't even deal with his own. "Did you ever tell her how you felt?"

Harley wiped a tear. "I don't think I fully realized it myself."

"She knew," Catfish said.

Catfish cleared the table of dishes and food. "I keep thinking about the notion the Staneks were behind the robbery. Doesn't sit right with me."

He watched Harley for some reaction. He was still slumped over the table, his head propped against the palm of his hand, the whiskey bottle at the fingertips of his other hand. He didn't move a muscle or say a word.

Catfish's questions had started at the Stanek farm, multiplied at the inquest, and remained unanswered. He eyed Harley. "Where's Duša Hook?"

Harley didn't respond.

Catfish chewed on a White Owl but didn't light it. The JP's answer was she'd run off with her brother, Andel, and the money, but that was too obvious.

He tried again. "How do we know that body isn't Duša instead of Miss Peach?"

"It's not," Harley muttered.

Catfish spat tobacco juice into a cup. "Don't you think it's peculiar that piece of cloth didn't burn up?"

"Huh?"

"Found it in the middle of all that burned debris. Nothing else around it but the money bag escaped burning up. How'd those two scraps of cloth survive the inferno?"

"They were charred," he spat back almost angrily.

"But the rest of her clothes and the rest of the bag were completely consumed? Leaving just enough to identify her and the money bag? I don't believe it. Here's what I think: the real killer burned the Stanek place to blame the Staneks for everything. It was staged like the robbery."

Harley's head still hung.

Catfish lit his cigar. If the body was really Duša Hook, and the other was either Old Man Stanek or Andel, then what happened to the third family member? Maybe the killer dumped his body someplace else to put the blame on him. But of course, even if the body was Duša, that didn't mean Miss Peach was still alive. The killer couldn't let her live to identify him. If he was willing to kill all the Staneks to cover his crime he wouldn't bat an eye at another killing.

Catfish expelled a cloud of smoke at the ice box in the kitchen corner. He had to be careful—shouldn't get Harley's hopes up too much.

Harley's head rotated back toward him. "Why would the killer, whoever it was, spare Peach?"

Good question. "Could be lots of reasons."

"Like what?"

The only reason he could think of was the killer wanted to do unspeakable things to her. She was younger and comelier than Duša, but Catfish didn't want Harley thinking about the killer saving her for sport. "I'll come back to that in a minute. Think about this with me, son: Where would the killer hold her if he wanted to keep her alive?"

Harley took a drink, but only a sip. "Probably the same place he'd hidden Toby. The shanty?"

Catfish yanked the cigar from his mouth. "He knows the police went there and found Toby. They might go back. Had to be somewhere else. No, this killer's got a lair somewhere else."

"Well, if that's right, we don't know where it is, and we'll never find it in time." Hopelessness glistened in his eyes again. "If she's still alive, which she isn't."

"Maybe we can find it." Catfish dropped his cigar in the cup and scooted closer to the table. "Do you think the killer snatched Toby off the street like he did Miss Peach?"

"Huh?"

"Here's what I'm thinking: We know he took Miss Peach at night on a dark street when she was alone riding her bicycle. And we know Toby didn't go out at night by himself on his bicycle. How'd he kidnap Toby? What if he lured him into a trap during the day?"

"How?" Harley asked.

"Maybe he got Toby to make a delivery to his lair and dragged him inside when he showed up. It's less risky than snatching him off the street in broad daylight, particularly if it's an out-of-the-way place."

"Where could it be?"

"Risher's Drug Store doesn't have any record of such a delivery." Catfish started pacing around the kitchen. "The killer probably called it in on the talking phone."

"Probably."

"Think about this." Catfish's mind raced. "How would Toby know where to go?"

"He'd memorized the city directory." Harley was getting more engaged. "He knew street addresses by heart."

"But how would somebody at Risher's communicate the address to him?"

"Miss Kate said they'd write the address for him."

Catfish snatched a pecan from the basket Mrs. Morrison brought, cracked the shell, and munched the nut. "Where would that paper with a written address likely be when the killer snatched him?"

"On Toby somewhere, but they'd have taken it. There wasn't one on him according to Quinn."

Catfish stopped pacing. That was it! "They'd only take it if they knew it was an address. Maybe they didn't realize what it was." That scrap of paper Quinn had found in Toby's coat pocket—he'd been pretty sure it was important but couldn't figure out how. It had to signify a location somehow. "Harley, you remember those numbers on the paper Quinn found in Toby's coat?"

Harley brushed his glass aside. "They were telephone numbers."

No, they weren't three different talking-phone numbers. It was a single address. Catfish was certain. "Do you remember

Miss Peach told us Toby somehow recognized a string of numbers like that as an address? It was Jake Levinski's."

He checked the city directory. *Levinski, Jacob (Lewine Bros., mgrs.), dry goods, clothing, boots, shoes, 521-523 Austin ave, watchmkr, jeweler, watches, clocks, jewelry, 407 Austin, r. sw cor N. 19ʰ, Morrow ave.*

Catfish thought aloud. "It says his dry goods shop is at 521 Austin, his watch shop is at 407 Austin, but his residence is listed as southwest corner of Nineteenth and Morrow. There's no exact street address given. When Miss Peach said Jake's name, Toby gave the shop's street address as it is in the directory but spouted a string of three numbers for the residence. He didn't have a street address to memorize, so he learned three other numbers instead, but they aren't in the directory. Where did they come from?" He froze. Of course. "Let's go to the office."

Chapter 48

"I should have made this connection before."

"What, Papa?"

Catfish shoved Miss Peach's notes from Dr. Wallace's examination of Toby in front of Harley. He pointed to the numbers Peach had written when she said Mary Sparks's name to Toby. He replied *51-31-2*. "Those numbers signify an address somehow, like Jake's."

Catfish went to the city map tacked to the office wall. "Look at the directory and tell me Mary Sparks's street address."

Harley found it. "Just like you said, it doesn't show a numbered street address. It's listed as *North Thirteenth between Burleson and West Avenue*."

Catfish put his finger on the block of North Thirteenth between Burleson and West. What did the numbers *51-31-2* mean? How would they represent this location to Toby? "It looks like when there's a name in the directory but no actual address, so he learned three numbers instead. That must have been how he learned the locations. Remember, Wallace said it was all rote. He had to have a number to memorize."

Where was the number from Toby's pocket, 58-15-13? Catfish perused the map from Risher's Drug Store on Austin Avenue toward the river. There was a small sketch of City Hall and of the bridge to the right and it sprang out at him like a hidden secret magically materializing from the mist—*58*—printed in large bold digits south of City Hall. His eyes flew to the map's legend. Those numbers labeled the city's Additions. Number *58* was identified as the *Original Town Addition*. The number 58 was printed over Third Street, between Franklin Avenue and Mary Street. He imagined that location and what was there—the Mitchell House, a few shops, the Waverly Hotel, the Cotton Belt depot. He grabbed the scrap of paper to make sure of the next number: *58-15-13*. Where were Additions 15 and 13? His eyes raced across the map and quickly fell on 13, printed in the same large, bold digits, over the block between Webster and Jackson Streets where Finks & Company was. The grocer? Toby must have made deliveries on Third Street somewhere and at Finks. Next was Addition 15 but where was it? Number 60 was the next large, bold number after 13 and 14 going south. That didn't make sense. Additions 1-14 were lined up north to south in order from Columbus down to Webster Street, but all the additions to the south of 14 were in the 60s or 70s. Where was 15? He scanned the entire map hurriedly once and again more slowly. A third pass showed no Addition number 15 anywhere.

Maybe Risher could help.

***

Like his previous visit there, Catfish found Risher in the back of his store near *Clark Stanley's Snake Oil Liniment*. "When we talked before you told me you didn't have any record of where Toby made deliveries on his last day. We're still trying to figure that out."

"I'll help any way I can."

Catfish dropped his hat on the counter. "When you told Toby to deliver something to a place that didn't have a numbered street address in the directory, how'd you tell him where to go? Did you give him the addition number by any chance?"

Risher's eyes popped wide. "How'd you know?" He motioned for them to follow. He led them across the store to a framed city map on the pharmacy wall. Catfish slipped on his spectacles. It was the same map as in their law office, published in 1891. What had he and Harley missed?

"I worked out a system. The customer would tell me where to make the delivery. If there was a specific street address, I'd write that down for Toby to learn. If it was only a location but no street number, I'd look on the map and find it. The map doesn't show street addresses, but it does show the addition, block, and lot numbers. Toby could learn numbers. As you suggested, I did give him the addition number."

"Fifty-eight," Catfish said, his finger flying to the spot on the map.

"Yes, but I'd give him the block and lot numbers too."

Of course. Catfish's index finger flew around the map. "Addition fifty-eight, block fifteen, lot thirteen." He stopped at a spot on the map near the river.

Harley slapped the wall. "That's it!"

Catfish couldn't believe it. Why hadn't he thought of it before?

Harley was already halfway to the front door.

"Wait!" Catfish shouted. "We can't go in alone."

Harley spun around. "Peach'll be dead if we don't."

Customers were staring.

Catfish caught up with him. These people were killers, and he couldn't bear to lose Harley too. Besides, he didn't believe in acting outside the law when the law could still act. They had to convince Quinn they were right. He wouldn't move on theories. "If Toby can recite the name from the number on the paper scrap, that's all we'll need to convince Sergeant Quinn to go in and look for her."

Harley pulled free. "You see Toby if you want. I'm going to help Peach."

Catfish called after him. "Don't go inside till I get there with Quinn. You can't—"

Harley brushed past a customer, knocking a package from his hands, and charged out. Risher's patrons gawked at the open door.

Catfish bolted out right behind him. He had to get Quinn.

Chapter 49

Deputy Buckram led Catfish and Sergeant Quinn to Toby's cell and took a position outside the door in the hall. Catfish kneeled in front of Toby where he sat on his bench, rocking.

"Toby, listen." Catfish unfolded the scrap of paper with the number. "I want to ask you about where you made your final delivery. When you were kidnapped."

Toby rocked.

Catfish recited the numbers slowly. "Fifty-Eight. Fifteen. Thirteen."

Toby stopped moving. "Jessie Rose."

Catfish clinched his fist. He'd been right. He straightened and turned to Quinn. "The sporting house."

"Miss Jessie's?"

The same place where Cicero Sweet killed the sporting girl. Catfish needed to be sure. He tried it a different way. "Jessie Rose."

"Fifty-eight, fifteen, thirteen," Toby said distinctly before going back to rocking.

Catfish jumped up. "The killer must be Big Joe."

"The madam's bouncer?"

Catfish wheeled around toward the hall where Deputy Buckram no longer stood.

"The deputy's brother."

Chapter 50

The blindfold over Peach's eyes was so tight it caused her head to hurt, but more maddening was the disorientation it induced. They'd grabbed her from her bicycle, stuffed a rag into her mouth, thrown a sack over her head, bound her hands behind her back, and jammed her into the floorboard of the carriage. From that point forward, she'd been unable to see or move freely. Had she been unconscious? Is that why she felt so filmy and odd?

They hadn't traveled long in the carriage, so she must still be in town. Farther away, church bells pealed, trains rumbled, whistles shrieked. Closer, yet still not in the same room, a man and a woman argued, her voice too faint to recognize. Had there been a woman in the carriage? When they brought her into the room and exchanged a blindfold for the sack over her head, she'd briefly seen the room but didn't recognize it.

It seemed as if she'd been here for days. They'd force-fed her bread and nasty beer once, but it was very little, and when she didn't keep it down, they didn't try again to feed her. Her wrists, her neck, her back, her every muscle, and every joint ached, but no matter how she tried she couldn't find relief. When she attempted to move, the cords cut more deeply into her wrists and her ankles. They'd also bound her waist into the chair so she couldn't stand. Her feet couldn't even reach the floor. The chair was hard and uncomfortable, but she couldn't shift her position to find relief. She tried tipping it over, but it was too heavy. Numbness had settled into her hands and feet hours earlier. Because they never allowed her to use a toilet, she'd urinated on herself. Oh, how humiliating! She cried, but even her tears had gone dry.

Exhaustion clouded her mind, but thinking was the only act of free will she could manage. She breathed deeply, deliberately, and let it out slowly. Sanity demanded the exercise of reason. She struggled through the enshrouding fogginess to free her mind for thinking rationally through the events of the last few hours or days. Or was it weeks? No, it couldn't be. She'd have passed out from hunger and thirst if it'd been that long. It was probably a day, maybe two. She'd heard trains. How many were there? What direction did they go? Was it a morning train or an evening train?

Of all the confused series of events, there was one moment which was patently distinct in her recollection. The face—the *two* faces, though both were the same—had flashed in front of her for an instant only as the carriage pulled beside her, but that was enough. The faces were so dreadfully familiar: Big Joe Buckram, with his hideous drooping eye, and his brutish brother.

Reality had spun and whirled as they dragged her first upside down and downside up. Had she struggled? Surely, she had. How could she not? Everything had gone dark, and she was smothering, her head trapped inside a wretched, foul-smelling cloth. She tried to scream but there was something stuffed into her mouth. No scream escaped. A ponderous weight on top of her—what was it?—crammed her face into the hard, creaking, bouncing carriage floorboard. She gasped for air. There were only the muffled sounds of the clopping hooves, the crackling gravel, the rattling carriage.

When the hideous ride ended, and they dragged her inside a building of some kind. Where did they take her? She had to reason that out, but where had the journey even begun? She was riding her bicycle home after the evening at Miss Kate's, past Harley's place, but what route did she take after that? Was she on Austin? Washington? The streets were a dark blur, and all she could remember was thinking about Harley.

Oh, Harley. Harley.

Why had those brutes taken her? Why? Why? If they intended to kill her—what reason could they have for that?—they would have done it before now. If not to kill her, then why? The memory of Big Joe's stinking, hot breath washed over her. His heavy breathing, his pawing hands. Was that their object? *Pray God, not that!* She gagged, but at least there was nothing inside to vomit because it would have choked her. She sobbed tearless cries. There was no escape from that unthinkable fate. She was hopelessly trapped.

The only freedom to move she retained was from her waist up. She bent forward and back. She shut her eyes tightly and tried to cry out through the gag, but she was still utterly, absolutely, maddeningly incapable of freeing herself. Forward and back.

She forced her mind away from the tempest which had swept her up and instead upon what was rational and orderly. Upon what was familiar and comforting. On what she could remember—the Bard would be there for her.

Forward she bent.

Thou shalt have freedom.

Back she rocked.

So, so, so.

Forward.

Thou shalt have freedom.

Back.

So, so, so.

She was very nearly rocking as Toby did, but it was all she could do. Was she mad like Toby? She twisted her head side to side. She was not mad, but she could not say the words. Poor Toby. He wasn't mad either. He must have felt just as trapped.

Toby, I understand!

She stopped rocking. She wasn't mad. She was not.

O, that way madness lies; let me shun that; no more of that.

Slowly, from the pit of her fear, she mustered defiance to take terror's place. *I will weep no more. I will endure.* Were she only free to shout the words.

Where was Harley? How quickly could he get there? He was—where?—at his home. He was reading. It was too far away to hear her screams. No, she had no screams. There was a deep, roiling rage that struggled to break free.

So, so, so.

Her cries for help were trapped inside, and he couldn't possibly hear them. But maybe he could sense them. Love made such possible. *Love looks not with the eyes but with the mind.*

She willed her plea out from that room, away from that place. *Oh, Harley!*

A distant door creaked open and shut. Muffled footsteps came closer. She drew herself stiffly erect now, no more rocking.

I will endure.

Another door, this one close, opened and closed. It was near. Heavy footsteps scraped across the wooden floor. She froze, utterly still except for a growing shudder she could not stifle. The grating tread of boots ceased; the reeking, musky presence loomed. Only his breathing sounded.

The hot breath struck her forehead, her nose, and her lips.

"It's me." A husky whisper, a foul wind assaulting her ear.

She forged rage into power and lashed out; the cords bit harder, but she didn't care.

Think you I am no stronger than my sex?

She twisted her head left and right, up and down. She kicked her bound feet against him.

So, so, so.

A huge, fleshy hand yanked up her hair and shoved back her head. His weight crushed down her legs, stopping still her motion. A close metallic snap. A blade, sharp against her cheek. Steel, cold against her neck.

Hell is empty; the devil is here.

A tremor coursed through her.

Please, God—

Chapter 51

Harley threw open the bawdy house door. He raced through the entry hall to the parlor doorway, hand gripping the pistol stuffed in his belt.

A woman in a sheer gown sprawled on the sofa.

"Where's Peach?" he demanded from the hallway.

"Who?"

Behind him, footsteps sounded on the staircase. "Mr. Calloway."

Jessie Rose swept down the stairs, her white lace gown swirling around her, a scarlet ribbon around her neck and a flower in her raven hair. "It's marvelous to see your handsome—"

"Where is she? Wh—"

More footsteps thundered outside, and something crashed through the still-open front door.

Harley whirled to confront a blur of motion. A huge man. Curly hair.

A blackjack.

Chapter 52

Where was Harley? Catfish should have gone with him.

He bobbed behind Sergeant Quinn as they peered through the front door window of Miss Jessie's Sporting House. Two armed officers crouched beside him. Behind them on Washington Avenue, people went about their business. Few paused to see what the police were doing at the sporting house late in the afternoon. Across the river, a train chugged into the depot.

He steadied himself with his cane in his left hand, his Iver Johnson pistol in the right. Being back here in this place again so soon was unnerving. He wiped away the sweat and the memories of investigating the murder of Miss Georgia: the red velvet upholstery of the parlor, the too-sweet smell of cheap perfume, the tinny tunes on the player piano, the banter of the sporting girls. Would Big Joe be lurking inside somewhere waiting for them? His brother, after his hasty flight from the jail, must have warned him by then.

Where was Harley?

Quinn dispatched one officer down Orman's Alley to watch the back of the house. He gestured to the other—"Let's go"— and eased open the door and crept into the entry hall, followed by the other policeman and Catfish.

Son?

From the parlor to the left, a clock ticked, but there was no other sound. Catfish followed the two officers to the open parlor doorway.

Harley lay crumpled face down, his arms splayed, his hat across the room.

"No!" Catfish rushed to him and with Quinn's help eased him over, supporting his head. Blood trickled from his nose and mouth. The pistol was still tucked under his belt. "Harley!"

Harley's eyes popped open. "Papa?"

Thank God! Catfish cradled Harley's head between his hands.

"What happened?" Harley croaked. His hand flew to his forehead. Already a purple knot was emerging. "Where's Peach?"

"Just got here." Catfish wiped away the blood. Thank the good Lord he was alive.

"I'm fine, Papa." Harley struggled free to prop himself up. "Find Peach."

Quinn tapped Catfish on the arm. "Listen."

The ceiling directly above the parlor was creaking. That was the bedroom where Cicero Sweet had shot Miss Georgia.

Quinn hurried to the stairs. He cocked his revolver, and the metallic click echoed in the stairwell. The other officer was right behind.

Catfish started to follow, but first brushed back Harley's disheveled hair. "Stay put, son. We'll find her."

Quinn had paused at the foot of the stairs. He signaled for Catfish and the other officer to search the first-floor hallway. The officer led. With every step they took, the floor beneath moaned.

Voices sounded from upstairs, and Catfish whirled around.

"Stay right there," came Quinn's shout from upstairs.

Footsteps pounded a hallway directly over Catfish.

"Let's go," shouted the officer with Catfish.

The first door on the right creaked open, and a man's head popped out. "What's going on?"

The officer leveled his pistol on the man. "Come out slowly."

A wide-eyed, fleshy man with hands held high stumbled out into the hall. The officer held his gun on him as Catfish checked the room. There was only a sporting girl, with sheets pulled to her chin.

From above sounded more footsteps and opening doors. Shouts from Quinn. A woman's voice, too. Not Miss Peach.

Downstairs, the officer shoved open the next door, but nobody was inside.

Footsteps raced upstairs, back along the hall toward the front of the building.

Catfish and the officer came to the end of the first-floor hallway. No more rooms, but there was a door that probably led to the outside.

A clattering on the stairs preceded Quinn and Harley's arrival.

Catfish had told Harley to stay put.

"Anything?" Quinn called.

"No, sir," the officer with Catfish responded.

Catfish brushed past him and flung open the door. It led not outside but directly into an attached wooden-frame building. He rushed inside. Boxes, barrels, furniture stacked all around. Two closed doors on the opposite side. He charged across the room, cane tight in his left hand in case he needed a club, pistol in his right.

He shouldered open the left door.

"Peach!"

Chapter 53

Harley rushed past Papa. Bound and gagged, Peach didn't stir. Her head dangled.

Was she alive?

"Peach!" Gasping for air, he clutched her shoulders. "Please!"

Her head twitched, her eyes fluttered.

He ripped the filthy rag from her mouth. "It's me. It's Harley. Can you hear me?"

Her eyes slowly opened. "Harley."

She was so pale. Her filthy blouse was ripped, her hair tangled.

"Thank God." He kept one arm protectively around her shoulders while Papa used his pocketknife to cut the cords binding her and gently eased her out of the chair and into his arms. Her weight cradled entirely on Harley, her head burrowed into his chest. Her trembling, her sobs, her tears voiced better than words how close he'd come to losing her. He shut his eyes before they teared.

"Shh. You're safe now," Harley whispered.

She burrowed more.

"You're safe."

He kissed her hair. Though tousled, it smelled so sweet.

***

A policeman brought the depot wagon around to the back door of Miss Jessie's, and Catfish helped Miss Peach inside for the trip to Dr. Black's home. She was weak but seemed to be physically unhurt except for some bruises, rope burns, cuts, and scrapes. She'd said Buckram had fled unexpectedly when his brother arrived. Before he could harm her.

"Don't worry, darlin', I told Harley that I'd take over both the talking phone and the type-writing machine duties until you're better."

She smiled weakly. Harley slid across the seat beside her and put his arm around her. Her head sagged to his chest.

Catfish leaned against the wagon. "Now, do I use one finger or two to punch those type-writing letters?"

She laughed. Though faint, it was good to hear.

He reached to pull the blanket over her legs. She wore bloomers, like boy's knickerbockers but baggy. Damp and filthy, too. "Have to buy you some new bloomers."

She gazed at them silently.

The pink stripes on white were as Harley had described them after the fire at the Staneks' farm. There was an irregular tear at the hem below her left knee, about the size of the charred scrap of cloth they'd found at the Stanek place. Without a word, he drew Quinn's attention to it, and tucked the blanket over her.

"You're gonna be fine."

"Thank you," her lips said silently.

The wagon rattled off.

Catfish pulled Quinn aside. "That proves Big Joe burned the Stanek place."

Quinn nodded.

"And made it look like Miss Peach died there."

"Why?" Quinn asked.

Catfish's head went side to side slowly. "Expect they had plans for her."

"The second body, the woman, must've been Duša," Quinn said.

"And I'll wager they dumped her brother's body somewhere else."

Quinn let out a breath. "All right. I'm going to look around and see what else I can find."

"Mind if I join you?"

Quinn motioned for him to follow.

Neither Big Joe nor his brother was there. Nor was Miss Jessie, though three of her sporting girls were. Each professed ignorance of what was going on and where the others were. An officer herded them into the parlor and kept them there. There were no carriages or horses out back, though signs of both in the dirt suggested a recent, hasty departure. None of the neighbors, all brothel dwellers, admitted hearing or seeing anything at Miss Jessie's or seeing anyone flee. Quinn sent an officer to check the train stations.

Catfish held his handkerchief over his nose as they searched the room where Joe had imprisoned Miss Peach. He found two blouse buttons on the floor beside the chair. The threads had been cut. It appeared Big Joe lived in the same squalid wooden building, though in the adjoining room. His quarters were small and sparse. There were a few clothes and a partially full chamber pot, but not much else. No blackjack; no weapon of any kind. No money.

They ended the search in a room upstairs in the back of the main building. It was bigger and more lavishly appointed than all the others. The bed, unlike the iron-frame ones in the other rooms, was a finely carved four-poster with a duvet and silk-cased pillows. It had been made and the pillows carefully placed. There were silver mirrors, combs, and brushes scattered on the dressing table. The empty wash basin was fine china. A large armoire housed a wardrobe full of dresses any fine lady would admire. There was a gaiety to this room that no other room in the house matched. Miss Jessie's room.

They searched the drawers for the Colt pistol Miss Jessie had wielded when Cicero shot Miss Georgia, but they found no guns. In a Saratoga trunk they found several yards of crêpe de Chine, six hand-painted black satin fans, an assortment of plumes, feathers, pompons, and ribbons, a stack of laundered men's shirts, and an odd lot of other things—an empty pocket book, a French leather cigar case, a pair of shears, a briar wood pipe, amber hair pins, a fancy lace handkerchief, a pair of long suede gloves, a bottle of Lubin's lavender water, a gentleman's shaving brush and razor, white pearl opera glasses, and a peculiar instrument labeled *Dr. Scott's Electric Tooth Brush*. Yet, no fine gold or silver jewelry anywhere. Nor a handbag or any money.

Catfish confronted Quinn. "Between what you've seen here and what you found at Old Man Stanek's, don't you think you should dismiss the charges against Toby?"

"I'll have to ask Lieutenant Palmer. He's in charge of the investigation." Quinn started to say something else, hesitated, and began to trudge back down the hall.

He was almost to the top of the stairs when he finally came out with it. "If it was up to me, the boy would be free tonight."

Chapter 54

Judge Goodrich gaveled the courtroom to order. "I call cause number 147, *In re Toby Budge, also known as Toby Topper.* I understand this is a hearing on a writ of habeas corpus, brought on behalf of Mr. Topper." He looked over his spectacles at Catfish. "What says the petitioner?"

Catfish and Harley stood. "Catfish Calloway and Harley Calloway for Mr. Topper, Your Honor. We're ready to proceed."

To Harley's right, in a state of mind known only to him, Toby rocked.

"The state of Texas is ready," Chitty announced.

The judge examined a document. "My docket sheet in *State of Texas v. Toby Topper* shows the insanity hearing was cancelled at the defendant's request, and that the case is set for trial on the murder charges in the July term. Why are we here in May on a habeas corpus, gentlemen?"

Catfish planted his feet squarely between the prosecution and defense tables, his back to Chitty. "The State has indisputable proof Toby Topper is innocent, yet they've failed to release him. The prosecution hasn't replied to my repeated requests he be freed. Detective Palmer, who's in charge of the police investigation, refuses to meet with me about it. We believe Toby's being unlawfully incarcerated, Judge."

The judge peered at the two prosecutors. "What do you have to say?"

The walrus, not leaving his chair, blinked at his more senior partner. Arrogance radiated from them like heat from a kettle.

Chitty stepped forward. "Mr. Topper was indicted by the grand jury. He's been tried and convicted once, as the court knows, and is set for retrial after the appeal." He turned to Catfish and acted as if he didn't know why there would be any question. "We have no reason to release him."

"I'll be happy to advise the court of the reasons," Catfish said, without facing Chitty, "but we also have proof if the court wants to hear it first."

"I'll hear what proof you've got."

"We call Sergeant Dennis Quinn," Catfish announced.

Catfish had subpoenaed both Quinn and Palmer. Palmer, Schoolcraft, and Hamp Boswell occupied scoundrel's row of the spectator gallery. Quinn made his way to the witness chair.

"Sergeant," Catfish began, "I want to ask you some questions first about what you found in the burned out Stanek house. Did you discover anything related to the robbery of the American Express wagon?"

A subpoena duces tecum had required them to bring to court all the physical evidence in their custody relating to the charges against Toby Topper, including what they found on Toby, what they seized from Miss Jessie's, and what they took from the Stanek place. Catfish had asked the court reporter to mark as exhibits all the items brought pursuant to the subpoena, and they were arrayed on the reporter's desk.

Quinn gestured toward the exhibits. "I did. This piece of canvas cloth marked Exhibit 1 appears to be the remains of the stolen money bag."

Catfish strode to the reporter's desk and held the exhibit for Quinn to see.

"Please read the lettering on the cloth for the court."

"A-M-E-R."

Catfish passed the exhibit to the judge. "Sergeant, do you believe those letters were all that remained of the name American Express Company?"

"I do."

"Other than the two dead bodies, what else of significance did you find out there?"

Chitty rose. "Excuse me, Your Honor, but I have to object to Mr. Calloway proceeding in this manner. He's attempting to litigate the merits of the underlying murder charges by habeas corpus. That's not the function of this proceeding."

Catfish knew that was coming. "I—"

"Hang on, Mr. Calloway," Judge Goodrich said. "I have no intention of trying the murder case today, gentlemen, but I do intend to satisfy myself there's enough evidence to continue lawfully to bind Topper over for trial."

"But—" Chitty began.

"Overruled. Proceed, counsel."

Good—the court would at least hear them out. He'd feared Goodrich would put it off until the trial in July, but he'd promised Miss Peach he would do everything he could to free Toby sooner. It was less than two weeks after they'd rescued her, and she was recuperating at home in Eulogy with her parents.

"Sergeant," Catfish said, "what else did you find at the Stanek place?"

"There was a scrap of cloth that had also been burned. The court reporter marked it as Exhibit 2, I believe."

"Please tell the court what significance you think that cloth has." Catfish lifted the exhibit for Quinn to see.

"Yes, sir. Miss Peach, who is Mr. Calloway's stenographer, was kidnapped not long ago, and she was wearing clothes made of the same cloth. I verified that when we found her. I saw where this cloth had been torn from her pants."

"Where did you find her?" Catfish asked.

"She was bound and gagged inside Miss Jessie Rose's bawdy house on Washington Avenue."

"Why'd you find that piece of cloth significant?"

"It tied together three separate events: the fire at the Stanek place, the American Express robbery, and the kidnapping of Miss Peach."

"Explain for the court how it tied the robbery to the fire and the kidnapping."

"There had been a threat to Miss Peach."

Catfish retrieved another exhibit for Quinn. "I want to show you what the reporter has marked as Exhibit 6. What's this?"

"This is a note which you gave me that your son found at your office the morning after Miss Peach disappeared."

"Read it for the court, please."

"It says 'idiot die peech live—not tell police.' Miss Peach's name is misspelled."

"Who'd you think the word idiot referred to?"

Quinn pointed at Toby, who remained lost in his own world, rocking back and forth.

Catfish handed the exhibit to the judge. "And when you read that note, Sergeant Quinn, what did you think about it?"

"That somebody was threatening to kill Miss Peach unless you backed off of your defense of Mr. Topper and let him hang."

"And when, in relation to my giving you that note, did we find Miss Peach at the sporting house?"

"The very next day."

Catfish leaned against the rail of the jury box from where he could address Quinn but also watch the judge's reaction. Goodrich was smart and didn't look confused. "Sergeant, what else did you find at the sporting house which you felt was related to the American Express robbery?"

"Well, it was mostly what I didn't find. Neither the madam nor her strong-arm man, Big Joe Buckram, was still there. It looked like they'd fled in a hurry."

"In your opinion, how might they have been warned to take off?"

"I object," Chitty said. "Speculation by the witness."

"Overruled. You may answer."

"Joe Buckram's brother is a McLennan County deputy sheriff who's been working as a guard at the county jail. He's been in charge of Mr. Topper while he's been confined there. I accompanied you to the jail that day right before we found Miss Peach. We went there to see if Mr. Topper knew the address signified by a string of numbers on a note we found in his pocket when we arrested him. When you read off the numbers, Mr. Topper said 'Jessie Rose.' At that moment Deputy Buckram apparently slipped away and warned his brother."

"So, you think Deputy Buckram was in cahoots with his brother, Big Joe Buckram, and Miss Jessie Rose?"

"I do."

Judge Goodrich made a note but was inscrutable as to what he thought of the testimony.

"It's been a fortnight since we rescued Miss Peach from her kidnappers. Seen any of 'em in Waco since?"

"No, sir."

"Tell the court, to your knowledge has anybody around here seen 'em?"

Quinn looked back at Judge Goodrich. "I don't believe they're still in Waco, Your Honor."

"You said you searched the sporting house," Catfish said. "Find any of the stolen money there?"

"No, sir. Neither did Lieutenant Palmer."

That was a surprise. Catfish didn't know Palmer had searched the house too. "When did Lieutenant Palmer go there?"

"The next day, along with Detective Schoolcraft. He told me I didn't need to go, but they conducted another search." Quinn glanced at scoundrel's row. "There's another box of things they found."

Catfish whirled around to face Schoolcraft and Palmer. Neither detective returned his gaze. So, they'd searched the house and there was evidence they didn't bring to court. He turned back to Quinn. "Where's that box?"

"Lieutenant Palmer instructed me this morning to leave it at the office. He'd told me before they didn't find anything significant. I'd looked over everything in the box myself, and I agreed with him."

Catfish squared himself toward the two detectives, not lifting his eyes from Palmer. "I subpoenaed everything. Where is it?"

Palmer didn't stand. "Quinn's right. There's nothing important there."

Catfish's stare didn't leave Palmer. "Judge—"

"Lieutenant Palmer," the judge said sternly, "go get it."

Palmer slowly got to his feet, glancing at Schoolcraft, whose expression didn't change. "Yes, Your Honor." It shouldn't take him long since their office was only a block away in City Hall.

Catfish eased back against the jury rail and turned again to Quinn. "Did you discover that note with a number on it in Toby's pocket?"

"It's in the coat pocket," Quinn answered, pointing at the coat on the reporter's desk.

Catfish rifled through the coat, pulling the lining out of each pocket. No note. Somebody deliberately hadn't brought it to court. "It's not there. When did you last see it?"

"You and me looked at it when you were in our office. I think Lieutenant Palmer took the coat from you, but I don't know what he did with the note in the pocket."

It had to have been that conniving cockalorum, Palmer. "I'll ask him about it when he gets back, Judge. In the meantime, sergeant, did you see the number yourself?"

Quinn faced the judge, not trying to hide anything. "There was a string of numbers written on a scrap of paper. I don't remember the numbers exactly. We didn't know at the time they had any significance."

"Sergeant Quinn," the judge said, "even if you can't remember the numbers, were they a street address?"

"No, sir."

"Judge," Catfish said, "it was a series of three numbers—fifty-eight, fifteen, and thirteen. They represent the addition number, block number, and lot number of Miss Jessie's sporting house. That's how we found Peach there." He eyed Schoolcraft. "If they hid it in the other evidence box, you'll see for yourself, Judge."

"He's right about the number, Your Honor," Quinn volunteered.

Judge Goodrich, still inscrutable, scribbled some notes.

"That's all I have of the sergeant," Catfish said. The judge seemed to be following him so far. "I'm sure I'll have questions for Lieutenant Palmer when he returns."

The judge looked to Chitty. "Questions?"

"Sergeant," the prosecutor said, "upon whom did you find the recovered American Express money?"

"Mr. Topper."

"Upon whom did you find the pistol which had been fired twice?"

"Mr. Topper."

"Upon whom did you find the top hat and brown coat which the eyewitnesses saw the shooter wearing?"

"Mr. Topper."

"Upon whose bicycle did the shooter ride when he conducted the robbery?"

"Mr. Topper's."

"Did any of those facts change when you discovered the involvement of the madam and her man in the robbery?"

Quinn glanced at Catfish. "I suppose not."

"Well, none of the witnesses described Miss Jessie Rose or Mr. Joe Buckram or Deputy Buckram as the actual shooter, did they?"

"No."

"So wouldn't you conclude, Sergeant, to use Mr. Calloway's words, Mr. Topper was also in cahoots with them?"

"I don't know about that."

"Well, the fact the madam and the Buckram brothers might be involved in the crime doesn't preclude Mr. Topper from also being involved, does it?"

"It doesn't, no."

"That's all," Chitty announced dismissively. "Your Honor, none of this is a reason Mr. Topper should be released."

"Mr. Calloway?" the judge asked.

"We demand our client's release, Your Honor. The prosecutor now knows beyond doubt he's innocent. The Buckrams set Toby up to take the blame, so as to end the need for any further investigation by the police and cover their own involvement. They lured Toby to Miss Jessie's sporting house to make a delivery—that's what the numbers did—and kidnapped him there. The madam had to be complicit. Sergeant Quinn and I traced those numbers right to her door, and we found Miss Peach inside, like a prisoner at Andersonville."

Chitty didn't rattle easily. He smiled. "That's quite a tale. We're willing to concede the possible involvement of the Buckrams and perhaps even the madam, but that in no way exonerates their accomplice, Mr. Topper."

"You know it does," Catfish fumed.

The judge extended the flat of his hand toward Catfish and turned to Chitty. "Explain yourself."

"It seems clear to us the Buckrams and maybe the madam employed Mr. Topper to actually carry out the robbery for them," Chitty said. "Eyewitnesses identified him there. His bicycle was found by the bodies. The police caught Topper with the gun and some of the money on his person. That money was Topper's cut."

"They set him up," Catfish hissed.

The walrus rolled out of his chair and chimed in for the first time. "We agree they set up Stanek. They knew Topper had been caught and decided to make it look like he was working with Stanek rather than them. Topper was their accomplice and there is no evidence they set him up too."

Catfish edged closer to the bench. "There most certainly is, Your Honor. No eyewitness saw his face up close on the bridge. The Buckrams kidnapped him, and one of them rode his bicycle and wore his top hat to the bridge. Then they knocked him out, dumped him in the shanty, and planted the gun and the money on him."

"It's just their theory," the walrus barked. "Where's the proof they set him up?"

"They hired Jaybird to represent him, knowing the boy would be convicted without much of a fight. They paid him with one hundred dollar treasury notes stolen in the robbery." But they were right about one thing: Catfish couldn't prove who hired Jaybird. If he'd only had that.

Chitty made a show of disdain for the argument. "A far-fetched theory, Judge Goodrich, but there's no evidence the Buckrams hired Mr. Jaye. And if there was, it would be for the jury in the murder case to decide, not for the court in a habeas corpus proceeding."

The judge rocked back in his chair and looked at Catfish. "You have any evidence? Will Mr. Jaye testify the Buckrams or the madam hired him?"

Catfish shook his head. "He thinks it was Toby's father, but it can't be because Mr. Budge died before the robbery. Jaybird doesn't know who paid him. It was done by mail."

Chitty swatted air toward the defense table. "Just as I said. They don't have a scintilla of evidence anybody kidnapped Topper."

"No other witness to it?" the judge asked Catfish.

"No eyewitnesses; it's circumstantial. As I said, Judge—"

The judge stopped him. "It appears to me this is all something to be determined at trial and not on habeas corpus."

"Exactly," Chitty said.

Catfish glanced at Harley. They'd hoped Chitty would concede Toby had nothing to do with it. Should have known better. "Your Honor, we beg you to wait until Palmer gets back with the rest of the evidence." He pointed accusingly at Chitty. "They deliberately held that evidence back despite a subpoena."

Chitty fumed. "We did—"

Catfish ignored him. Something was in that box of evidence

they didn't want him to see, and he wouldn't give up until he knew what it was. "They're hiding something, and we have a right to see it. If the note from Toby's pocket is in that box, that proves they intentionally tried to conceal the truth from the court."

"Preposterous," Chitty snorted.

"The number is proof the Buckrams lured Toby to Miss Jessie's."

Chitty threw his hands up. "If it's anything, it's proof he went there to meet the rest of the gang and plan the robbery."

The judge drummed his pen on the bench. After a moment he looked up. "We'll wait. Palmer should be back with the box soon."

Catfish sighed with relief. They still had a chance.

A new voice rose from behind. "If I might say something, Your Honor?"

Everyone turned to see who spoke. On scoundrel's row of the gallery, Thaddeus Schoolcraft sat alone. He stood.

"I object to that," Catfish cried.

Schoolcraft's eyes cut to Catfish's, but there wasn't an iota of malice anywhere on his own face. "You should wait until you hear what I have to say."

Chapter 55

Incredibly, the judge appeared perfectly willing to listen to that scalawag. "Come forward, Detective."

Schoolcraft made his way inside the bar. "I have pertinent information for the court."

Catfish clinched his fists. The last pertinent information he'd passed on—that the tipster spoke with some kind of European accent—had proved completely wrong. "I demand he be under oath, Your Honor."

"Willingly," Schoolcraft said, raising his hand without being asked. Gone was his customary haughtiness, but hopefully Judge Goodrich would see right through such play-acting.

After he was sworn Schoolcraft took the witness chair. "I can corroborate Mr. Calloway's theory."

Catfish gaped at him.

Chitty scrambled forward. "What are you—"

"Wait," the judge instructed Chitty. "I want to hear him out."

Hear him out? The bile rose in Catfish's throat. Schoolcraft wore lies like other men wore clothes. Whatever nonsense he was about to spew couldn't be trusted.

"I have long been embroiled in an unpleasantness with Mr. Calloway, but I've never borne him any personal animosity," Schoolcraft began, feigning sincerity. "It's always been the product of my zeal in the pursuit of justice. Indeed, I have much respect for Mr. Calloway because I believe he shares that aim."

Catfish stood dumbfounded. What gambit was Schoolcraft playing? He glanced at Harley, who had no answers.

The rear door creaked open, and Palmer hustled in carrying a box. The turncoat Boswell tagged along behind like a suckling calf after its mother.

Schoolcraft motioned them to the front. "If I could have the box, Your Honor."

"Bring it up."

Schoolcraft dug through the box and pulled out a paper. "This is the note with the number on it."

"Why's it in there?" the judge asked.

"If I might begin in the beginning," Schoolcraft said, still dripping false candor. "I accompanied Lieutenant Palmer to the bawdy house after I heard Miss Peach had been held captive there. I knew American Express would be very interested in pursuing the true culprits. I asked the officer if we might go there and see what we could find. We found some things in a drawer downstairs near the telephone that I don't believe even Mr. Calloway knows about."

Now it was coming. Catfish thrust up his hand. "I object—"

Schoolcraft twisted around. "Wait! I'm helping you."

Catfish stared back. What was happening? Harley tugged his sleeve.

The detective pulled a book from the box. "I found this city directory and at first gave it no thought, but a note tucked into the book caught my attention." He removed the note from the book and handed it to the judge. "On the note there is a name handwritten in pencil: *Risher*. I knew Mr. Topper made deliveries for Risher. Written below the name, as you can see, Judge, is the number 148. I knew it to be the telephone number for the drugstore. What caught my eye next was the directory page the note marked."

Catfish sank back into his chair.

Schoolcraft handed the open directory to the judge. "It wasn't the page where Risher was listed, but instead was a page in the *Business Directory* section of the book. The right-hand column, as you can see, is the listing for attorneys. At the bottom of the page, between *Herring & Kelley* and *Judge Warwick Jenkins,* is a name circled in pencil: *J. Birdsong Jaye.*"

The judge examined the page and shoved the book across the bench for them to see. Harley hopped up and got it. The note *did* say Risher, and Jaybird's name *was* circled. If it was in the drawer by the sporting house talking phone that was the very proof he needed that Buckram or Jessie hired Jaybird. Why had Schoolcraft turned suddenly honest?

"After we returned to Lieutenant Palmer's office, I asked him if I could see the evidence they had taken when they arrested Mr. Topper," Schoolcraft said. "I too examined the brown coat and found those strange numbers."

Catfish braced himself for some deceitful explanation, but his expression was still uncharacteristically benign.

"I didn't know at the time what it meant, but when I heard Mr. Calloway a few minutes ago explain what the numbers meant, it all came together for me. As a detective myself, I have considerable experience with criminal enterprises. I came to the same conclusion as Mr. Calloway but unfortunately much later than he did. The numbers on the paper, the name circled in the directory, the druggist's telephone number, the kidnapping of Miss Peach, the fire at the Staneks, the scraps of burned cloth, the sudden disappearance of the Buckrams, the imbecility of Mr.

Topper all point to one inescapable conclusion: Joe Buckram and his brother framed Mr. Topper to cover their own crimes."

Catfish's head was spinning.

Chitty stood rigidly, gawking at Schoolcraft in disbelief. "What are you doing?"

Schoolcraft refused to look at Chitty. "I have a conscience, sir, and I can't let an innocent man hang for the misdeeds of two criminals. It's my intention to track the Buckrams and see they're brought to justice."

Harley pressed Catfish's arm and whispered to Toby, "You're going free."

Toby rocked.

Judge Goodrich slammed his docket book shut and rocked forward on folded arms, eying the prosecutors. "Gentlemen?"

Chitty and the walrus just stood there.

"If it helps," Schoolcraft added, peering at them, "I intend to speak with my counterpart at American Express and recommend we not proceed further with the case against Topper. I'm confident he will agree."

Chitty finally gave a single, curt nod.

Catfish never imagined he'd say *God bless Thaddeus Schoolcraft*.

Chapter 56

"Have you seen my giraffe, honey?" asked the toothless little lady with the wrinkled face.

Speechless, Peach looked helplessly at Harley.

"Did you say giraffe, ma'am?" he asked.

"I can't seem to find him anywhere." The lady gazed down the hall, quite befuddled. "Clarence!"

Harley smiled reassuringly. "I'm sure he's safe outside somewhere."

Peach slid her hand under his arm. He had such a kind way with people.

An attendant scurried up. "Mrs. Pontefract, I need you to come sit over here, please. We'll find Clarence after the program."

The attendant led the tiny lady to a chair next to a man in a wheeled chair. His arm dangled over the side, almost touching the floor, and his head sagged to his chest.

Mr. Calloway pointed down the hall. "They're bringing Toby in."

They took their places in the large sitting room. Another attendant led Toby in and stood beside him at the front. Toby rocked in his usual way.

Once he was released from custody by the sheriff, Toby had nowhere to go. At Peach's suggestion she, Miss Kate, the

Vaughns, and Mr. Calloway collaborated to send him to the new private asylum in Marshall, where Dr. Wallace assured them he would get the care he needed. Even American Express had contributed a modest sum to his care. The home was a wonderful, caring place, and Toby seemed as happy there as he was anywhere. It was all so hard to believe.

Peach too had been recuperating since her ordeal. Physically, she'd healed quickly, but emotionally, she still struggled sometimes. Never had she been terrorized by such realistic nightmares. Two restorative weeks at home in Eulogy with her family had helped immensely, and she was slowly regaining her aplomb day by day. She rested, she took walks, she read. Her father took her riding across the rolling countryside. Her mother sat with her on the porch talking of matters important and not. Just being in the company of such love was wonderfully strong medicine, but she missed the Calloways terribly the whole time she was home.

She'd missed Harley more than she could possibly have imagined. It was so hard to be apart at such an important time for him. The part he played in gaining Toby's freedom, especially his brilliant victory in the Court of Criminal Appeals, enhanced his standing among lawyers, and restored his badly shaken self-confidence. She wrote him every single day, sometimes twice when some important thought occurred to her after she'd posted the first. A single letter from him—and she received many—did more to advance her recovery than any full night's sleep.

She wrote Harley she wanted to see Toby as soon as she was able. Harley and Mr. Calloway had picked her up in Eulogy, and the three of them took a train to Marshall in east Texas. Their reunion was so restorative. Mr. Calloway always made her laugh, and his knees seemed to be completely better. He wasn't even carrying his cane. And Colonel Terry came too, administering his own slobbery curative.

Reuniting with Harley had been unexpectedly thrilling—but truthfully now, hadn't she anticipated it fully in her last thoughts every evening and her first each morning? To walk side by side, to talk intimately, to embrace, to be so completely joyful. Each moment inspired in her the recollection of a dozen bits of verse. How could a poet have known so well how she would feel?

If only she was certain how Harley felt. She thought she remembered him saying he loved her when he freed her from her bondage, but she wasn't sure. Whether he did or not, his eyes, his face, his voice, his touch all said that and more. He seemed more affectionate now.

The director of the Valle Loma Asylum stood before the small audience. "And now, Mr. Toby Budge will present some sonnets from Shakespeare."

Peach, Harley, and Mr. Calloway clapped enthusiastically. When the other spectators—patients all—settled as much as they could, the director prompted Toby with the first line of Sonnet 75.

He recited it beautifully and performed ten more, each without the slightest misstep or imperfection. Peach couldn't put her finger on why she thought so, but Toby looked utterly joyful as he recited, especially when the audience clapped—and they did so, quite genuinely. Other inmates responded in their own ways. They acted joyful too. One hummed some unknown tune as Toby recited. It was discordant with the rhythm of the verse, but nobody cared. She smiled and swayed her head as she hummed.

Peach never managed to catch Toby's eye, but that was fine. It was unnecessary.

"Do we have any requests?" the asylum director asked, looking toward the three visitors.

"Sonnet 29, please," Peach called.

The director began turning pages in the book of sonnets which used to be Peach's. "Yes, let me find it."

"Don't bother. I know it," she said. "'When in disgrace with fortune and men's eyes. . .'"

Toby stopped rocking and addressed the floor to his front as if it were his dearest friend.

"'I all alone beweep my outcast state,
And trouble deaf heaven with my bootless cries,
And look upon myself and curse my fate,
Wishing me like to one more rich in hope,
Featured like him, like him with friends possessed,
Desiring this man's art and that man's scope,
With what I most enjoy contented least;
Yet in these thoughts myself almost despising,
Haply I think on thee, and then my state,
Like to the lark at break of day arising
From sullen earth, sings hymns at heaven's gate . . .'"

Toby's head tilted up. His eyes met Peach's directly.

"'For thy sweet love remembered such joy brings
That then I scorn to change my state with kings.'"

Tears streaming down her cheeks, she touched Harley's sleeve. Toby had made an error. He'd never done that before. He'd recited that sonnet to her a dozen times, each time with perfection, but this time, he'd made a mistake.

She dabbed her eyes and wondered if he'd do it again. "'When in disgrace with fortune and men's eyes. . .'"

With that prompting once more Toby recited the three quatrains perfectly. Again, he met her eyes directly in the first line of the couplet. Again, he erred at its end. The couplet was supposed to be *For thy sweet love remembered such wealth brings.* But Toby kept saying "joy" instead of "wealth." How so unlike him to make a mistake, yet he made it twice.

Or was it a mistake?

As soon as he concluded, Toby's eyes left hers and he began to rock, staring once more at the floor.

She reached for Harley's hand and squeezed it tightly. That had been no mistake. The savant had composed a new couplet, changing it to suit his state.

As the lark still sang in her heart, another tear dropped. She closed her eyes. They were all there—the Mr. Calloway she so admired, the Mr. Calloway she so loved, the trapped soul they together set free.

***

Catfish glanced back to the depot where Harley and Miss Peach sat arm in arm on a bench. They were all going home.

"A fine day to be in love, isn't it, Colonel?"

Colonel Terry, trooping along beside him, answered with an arch-eyed glance but didn't break his stride.

The train wouldn't leave for an hour, so they went for a walk along the railroad right-of-way. Beyond the houses on the edge of town, a cool breeze blew through a break in the tall pine forest. Between the tree line and the track, a field of fire wheels blazed red, orange, and yellow. A pair of hummingbirds buzzed by. The buttercups had already withered for the day, awaiting new blossoms that evening. A few early bluebells and a scattering of Mexican hat dotted the bar-ditch with color. Been a wet spring in east Texas.

He'd gone almost his entire life before ever noticing some

bluebells were white. Martha never missed small wonders like that—*God bless her*—but he'd always been too busy to notice. Such a shame.

His mind wandered from wildflowers back to the asylum. He'd thought it would be a sad place, maybe even frightening, but it wasn't at all. Each of the inmates looked to be content in whatever world the person inhabited. They'd take good care of him there yet give him what freedom he could handle. Catfish had stopped by the local hardware store after the program at the asylum and bought a bicycle for Toby. This one had the latest Morgan & Wright pneumatic tires, not patched, and it wouldn't need a wicker basket for making deliveries. This one would be just for the joy of riding.

He kneeled beside the track to pick a fire wheel, and the fresh scent of the flowers washed over him until he surrendered to the moment. The colonel nuzzled against him as if to suggest they linger a bit, so he sat cross-legged, pulled his companion close, and closed his eyes as the south breeze brushed his face. He knew Martha would tarry there too. *Darlin', we saved that boy, and it was righteous work. I wish you'd been there for Harley's argument to the court of appeals. It won the day. Oh, and Miss Peach— Harley's sweetheart. She showed such determination that Toby was innocent. I believe, dearest, if I'm the voice and Harley's the brains of the firm, then Miss Peach gives us heart. So, I've been rethinking my decision to get out of leading the defense of murder cases. It just seems as if that's what I'm supposed to be doing. I know you'll understand.*

He dropped the fire wheel into his pocket. Martha used to press flowers between the pages of a book. A jigger to remember Toby by.

A train whistle shrieked in the distance, so he struggled to his feet, and they headed back.

The third-floor turret of the asylum poked skyward among its neighbors. A fine place for Toby. The director of the asylum had told Catfish about a donation of two hundred fifty dollars by American Express for Toby's care. Mighty decent of them.

He also said Thaddeus Schoolcraft had sent a personal donation of one hundred dollars. Not sure how he could have been so wrong about that man.

Chapter 57

Thaddeus Schoolcraft caught his face in the mirror and gave it a jaunty wink, slicked his hair, and wiped his horseshoe mustache smooth before tossing his mail on the desk, hanging his bowler on the hook, and dropping his blackthorn cane into the stand. He settled into his chair to examine the mail.

There were several letters. The one from Ft. Worth smelled of fine perfume. He sniffed but didn't open it. He pictured her—black hair, a scarlet ribbon about her neck, alluring eyes peering over a black satin fan, the enchanting intonations of St. Tammany Parish. She probably signed the letter, as she always did, with the single initial *G.* He never much cared for the name Jessie—it was quite common—and she never used it with him.

Dearest F, her letter probably began. He tossed it aside. He'd read it later.

Instead, he ripped open the box she'd also sent and beheld the freshly typed draft of his new dime novel, *The Adventures of Thaddeus Schoolcraft, Railroad Detective—The Suspension Bridge Robbery—BY MIRIAM GARTRELL GISELLE.* He'd been relieved when he learned she hadn't left it in the house when she'd fled.

He turned to the last page.

The vicious, bloodthirsty imbecile's twitching body swayed in the crisp fall breeze. Nearby, his corrupt, old white-haired lawyer chafed at being thwarted once again. Detective Schoolcraft, from his place at the center of the scaffold, declared boldly to the gathered masses, "Justice is done."

That ending would now require some re-writing because of Calloway, but he had an even better one in mind. He savored the memory of the climactic moment when he had announced the solution of the crime, the looks of astonishment on every face—certainly Chitty's and Palmer's, but especially on Calloway's. It was delicious. If he hadn't been so quick to think of a story, Calloway would have caught him when they discovered the directory with Jaye's name circled.

He flipped through the draft and put it back into the box. It would make a more handsome profit than the first book. He must remember to send a signed copy to the governor as he promised. And to young Boswell's father, the banker in Austin. His gift to the clerk of the Court of Criminal Appeals hadn't born fruit, but it didn't matter in the end.

He opened his desk drawer and removed a tin box. Inside lay an envelope with a return address of Beadle & Adams, Publishers of New York, addressed to *Miss Miriam G. Giselle, Washington Avenue, Waco Texas.* On the reverse side of the envelope, he admired again the two messages he composed after the Calloway whelp convinced the meddlesome court of appeals to interfere. He hadn't even thought of using the Staneks until then. The first message was an adequate feint for a time: *stop protecting killer or you regret—idiot must hang.* It was pure luck when Stanek used the word "idiot" to Calloway. It was hard to conceal his delight when he heard. But when he later got word the Calloways were abandoning the insanity defense and focusing instead on proving Topper wasn't the killer, it became obvious stronger measures were required. The kidnapping had been an essential adjustment to his plan.

He admired the text of the second message he composed and sent along afterward. It was brilliant: *idiot die peech live*. He'd written "peach" on the envelope originally but changed it—an exquisite touch—before Buckram copied it in his own hand. Everyone readily believed it was Stanek at first, but when Calloway caught on to Buckram, they just as easily believed someone as stupid as Buckram would misspell her name. He was concerned at first when he heard the police had searched Giselle's whorehouse, but happily they missed the envelope with the two threats. Palmer was easily manipulated to let him inside after they shut the place down. The fool hadn't noticed him take the envelope from Giselle's desk drawer and slip it into his pocket. He couldn't secret the city directory away, but he'd had another idea about it and so had left the note with Risher's number marking the page of Jaye's listing. What foresight he'd had to preserve it. In court Calloway had come uncomfortably close to upending his plan but his own quick response saved the day, naturally.

In the beginning, he hadn't cared whether Topper hung or went to prison or to an asylum as long as everyone believed he was the robber, which they did. But when Calloway stuck his nose into the case, he wanted the freak dead and his lawyer ruined. Upon reflection, in the revised ending of his book, he would free the pitiful imbecile himself and bring both Buckrams to the scaffold in California. American Express and the KATY would be so grateful.

He burned the envelope and returned his attention to the tin. It was time for the accounting.

One by one, he removed the hundred-dollar notes and tallied them on his ledger. Of course, on the expense side he'd paid five of those hundred-dollar notes to the incompetent lawyer. Two thousand dollars had been planted with the idiot at the shanty, and four hundred had gone to pay off the Buckram brutes. By that time they were in California. The five hundred dollar reward American Express paid to the informant was income to him rather than an expense. His kind and generous donation of one hundred dollars to the asylum wasn't actually an expense, since American Express paid that out of its own kind and generous donation of five hundred more, and so he recorded $150 on the income side of the ledger.

But he did lay out $27.50 to buy a new silk reception dress from Bloomingdales for Giselle to replace the one she'd hastily left behind in Waco. Pity she'd been in such a panic after Deputy Buckram had arrived with the warning.

He calculated the final tally for the American Express entry in the ledger: $22,722.50. He divided that number by two, as he promised Giselle, and recorded the five thousand he would actually give her. It wasn't the exact amount he promised her, but she would understand how quickly expenses mount. He'd bring her a cheap bauble and tell her he had to pay the perfidious Boswell for his intelligence about Dr. Wallace. She needn't know he freely passed it along out of his natural animus for the Calloways. And anyway, all she did was mail a letter to Jaye with his fee.

He added his cut to the grand total for the year 1895. It was a handsome sum. Well over eight times his paltry railroad salary.

Thaddeus Schoolcraft, railroad detective, rocked back in his chair. He would settle Calloway another day. And his whelp too. Like he'd settled the other Calloway son nine years ago.

Quick money was easy to make; revenge couldn't be rushed.

Author's Notes

One must start with the bridge. The famous single-span suspension bridge where the American Express robbery occurred still stands astride the Brazos River. At the time of this writing, it is under significant restoration to be completed in 2022. It was originally a toll bridge primarily for cattle on the Chisolm Trail to cross the river. The 475-foot wire rope spans were made by the John A. Roebling Company of Brooklyn Bridge fame. By the time of Toby Topper's case the bridge was paid off and operated by the county. While it will soon be open again for foot traffic, in 1894 and 1895 it accommodated not only pedestrians but also wagons and animals, though cattle drives no longer made the trek. Springing across the river from Waco's Downtown Historic District, the bridge is on the National Register of Historic Places and is a Texas Historic Civil Engineering Landmark.

In addition to the bridge, several other places in the story also survive. Harley roomed above what is now Barnett's Pub, at 420 Franklin Avenue. Jacob Levinski's lovely house is at 19th and Morrow, now with the address 724 N. 19th Street. The Methodist Home still nurtures orphans, though the original structure which Catfish visited was replaced by the present brick buildings. A short trip down I-35 brings one to Austin, where the Driskill Hotel still caters to influence peddlers, politicians, and even ordinary guests. The state capitol is a short distance up Congress Avenue, and visitors can tour the old Court of Criminal Appeals courtroom, where Harley so magnificently argued and won Toby's appeal. It appears today much as it did in Harley's day.

Miss Kate, Peach's aptly named friend, was a dynamic personage in Waco and beyond from the late 19th until the mid-20th century. While her home on Mary Street no longer stands, admirers of the remarkable Kate Friend will find other solid evidence of her impact. She was an internationally renowned Shakespeare scholar who was responsible for the well-hidden Shakespeare monument located near the intersection of North University Parks Drive and Colcord just beneath the water treatment plant. The Waco Shakespeare Club, founded by Miss Kate about five years after Toby Topper's case, erected it in 1916 to memorialize the Bard on the 300th anniversary of his death. Thus sayeth the inscription on the obelisk:

> *Shakespeare! Deign to lend they face,*
> *This romantic nook to guard,*
> *Where untaught nature sports alone,*
> *Since thou and nature are but one.*
> *1616-1916.*

A romantic nook indeed, it does bear his face and is worthy of a picnic and sonnet-reading on a pretty day.

Another reminder of Kate Friend's accomplishments sits just outside Waco's modern city hall. Miss Kate was a great animal lover, and under her leadership the Humane Society placed a massive fountain for both horses and dogs on the town square outside the old city hall. Several early photos depict buggies stopped at the fountain for the horse's refreshment. The Humane Society erected a monument for Miss Kate at Waco's Oakwood Cemetery: "TEACHER, EDITOR, PUBLISHER, WRITER, SCHOLAR, LECTURER, CLUB WOMAN, RELIGIOUS, CIVIC & POLITICAL FIGURE. MOST RENOWNED HUMANE FACTOR IN TEXAS AND THE NATION."

Toby Topper's sanity is a central issue in this story, and two characters influencing the outcome of that issue still stand tall in Waco, or at least in Oakwood Cemetery. Dr. David R. Wallace testified as an expert witness for the defense. He had, as Peach described, presided as superintendent of the Texas State Lunatic Asylum and later of the North Texas State Lunatic Asylum. He was a pioneer in mental health care who came to be known as the father of modern psychiatry in Texas. His 1921 grave in Oakwood is marked by a life-size statue which faces his "friend for eternity," Senator Richard Coke. The famous Coke was a soldier, a lawyer, a trial judge, a Texas Supreme Court justice, twice the governor of Texas, and a three-term U.S. Senator. He too is memorialized by a life-size statue, and it faces Wallace. Giants, then and now.